MW00561381

THE DISAPPEARED

THE
DISAPPEARED

REBECCA J. SANFORD

**BLACK
STONE**
PUBLISHING

Copyright © 2024 by Rebecca J. Sanford
Published in 2024 by Blackstone Publishing
Cover and book design by Sarah Riedlinger

All rights reserved. This book or any portion
thereof may not be reproduced or used in any manner
whatsoever without the express written permission
of the publisher except for the use of brief quotations
in a book review.

Any historical figures and events referenced in this book
are depicted in a fictitious manner. All other characters
and events are products of the author's imagination, and
any similarity to real persons, living or dead, is coincidental.

Printed in the United States of America

First edition: 2024
ISBN 979-8-212-38536-7
Fiction / Historical / General

Version 1

Blackstone Publishing
31 Mistletoe Rd.
Ashland, OR 97520

www.BlackstonePublishing.com

For the Grandmothers

Truth is the daughter of time, not of authority.

—Francis Bacon

PART I

PART I.

CHAPTER 1

Lorena kept her head down as she hurried past the *kiosko* stacked with government-backed newspapers. She focused on the little flowers stitched into her leather clogs, on their *clop-clop-clop* sound against the hot pavement. At the corner, a cluster of military officers loomed. They were everywhere now, black-booted and dressed in olive uniforms, boasting submachine guns like trophies. Lorena ran her index finger along the laminated edge of the identification card in her pocket and lifted her gaze to the nearest soldier's face. He was slightly younger than her—early twenties, maybe—with deep-set eyes and a bottom lip that jutted out. She imagined encountering him in another time or place, recast in a role that wasn't on the opposite side of *el Proceso*—the government's "reorganization process." He might have seen her differently then, as a woman rather than a possible subversive. Perhaps he would have made a pass at her. Perhaps she would have laughed him off sharply enough to damage his pride, and he would have been the one at her mercy instead of the other way around.

The idea passed quickly as the young man glanced back and forth between her face and the identification card he now held in his hand.

"Lorena Ledesma," he read aloud, emboldened by the authority of his misbuttoned uniform.

She nodded obediently. Lorena Ledesma: a devoted citizen, a faithful wife, the mother of a young son. A loving daughter hosting dinner for her extended family that very evening, she explained to him, just on her way to the grocery store to pick up some meat for the empanadas.

He leered at her with an intensity she doubted he could've summoned if he weren't holding the gun. Perhaps he'd caught sight of her coming out of the university, where classes had been canceled to thwart the spread of radicalism. *Please*, she thought. *Just let me go home.* If she could just get through one more dinner, one more day, something was bound to happen to break this ominous tension.

"Your errands are done," said the officer at last, giving her the ID. "Go straight home. Hurry up, and mind curfew tonight."

She took it, irate but relieved, and dropped her eyes again. Her cotton blouse clung to the sweat spreading across her back. The cinnamon scent of a lonely churro cart faded behind her as she boarded the bus for Barrio Norte, its arrival a small miracle given the recent unreliability of public transport. Inside her clogs, her feet had begun to swell.

When the bus door shrieked open at Alvarez Thomas Street, Lorena disembarked and made her way past stone facades and gates of finished wood. She was a fool for going back to the university in the first place. It wasn't as though she expected to find Claudio there, in the faculty lounge where it had all started, but she'd still wanted physical proximity to his memory. It had been weeks since she'd heard a single word from him.

She unlocked the front gate and went inside. José was in the kitchen fixing a drink, his shirt unbuttoned in the heat. Every evening lately, he poured a stiff drink at an early hour, as though he'd been fighting fascists with his bare hands all day rather than philosophizing with furloughed political science professors. She kissed him chastely and began slicing vegetables. The cat weaved between her ankles.

"What time does your mother arrive?" he asked.

"Seven," she said. "I told you that already."

"You didn't."

"Well, it's seven." Lorena was exhausted and her legs ached, but she wiped down the counters and fired up the stove. Making José feel like the man of the house was a small penance for the things she hid from him, and it offered protection: the work of an ordinary housewife was unsuspicious.

By the time Esme knocked on the front door, the aroma of sizzling peppers and spices wafted through the place.

"Come in, Mamá," Lorena called from the kitchen.

Esme appeared cradling her groggy two-year-old grandson, Matías, in one arm.

"How are you feeling, my love?" Esme asked, cupping her daughter's face with her free hand. Her palm was smooth and warm. "You still haven't put up your Christmas decorations."

Lorena pried her son's fist from a lock of his grandmother's hair and nuzzled his soft cheek with kisses. The boy wriggled from Esme's grasp and hefted his weight toward his mother.

"I'm fine," Lorena lied, cuddling her boy. She kissed Matías again and set him down on the tile, where he immediately tottered toward the patio. Lorena twisted her dark hair into a loose bun and tucked it in place. "I haven't had time yet, but I'll get to it."

"Immaculate Conception Day was Wednesday." Esme set her pocketbook on the counter and fanned herself with one hand. "Children need Christmas. They need celebrations, things to look forward to—especially these days, God help us."

Lorena glanced around. The heavy wooden shutters along the front of the house were unlatched, exposing thick wrought iron bars over the windows. French doors opened from the kitchen to a back patio where blades of grass thrust between cracks in the concrete to graze Matías's pudgy bare feet. The stone pavers were still warm from the day's sun, which had just begun to set. A pang of longing struck. She missed her father.

Esme followed Matías outside. The bamboo patio chair creaked as she settled into its faded cushion.

"You want a glass of wine, Mamá?" Lorena asked.

"Just some water, dear." Esme sighed. "Have some, too. You look tired. You need to stay hydrated in this heat."

In the living room, the turntable's needle steered through the prelude to one of José's favorite songs. He emerged, drink in hand, and joined his mother-in-law on the patio.

"Good day today?" he asked, leaning down to offer his cheek.

Esme kissed it fondly. José took the seat next to her, lifting his feet to the ottoman and humming softly to the music. Resentment filled Lorena as she fetched a glass of water and delivered it to her mother.

"Matías was an angel," said Esme, who helped take care of her only grandson a few days each week. "As he always is. We tried to go to the park, but—" Esme sighed, lamenting some earlier event, and took a long sip of water. "What can you do? What can anyone do about such madness in the world? It's in God's hands, I suppose."

In the kitchen, Lorena stuffed half-moon pockets of dough with cheese and vegetables, crimping the *repulgue* the way Esme had taught her as a girl, but with far greater force. Her late father, Gustavo, a union leader and Peronista, would stir in his grave if he heard Esme dismissing the current state of his country. Lorena shifted from one sore foot to the other. A revolutionary's drumbeat echoed in her memory. Esme and José preferred to sip drinks and downplay the junta's fascism. Lorena straightened her spine; she would never be subdued. She would never abandon her father's fight—the people's fight—and she knew Claudio wouldn't, either.

"Mamá, dance!" Matías squealed, stomping into the kitchen and wrapping his arms around his mother's legs. He gazed up at her adoringly.

"My love," she said, softening. She reached down to tousle his hair, then paused, her hands wet with empanada filling.

"José," she called, "can you help with Matías?"

José turned his head in her direction without getting up, then dropped a hand to pet the cat's head. He took a slow sip of his drink.

Lorena stuck the empanadas in the oven, wiped her hands on a towel, and carried Matías back out to the patio, where she danced with him a bit before guiding him toward Esme's lap. The boy hopped back down and followed Lorena to the table, grabbing at the flatware as she arranged the place settings.

"Any word from Claudio?" Esme called over a lull in the music.

Lorena stopped folding the napkin she was holding and glanced up to catch—then avoid—her husband's eye.

José shook his head. "God only knows what he's gotten himself into."

Lorena's jaw constricted. "I'm sure he's fine," she said quietly. "He knows what he's doing."

José glared. "He's reckless as ever."

"You haven't seen him?" Esme asked.

Lorena straightened a fork at one of the place settings.

"No," José said quickly. "We're not involved."

Claudio is not our concern anymore, José would insist. *You need to stay calm, Lorena. Stop getting so worked up about things you can't control.* But Lorena didn't want to keep calm. She wanted to set the streets on fire until her country belonged to its people again, and from the look on José's face, he knew exactly how she felt.

"Let's eat," she said, smiling tightly.

Since the coup last March, General Jorge Videla had been running the country with tight control. Tanks were parked outside the Casa Rosada—the Pink House, Argentina's presidential residence—bolstering the right-wing dictatorship's message: the time for resistance and uprisings was over. Any perceived subversion was snuffed out by the junta. Leftist militant groups like the Montoneros and the People's Revolutionary Army had lost support, and their members—like Claudio—were going underground or into exile. Guerrillas were eradicated and people suspected of subversion were going missing. There was no tolerance for public spectacles like the union demonstrations her father had organized for years. *Fall in line*, Videla had warned citizens explicitly, *or pay the price and become invisible.*

Lorena brought out the platter of empanadas and a bottle of red wine as they settled around the table. Matías perched on Esme's knee while she said grace. Across the patio, the neighbor's back door slammed. José opened the bottle and poured, then took a bite.

"No meat?" he muttered.

Lorena's cheeks burned. "I couldn't get any." She envisioned the young officer's smug face and tore off the tip of an empanada with her teeth.

"They're delicious, sweetheart," said Esme.

"Yes, very good," murmured José, a small kindness that reminded Lorena of a time when there hadn't been such tension between them, before his complacency had become intolerable. But when he swiped a napkin across his mouth and patted Lorena's hand, her fury returned. *We have a family now*, José would remind her, as if that wasn't all the more reason to take a stand for their country.

After they finished eating, Lorena cleared the table and set down a tray of coffee and *alfajores*. José moved his hand to the small of her waist. She flinched, then closed her eyes as his fingertips found the broad part of her hip. His touch was reverent, tentative, as though he was uncertain of her body's full capabilities or his own capacity to handle them. Lorena breathed through a quiver of anxiety.

"You all right, dear?" Esme asked.

Matías, who was overtired and tearful, curled up on his grandmother's lap and reached for her earring.

Lorena let out another breath, opened her eyes and met Esme's. It seemed her mother could see straight through to her fraying soul.

"Everything's fine," said Lorena quietly. She watched with a pang of envy as Matías nestled into Esme's lap. How she longed to be comforted in such a simple way, to return to a time when her mother's touch was all it took to erase every mistake she'd ever made.

Later, as she put her boy to bed, Lorena studied his long lashes, the tiny lids eclipsing his brown eyes, his soft, dark hair like José's. Matías reached up and wrapped his hand around Lorena's finger, but the sweet gesture seemed too mature, as though he was holding onto her, already wise to the possibility of her absence.

It was past curfew. Esme retired to the guest room, and José took his book to bed. Alone, Lorena moved through the house, adjusting the open windows with precision. Warm summer air bled in. The balance of muted street sounds and the soft, sleeping breath of her family gave her the sense that everything was momentarily in its proper place. She yearned to miniaturize it all, to package them up and keep them safe. In the hallway, the fan was a rickety metronome, the tiles cool beneath her bare feet.

The cat hurtled from the kitchen windowsill and landed on the patio with a soft trill. In the moonlight, laundry fluttered on the line and palm fronds rustled in the breeze. Where was Claudio tonight?

In the bedroom, Lorena pulled back the ivory coverlet and slid between the sheets. José's skin felt warm and welcoming. She pressed her body against him and, through the thin material of her nightgown, felt the shift of his shoulder blade. She kissed his bare shoulder. She'd almost forgotten the taste of his skin. She hadn't held him in months, but now she realized that focusing on his body distracted her mind. *Please, God,* she prayed. *Give me strength to handle this. Help me to know what to do.*

Through the open windows, the city streets fell quiet. She closed her eyes and tried, just for a little while, to make everything go away.

———— · ⟡ · ————

In the darkness, a thud jolted Lorena awake. Adrenaline surged through her chest. Before she could orient herself, her mind went instinctively to Matías. Her eyes adjusted as José sat up in bed, running his hand absently over his face and through his hair. It was past midnight. A series of thuds sounded from the front entrance of the house.

Lorena flung the covers off her legs and fled to the baby's room. When she reached his crib, she found him still half-asleep.

"Mamá?" Matías groaned as she picked him up. Cradling the warmth of his small body, she headed toward the guest room.

"Mamá?" Lorena echoed her son as Esme emerged. The sharp banging was startling. Matías began to cry.

"What's going on, Lore?" asked Esme, shoving her arms through her robe. The front door shuddered, each pounding more forceful than the previous.

Claudio, thought Lorena.

José tugged an undershirt over his head as he made his way down the shadowy hall. His bare feet were silent on the tile floor.

"José," Lorena hissed. "Wait."

But when José turned around, Lorena couldn't articulate her fears, managing only to hold her husband's gaze. She imagined the state Claudio might be in, the help he might need. *Not now*, she thought. *Please, not with Mamá here. Not with the baby. Not like this.* Matías wailed at the banging. It didn't stop.

"Coming!" José shouted.

The heavy metal latch screeched as José opened the door. Shadows merged the profiles of two unfamiliar men at the threshold. Behind them, a third silhouette filled the gap between their shoulders.

Lorena came up behind her husband, bouncing Matías on her hip frantically to soothe him. Esme began to follow, but Lorena flicked the air with her free hand to keep her mother back. *Keep calm*, she thought, but her heart pounded.

"José Ledesma?" barked one of the officers in front. He wore a thick shirt, belted pants with pocketed thighs, and calf-high black boots—the same uniform of the junta Lorena had passed near the churro cart that afternoon. The other two men wore plain street clothes and brandished rifles.

José turned to look at Lorena, then back toward the men.

"Sí," he said in a near whisper, stepping back.

The officer shoved José's chest with the side of his rifle, thrusting him against the foyer wall with a crash, then belted him across the torso with the gun. José's single high-pitched cry pierced the air. For a moment, Matías went quiet.

"Is this your wife?" the officer snarled, nodding toward Lorena. He leaned into José, who looked wordlessly at the floor. "Lorena Ledesma?"

The resonance of the officer's voice sent a cold terror through Lorena's chest. She held Matías tighter.

"We've done nothing. You've got the wrong house," José uttered, his voice shallow, the breath emptied from his lungs.

Lorena bolted back to Esme, who clutched her chest and covered her mouth. Their eyes locked. Lorena was close enough to feel the warmth of Esme's body, the brush of her mother's cotton robe against her own bare calves. Esme reached for Matías, enveloping him with both arms and cradling the back of his head.

Lorena lurched back toward the entryway, a trailing arm outstretched to shield her mother and son. Matías reached for her as she moved away, but Esme held on tightly until he buried his face in his grandmother's soft shoulder.

The officer relinquished his hold on José, but one of the other men seized him by the shoulder and kneed him in the gut. José yelped, slinging his arm across his waist as he crumpled to the floor.

The lead officer dashed toward Lorena, yanking her arms behind her. Lorena's swirling hip slammed against the wooden sideboard that she and José had bought in Palermo, sending a basket of hollow gourds clattering to the floor.

"Let's go," the officer spat. He pushed Lorena down the hallway toward the bedroom. She took quick inventory of him. Would he rape her, right here in her home, in front of her husband, mother, and son? He gestured back for the third comrade to enter the house. Their boots were like hooves against the tile. He shoved Lorena through the bedroom door.

"Get dressed," the officer demanded.

Crashes reverberated from the living room.

"We haven't done anything," she whispered, wincing in fear. But it was a lie. What she'd done hardly seemed enough to bring the junta into their home, but she knew they were here now because of her—because of what she'd done with Claudio.

The officer looked down his nose at her, disgusted. "Put some clothes on," he said.

Shame, then rage, seeped through her fright. She crouched next to the full laundry basket at the foot of the bed and pulled out a pair of drawstring pants she wore to clean the yard. The closet door was partially open. The bedsheets were pulled back. There was a faint valley in the pillow where José's head had rested just moments earlier. There was nothing within her reach substantial enough to inflict pain, and she knew she would be killed before she could cause any real damage.

"Who sent you?" José shouted from the foyer as Lorena slipped the pants over her bare legs.

"Shut up," she heard one of the men growl. "We ask the questions."

They'll realize we're not worth their time, Lorena thought. *They'll take us in for questioning and let us go. We'll be home before morning.* She slid on the shoes she'd discarded when she got home, ages earlier.

The officer butted his rifle against her arm, prompting her back into the hall. Esme receded toward the guest room still holding Matías.

The third man was standing in the living room, surveying it. Fragments of a shattered vase speckled the floor. Couch pillows were shredded, their innards strewn. A wall tapestry had been torn down, dumped in a rumpled pile.

"Let's go," the lead officer ordered. For the first time, Lorena noticed his features—his burlap skin reddened by razor burn, his small eyes the color of lentils.

"Mamá!" Matías cried from Esme's arms.

"Please," Lorena pleaded with the officer as he shoved her toward the door. "My son."

Fueled by adrenaline, she broke free of the officer's grasp and sprinted the brief distance to Esme. Tearfully, she pressed her lips against Matías's face, rubbing his plump arms and legs maniacally. She ignored the approaching boot steps until the officer yanked her away by her hair.

"I'm coming back, Mamá," Lorena said to Esme.

Matías began to whimper.

"What's their crime?" yelled Esme, her voice breaking. "Why are you doing this?"

The officer jerked his head toward the door, then took an ominous step toward Esme.

"Leave the boy and the old woman," he said to the third man.

"We're coming back," cried Lorena.

Before she could utter another word, Lorena saw the second man lift José from the floor. His arms were bracketed behind him, his shoulders hunched, vulturelike. The third man produced a dark sack and plunged its opening over José's head. She saw the stubble on her husband's jaw, the place where she'd kissed him just hours earlier.

Then her entire world went black behind the tight warp and weft of material that reeked of sinister things: gasoline, rubber, something metallic.

Matías's cries faded as the clomping boots led her out to the street. She could still feel the warmth from his small body against her chest, the weight of him in her arms just moments earlier. A lump filled her throat. She envisioned him wriggling from Esme's embrace, crawling toward the front door with his little hand outstretched. He would twist his body defiantly when Esme swept him up to comfort him. He would see Lorena being marched away.

Her soul tore with every inch she moved away from Matías. A part of her became crippled, debilitated. But another part was starkly alive, walking in her nightgown and drawstring pants, her swollen feet still in her own shoes. In the warm air outside the house, she was being prodded toward the street by brutal men hell-bent on carrying out their orders. Her rational mind still worked devastatingly well.

The two men in plain clothes had to be Triple A—the Argentine Anticommunist Alliance, a paramilitary group—and it was possible that they'd seen her go into that apartment with Claudio months earlier. She'd only been inside for an hour, maybe two, and she'd been so careful—but the junta had eyes everywhere.

Please, God, she prayed. What would happen to Matías? Was Esme strong enough to keep him safe? *We could be home by morning. We have to be.* But the hood over her head told a different story.

Crushed between the two men, Lorena heard the muffled sound of José's voice somewhere up ahead. A grumbled threat silenced him. She longed to collapse against his chest, to find safety there, but in the next terrible instant, she longed for Claudio instead. Claudio would know what to do—he'd have found a way out of this already.

A car door clicked open. Someone put a hand on Lorena's head and shoved her inside. She was in the backseat between two of the men, the sides of her arms and thighs pinned by their hard bodies as the engine started.

No one spoke; only her sniffling could be heard in the silent vehicle. From the turns she could sense, they seemed to be headed north. The darkness was insufferable. Was José with her in the car? If she spoke, could he answer?

In a tiny, halted voice, she said his name, off-pitch.

"José?"

A blinding white light flashed behind her eyes. The shock of the force against the side of her head eclipsed the pain.

Please, she prayed. *Please keep Matías and my mother safe. That's all I ask.*

The white light began to glow, illuminating both her hope and vulnerability. She tried blotting it out with reason—*we'll be home by morning*—but as the car swerved, her consciousness descended a tunnel toward the brightness, through a terrifying premonition of the hours, days, and weeks ahead. There, in the radiance of her own intuition, she was paralyzed by questions even her worst fears couldn't answer yet. If the junta learned of her secret, God only knew what they would do to her. All Lorena could conceive of now was how much infinitely more she had to lose.

CHAPTER 2

NEW YORK CITY

JUNE 2005

Rachel arranged the hand-labeled cheeses and truffled quail eggs, lined up a row of liquor bottles, and placed sprigs of dill on the crème fraiche with fond thoughts of her mother's herb garden. A digitized rendition of Bach's Fugue in D minor rose from her pink Motorola RAZR, and she grabbed the quaking thing off the kitchen counter, flipping it open distractedly without bothering to check the incoming number.

She expected someone to wish her happy birthday. Instead, over the music from her living room, where a dozen people were already packed into the six-hundred-square-foot apartment she shared with her roommate, a woman's vibrant voice rang out through the receiver.

"Is Rachel Sprague available, please?"

Rachel moved to the kitchen sink to unwrap a bouquet of flowers and fill a vase with water. She propped the phone on her shoulder and wrestled with the leaky dual spigot. "This is she."

"Rachel? My name is Dr. Marisol Rey. We haven't spoken before. I wasn't sure I had the right number. Did I get you at a bad time?"

A distant siren cut through the music as a friend squeezed past Rachel to grab the vodka from the makeshift bar. A few feet away,

Rachel's roommate plucked a grape from the cheeseboard and loaded a cocktail shaker with ice, rattling it adeptly.

"It's not the best time," Rachel said.

"I apologize for calling you out of the blue," the woman went on. "It's just that I have some important information I wanted to share with you."

The door buzzer bleated. Nearby, a bottle of chardonnay blubbered out a rising scale as wineglasses were filled and distributed. Guests were cramming in, glossy gift bags dangling from manicured fingers. A flush crept across Rachel's neck.

"Dr. Rey, did you say it was?" Perhaps she'd missed an appointment. She called to mind the list of practitioners' names engraved on the brass doorplate of her doctor's Park Avenue office, but *Rey* didn't ring a bell.

"Please, call me Mari," said the woman.

"Where did you say you were calling from?"

"Well, I'm from Miami." The woman sounded uncomfortable. "But I'm here in New York right now. I work for an organization in South America."

Rachel wished she hadn't answered. "How can I help you?"

"Well, like I said, there's some information I want to share with you. I was wondering if we could arrange a time to talk in person. I know it's short notice, but if you're free tomorrow—"

"What kind of information?"

The woman cleared her throat. "It's in regard to your identity."

Pinpricks traveled over Rachel's chest. She paused for a moment, glanced at the tap water dripping from her long, slim fingers—her mom always called them pianist's fingers, though she never played—and wondered fleetingly if her debit card had been stolen.

"Hold on just a minute, will you?" Rachel yelled into the phone, then shook her hands dry and headed for the door.

Outside her first-floor apartment, plane contrails scraped the late sunset. The summer sky trapped stale heat. Rachel shifted her weight from one heel to the other, flattened her free hand against the concrete balustrade, and lifted the phone to her ear.

"Hello? Are you still there?"

"Yes, hi," said Mari. "I'm here."

Rachel leaned into her palm. Near the entrance gate to John Jay Park across the street, a crescendo of laughter rose from a group of teenagers.

"What is it, specifically, that you're looking to share with me?" She turned to face her apartment window. Propped on her kitchen windowsill was the thick floral card that had arrived earlier that afternoon, filled with her mother's disciplined handwriting: *Happy birthday, sweetheart! Wishing our favorite girl an unforgettable year. Love you always, Mom & Dad.*

"It's about your adoption."

Rachel's heart knocked against her rib cage. One spaghetti strap slid off her shoulder as a merciful breeze billowed her dress. Her mind raced, lifting all the stones she'd turned countless times throughout the years: the private investigator her father hired when she was sixteen; the story of how she'd been left on the front porch of the family center; the only remnant of her abandoner, a pale square of cotton fabric no bigger than a large scarf—still Rachel's most beloved possession.

Rachel's pitch rose. "Are you sure you have the right person?"

"Actually, no," said Mari. "We're not sure at all. That's what we're hoping to find out."

"Who's *we?*"

"It's—there's so much to explain. Why don't I give you my contact information? You might be more comfortable reaching out to me directly when it's convenient for you."

Rachel failed to see how any outcome of this conversation could be comfortable or convenient. Her living room window was lit with her friends' silhouettes, market lights strung from her potted palm, the muted bass from a Mariah Carey song emanating from the speakers. She'd had lavish birthday celebrations every year of her life—to overcompensate, it seemed now, for the fact that she'd never been entirely certain of her actual date of birth—and suddenly it was as though the woman on the other end of the phone had called her out on this lie, exposing the pretense of her party right in the middle of the celebration.

"Can't you just tell me over the phone?" Rachel asked.

Mari paused for a long beat. "I think it's better if I speak with you about this in person."

Rachel shut her eyes, impatient, confused. Up the block, horns clamored as cars nudged each other along York Avenue.

"Okay," she conceded. "Tomorrow's fine. Meet me at the farmers' market in Union Square." She was going there anyway.

Mari agreed on the time, gave Rachel her contact information, and they hung up.

Rachel sat down on the front steps of her apartment building and let her heart rate slow.

It was summer, she thought suddenly, *but the leaves started changing early.*

She hadn't thought of this in years. It was the beginning of a story her mother had told her every night of her childhood, recited like a fairy tale, describing in detail the day Rachel had been found: a little miracle sent straight from God, as the story went, with her birth parents depicted as angels—vanished but omnipresent, ever loving. Even now the idea of her biological parents held a mysterious, supernatural quality.

She wrapped her arms around her torso, fighting the instinct she never fully allowed herself to feel. There, in a dark place she kept tucked away, was an unspoken truth: the notion that she'd arrived at her life unnaturally. It wasn't unworthiness—she knew she'd been "chosen"; this had been drilled into her to no end. It was the exhausting obligation to feel grateful for this, and the suffocating expectation to be content occupying only the smallest region of who she was—a domain that had been carefully illuminated, plotted out, and defined for her. She lived within the parameters of the life she'd been given, but she knew there was a broader landscape beyond them, vast parts of her history that were unexplored. She'd been restricted, sequestered, cooped up inside herself for as long as she could remember. It kept her from growing.

What else was there, inside of her, and why did it feel so forbidden? The phone call sparked her latent desire to know the truth.

Beside her on the stoop, Rachel felt the sudden scorn of a familiar presence, the ghost of the biological daughter her parents never had: tall and blond, with some horticultural name like Dahlia or Iris. A girl to whom Rachel played a distant second fiddle, who fit in perfectly where Rachel didn't and never failed to remind her of it. A girl who would have been more than satisfied with a life like Rachel's.

She stood up and brushed off her dress, ignoring the blond ghost. Rachel turned toward the celebration brimming on the other side of her apartment window and took a step, but the questions for Dr. Marisol Rey had already begun crowding her mind, piling up like rocks along an endless shore.

CHAPTER 3

Matías drifted off in Esme's lap on the narrow bench in the police station hallway. She swept a lock of damp hair across his forehead.

"Next," an officer barked from behind the pass-through window.

Esme roused her grandson and hurried to the counter.

"Good day, officer." She produced the wedding photo she'd taken from the broken frame in Lorena's living room. Her hand was shaking slightly. "This is my daughter and son-in-law. They were arrested late last night. I'm trying to find out where they're being held."

The officer glanced at the photo. "Name?"

"María-Lorena Arias de Ledesma." Esme pointed to her daughter's face in the photo, the tip of her fingernail on Lorena's bridal veil. "And her husband, José Ledesma. My son-in-law."

The officer peered at her. "*Your* name, señora."

"Oh." Esme hesitated. She looked down at Matías, who rubbed his eyes. She shouldn't be here. It was all wrong. "Esmeralda Arias," she said, presenting her identification card.

The man jotted down her name. Maybe the junta would return to her house tonight and kidnap her too. Esme draped a protective arm around Matías's shoulder as the officer ran his eyes over a page in an open binder.

"Ledesma," he said. "They're not here." He slid the binder to the side, handed back the ID card, and looked past her. "Next?"

A man too young to be leaning on a cane rose from the bench and approached the window.

"Wait," said Esme. "Please. I just need to know where they are. They were taken last night from their home. This is my daughter's boy—he's only two. Can you help me?"

The man's forehead lifted. "Write down their names," he said, irritated.

Trembling, she did as she was told. "Will you tell me where they are?"

"I've already told you what I know. They're not here."

"Where could they be, then?"

The cop shook his head. "I have no other knowledge as to the whereabouts of your family. I'm not sure why you'd think I'd be withholding that information."

Esme's mouth went dry. "No, not withholding, señor. Of course not. It's just that it was the authorities—"

"You're certain they were detained by officers in uniform?"

Esme nodded. "Military police." She swallowed. "At least some of them. Well, one of them, at least."

The man raised an eyebrow. "What was the officer's name?"

Esme's voice rose in pitch. "I don't know."

"Do you have his identification number?"

Her chest tightened. "No."

"And you're telling me this happened in the middle of the night?"

"Yes, that's right."

"Are you sure this is a police matter? Perhaps your daughter and son-in-law had other involvements." He peeked over the counter at Matías. "It doesn't seem responsible to me—especially with a young child—but I can't speak to the choices of others these days, now, can I?"

Esme's grip on her purse straps tightened. "They were *taken*," she said, trying desperately to maintain her poise. Lorena and José had been wrongfully arrested, which meant that they would be accounted for, surely, in a jail somewhere. There were missing person flyers throughout the city, stories of people who had disappeared without a trace. Esme pushed them from her mind. It was the only way to ward off the terror expanding in her chest.

"Were there any other witnesses to this supposed arrest?" the officer asked.

Esme looked down at Matías, as if he could help. The commotion in the night was loud. Could a neighbor have overheard? There was a family next door, to the right of Lorena's house. She'd seen them in church with their teenage daughter. But they gave disapproving looks when Lorena served dinner on the patio, especially when Claudio was there. *Damn you, Claudio Valdez.* Lorena was galvanized by the man; he wore his insurgency like a strong cologne. For all Esme knew, the neighbors had been the ones who reported José and Lorena to the authorities just for fraternizing with the likes of Claudio. Even if they'd heard the arrest, she knew the neighbors wouldn't admit to it. She couldn't blame them. It was far too risky.

"I was there myself," said Esme, her voice growing desperate. "I witnessed it with my own eyes."

The officer seemed energized now. "And yet you seem to have no useful information as to the parties involved. What were the charges?"

"I don't know," said Esme. She recalled the green Ford Falcon she'd seen drive off from Lorena's house, its license plate covered. She never should have come here.

"Innocent people are not typically arrested," the officer countered.

"They haven't—" Esme's breath quickened. "They're good people, señor. This is just a mistake. If you could just tell me where they *are*—"

"Please be conscious of your tone and of what you are suggesting"—he glanced down at his notepad—"señora Esmeralda Arias," he warned. "I've told you that your daughter and son-in-law are not here. They are not in custody with us. You are free to check with the other local stations, but for now you must please be on your way."

Esme took a steadying breath. *God, help me.* If she lost her wits now, it would only take the slightest flick of a pen for her name to end up on the wrong list.

Matías picked at a piece of chipping paint from the concrete wall beneath the window. Esme brushed his little hand away. The man with the cane cleared his throat and shuffled closer to the window.

"Thank you for your help," Esme hissed, turning away with her chin in the air.

———— · ✵ · ————

There were two other police stations within walking distance, but neither had a record of the arrest either. Again, Esme was asked to provide her name and address; again, she managed to uphold her manners. Before long, Matías was exhausted and crying for his mother. Esme carried him back to his pillaged home, fed him lunch, and put him down for a nap.

Once Matías was asleep, Esme paced the house, wringing her hands. Going to the police stations had made her feel like a criminal. She was more afraid than ever. She recalled the days when Lorena was a toddler, when Gustavo was still working and Esme had taken care of her friends' children, her home filled with the sounds of little ones. Lorena had been a leader even then, her clear voice rising above the other children's. Esme never would have admitted it to Gustavo, let alone Lorena, but she was relieved when the military took over. She had been as tired as everyone else of the civil unrest and guerrilla attacks. Someone had to take control. But it was never supposed to be like this.

Esme lifted the tapestry from the living room floor now, a sob rising in her throat. She choked it back down. She couldn't let this overcome her. She had to clean up and go back out quickly. She had to be smart and find out where they'd taken Lorena. There was no time to waste. Matías needed his mother.

———— · ✵ · ————

When he awoke, Esme took him to the bus stop, and they rode to three more police stations. Every officer she spoke to had no record of the arrest, but Esme was made to write her name and address in a register regardless. Matías squirmed and whimpered on the bus ride home. Esme kissed the top of his head, breathing in the lingering scent of Lorena. The lump in her throat hardened. She wanted to throw her head back and scream, pound her fists into the seatback, but a tall officer presided over the silent passengers. Matías settled to sleep in Esme's lap just as the bus door screeched open at Alvarez Thomas Street.

Evening fell. The cat mewed in the kitchen, eager to be fed. Esme gave Matías a bath, diapered him for the night, and sang him to sleep.

"Mamá," he said, just before his eyes finally closed. Esme's own eyes welled with tears.

When all was quiet, she sat alone on the bed Lorena shared with José.

Perhaps this was Gustavo's fault. Esme recalled her beautiful, bold adolescent daughter when she was first brimming with her father's ideals, back when their potency was still brewing, before Gustavo passed away and acrimony came to a boil within Lorena. Back when Lorena was just an idealistic kid—that's what they all started out as, these guerrillas and revolutionaries—when Lorena had first met José and the young Claudio Valdez. Claudio was every bit Lorena's equal in his intellect, his outspokenness, his radicalism and passion for social justice. Esme had done all she could to steer Lorena toward José, a boy who didn't foolishly take up fights, a boy who calmed and grounded Lorena the way Esme had grounded Gustavo.

Esme considered this now. Lorena had looked so unhappy at dinner. José was quick to answer on her behalf. *We're not involved.* She couldn't imagine José doing anything to risk bringing the junta into their home, but perhaps Esme had missed signs. Perhaps Lorena knew they were being targeted and Esme had missed her daughter's cry for help.

Her tears spilled over now. She longed for a friend—but who could she call at this hour? What friend would risk having their name added to a list just to console her? No one in their right mind would believe that Lorena wasn't to blame for her own arrest. Subversion was a contagion these days. All of Gustavo's friends who could have helped were unreachable now, underground or in exile. Esme collapsed to her knees by the bedside, the tile floor hard and cold against her shins. She covered her face with her hands and prayed through her sobs.

"Please, God," she wept aloud. "Protect Lorena tonight, wherever she is. Keep her calm. Keep her safe. Gustavo, my love, if you can hear me, your daughter needs you now. Please watch over her. Please help bring her back to me."

"'Buela," a small voice called from behind her.

Matías, who had escaped from his crib, stood in the bedroom doorway.

"Oh, sweet boy." Esme wiped the tears from her eyes and picked him up. "I'm sorry. You startled me."

"Mamá," he said.

"They'll be home soon, little one. They'll be home in no time." She carried him back to bed.

———— · ❖ · ————

Esme stayed at Lorena's house in case Lorena or José returned, and because it was familiar to Matías. On the second day, she went to four more police stations, none of which had arrest records for anyone named Ledesma. Matías developed a cough from being dragged around the city. They needed groceries. The living room floor was still littered with pillow feathers. Esme had to stay strong, vigilant, prepared.

Three days passed. On Sunday, Esme took Matías to church, where Lorena's neighbors eyed them warily. After the services, Esme approached the priest she'd known for years, a man of whom she never asked anything other than forgiveness at confession.

"Padre," she said. "I was wondering if I might ask for your guidance. It's a personal matter."

They sat in an empty pew as Esme explained, through sheepish tears, about the arrest and the fact that Lorena had not turned up in any of the local jails.

The priest took her hand and bowed his head. He was silent for a long time.

"I'm sorry you're facing this, my child," he said finally.

Esme dabbed her nose with an embroidered handkerchief. "Perhaps you might be willing to help me with a letter to the authorities." She dried her eyes. "My Lorena was baptized in this parish, you know. Perhaps if it came from the Church . . . "

The priest lifted his eyes, though not his head. "I remember your daughter."

Esme leaned in as the priest's brow furrowed.

"I haven't seen her at mass in years," he said.

Esme removed her hand from his and blew her nose.

"We don't always understand the Lord's intention for us," he went on, "but our heavenly Father always has a greater plan. Many of us have been pushed to the edge of our faith in these difficult times, but we must always trust in the Will of God, and in the leaders of our country."

Esme recoiled. "My daughter is a good woman, Father."

The priest closed his eyes patiently for a moment, as though Esme was missing the point.

"She was taken from her home." Esme's voice rose to a loud whisper. "Taken away from her son. And no one will give me any *answers*."

The priest glanced around with alarm as though Esme had cried out in blasphemy. Her handkerchief was damp with tears and mucus now. Matías shifted restlessly in the pew.

"I don't have answers," said the priest softly. "But I will pray for you."

Esme glanced up at the altar, at Christ on the crucifix with his punctured ribs, Pontius Pilate's *INRI* inscription. What kind of test of faith was this? She knew God. This was not God's plan for Lorena. Esme took Matías's hand and filled the church with the echo of her retreating footsteps as they walked away.

The deacon, a stout man with whom Esme always exchanged congenialities, was unlocking the offertory box near the entrance.

"Señora," he whispered. "If your children really were arrested, they have to be brought forth for charges. Go to the Ministry and ask where they are."

Esme gave him a watery smile, his brave kindness flooding her with warmth.

The next day, Esme knocked on the neighbor's door. The teenage girl answered. She looked younger than Esme anticipated, with a smattering of freckles across the bridge of her nose.

"Would you like to babysit?" Esme inquired politely. "Earn a little extra money? Matías is no trouble at all. Just a few hours while I run some errands."

"Where are his parents?" asked the girl. She was smarter than Esme had hoped.

"Not home right now," Esme said with a quick smile, reaching for her purse. She had a small savings from Gustavo's monthly pension checks. "How's twelve hundred pesos?"

———— · ❖ · ————

Once the freckled neighbor girl was comfortably situated in the house with Matías, Esme went straight to the Ministry of the Interior. Armed officers monitored the crowded lines inside the building. Esme held her head high and spoke to no one, eavesdropping on the muted whispers of others waiting in line. She was not the only one with missing loved ones.

By noon, the line had scarcely advanced.

"Ministry is closing for lunch," said one of the guards, ushering them out of the building and locking the doors. "Come back at two if you still require assistance."

Esme felt short of breath. As she walked past the cathedral to the Plaza de Mayo, a sturdy woman about her age approached and tapped her on the arm.

"Excuse me, señora," the woman said in a hushed voice. "I noticed you coming out of the ministry. Did you have a daughter who went to the national school? Pretty girl, with long dark hair—she was in the student government?"

Esme stared at the unfamiliar woman, overcome with hope. "Yes!" she breathed. "My daughter, Lorena."

"I thought I recognized you. I remember when your husband passed—such a tragic loss. My condolences."

"Did you know Lorena? Do you know where she is now?"

She placed both hands on Esme's forearm as if to settle her. "No, I don't. My name is Alba Ramos. I'm looking for my son, Ernesto. He was a friend of Lorena's once, I believe. They were in the student union together."

Esme thought she recalled the name, but she couldn't be certain. Lorena was social. She had so many friends at school.

The woman's eyes were sad but sincere. "My Ernesto was arrested at the bus stop near the Obelisco Norte on November twelfth." She quickly showed Esme a wallet-sized photo of a young man Esme didn't recognize. "We haven't heard a word since."

Esme apologized reflexively, but Alba seemed to seek no pity.

"Has Lorena gone missing?" asked Alba.

Esme let out a wavering sigh. "They took her in the middle of the night," she blurted. "Along with my son-in-law, José. Lorena's son is only two years old. I'm watching him now until they—"

"Shh," Alba hushed. "Let's keep walking. If we stand around talking like this, they'll arrest us for public gathering."

Esme's muscles tensed. Walking with Alba seemed risky. While it was a relief to talk aloud to someone about Lorena, Esme didn't want to be aligned with this woman and her plight. Even if Alba's son was as innocent as Lorena, which Esme wasn't certain he was, he'd been missing for over a month. Esme, on the other hand, would find Lorena any day now.

"My husband and I filed a writ of habeas corpus, but we're still waiting to hear back," Alba went on. "The police won't tell us a thing, of course. But if you file a writ for a judge to review, the judge can make demands of the authorities to produce the person who was arrested."

"How did you file the writ?" asked Esme. "That's what I came here to do. I need to know where they're keeping Lorena and José. They have to tell me that, don't they?"

"You'll need a lawyer to help you file it," said Alba, digging in her purse. "There's no sense in waiting around at the Ministry until you have one. Here." She handed Esme a business card. "This is the one we're using. His name is Marcos Suarez. He's filed writs for the families of other missing people. He knows what to do."

"Thank you very much."

"Good luck to you, señora. God bless you," said Alba, though she looked crestfallen. "May God protect your daughter and son-in-law. I hope you find them soon."

———— · ✦ · ————

By the time a full week had passed, Esme was crawling in her skin. She put up a small Christmas tree at Lorena's house and stared at it for a long time. She wrapped a few gifts for Matías—a Zorro doll, a plush bear—and stashed them in Lorena's bedroom closet. Seeing her daughter's clothes hanging there filled her with grief, then rage. It was torture: the uncertainty, the not knowing, the waiting up each night.

The lawyer, Suarez, didn't return her calls. She left messages with his secretary and those of two other attorneys—the ones with the biggest ads in the phone book—every morning. Esme constantly felt torn between the desire to go out and look for Lorena and the fear that she wouldn't be home if Lorena returned.

Eleven days after the arrest, government offices began shutting down for the holiday, and Esme had established a daily routine of calling the attorney's office and leaving messages. She called the babysitter, who could only stay for an hour, and returned to the Ministry of the Interior on its last day open. She had to appease the agonizing sense of impotence that arose from doing nothing else. Perhaps someone there could refer her to a lawyer who would at least return her calls.

At the Ministry, she saw Alba again. An officer was monitoring the line to keep order, so Esme just smiled at Alba and said nothing. Minutes after their eyes met, Alba began to cough loudly.

"Such a cold!" complained Alba once she'd gained composure. She rummaged through her purse, sniffling now. "You don't happen to have a tissue, do you?" she asked Esme. "Or a cough drop?"

Esme unzipped her pocketbook to check as Alba moved closer to her. In an instant, Alba reached over and pushed a small piece of paper into Esme's purse.

"Oh, here, look," said Alba, tugging a cloth from her own purse and dabbing her nose. "I've found one. Never mind. Thank you anyway."

Both women glanced at the stone-faced officer without making eye contact. When the ministry finally shut down before the full line had advanced, Esme rushed home and dismissed the babysitter. She opened the folded-up paper Alba had given her. It listed the name and address of a prominent café. *Please come for tea at four o'clock on the day after Christmas. There are other mothers.*

Esme folded the note back up hastily and stashed it in a drawer in Lorena's kitchen, repelled by its very presence. What was Alba thinking? Esme wanted no part of other women's troubles. She and Alba had nothing in common other than the fact that they were mothers whose children had gone missing. It was hardly enough of an alliance to put herself—or Matías—in danger. What would the junta do with a group of mothers conspiring to track down their arrested children when every bus-stop advertisement and television commercial explicitly prohibited organizing under penalty of law?

For five days, Esme's thoughts circled through the possibilities of Alba's note. *Other mothers.* It would likely only mean meeting a few women at a café, after all. It wasn't as though they were forming an underground militia. But perhaps Alba's son, Ernesto, had been a guerrilla or a criminal. Esme didn't want to know. The less she knew, the safer she would be. *Just meeting a friend for tea.* That's what she could say if the junta questioned her on the street. If the mothers talked quietly, perhaps no one would even notice them. She practiced it in the mirror above Lorena's dresser, pretending to be bored. *Just meeting a friend for tea.*

———— · ❖ · ————

Christmas marked the sixteenth day without Lorena. Esme helped Matías unwrap the gifts. He sat on the floor and knocked Zorro's head against a block, looking up at her with eyes that were too wise for his age.

"Mamá," he said.

Esme wanted to scream. Instead, she picked up the discarded wrapping paper, cut up a piece of fruit for Matías, and wiped down the kitchen table. She sat down and said her rosary, dabbing at her tears with a threadbare pocket square. She glanced at the drawer that contained Alba's note.

All the government ministries would be closed until January. None of the lawyers' offices had responded to her calls. If there was even the slightest chance that any of the other mothers knew how to access information that could be useful—where Lorena was being kept, under what conditions, whether, God forbid, she was still alive—Esme had to find out. She needed answers.

———— · ◈ · ————

On the day after Christmas, Esme dug the note from the drawer and called the babysitter again.

"I won't be very long," she told the girl.

As Esme crossed Avenida del Libertador, wind lifted bits of trash from the street around her. The plaza opened up to the yellow sky of late afternoon, where feathery palms rustled against stucco bell towers and spired cupolas.

"Where are you headed?" one of the officers asked Esme.

"Just there." She motioned toward the bistro at the edge of the plaza. "I'm meeting a friend for tea."

They checked her identification routinely, and she entered the café. Alba was sitting at a far table with one other woman Esme didn't recognize, who wore tinted glasses and a pretty floral blouse.

"This is Reina," Alba said casually, as though Esme were an old friend.

"Hello," said Esme, taking the third seat at the table. Alba's small talk with the waiter seemed exaggerated, overly polite. Up close, Reina looked to have been recently crying. Esme resisted the urge to leave.

"There are several of us," Alba whispered to Esme once the server was gone. "But I've kept this to a small affair, to give you a quick update. Reina's son, Paulo, was taken by the junta three months ago," Alba poured tea into Esme's cup and went on before Esme could ask questions or offer condolences. "Marcos Suarez helped her file a writ of habeas corpus."

Reina dropped her head. "It was rejected," she sniffed.

"Why?" gasped Esme.

Alba glared at her, a warning to keep her voice down, and coaxed Reina subtly toward composure, glancing around.

"The judge who reviewed Reina's filing wasn't willing to make demands of the junta," Alba's voice was eerily pleasant as she moved sugar cubes toward Esme's tea with a tiny silver spoon. "Sugar?"

Esme nodded dumbly. A tear streamed from below Reina's glasses, but she caught it swiftly with the corner of her scarf and flashed a weak smile at the passing busboy.

"No judge in their right mind is going to ask this military to produce missing people," said Reina. "It would put their family at risk."

Alba's expression remained stiffly cheerful as she lifted her teacup.

"But there are so many judges," Esme whispered. "You can try again. Surely there has to be a braver judge. We need to know where they're keeping our children."

Reina and Alba exchanged a doubtful look.

"Reina hasn't heard from Suarez in weeks," Alba said through her teeth.

"I'm not surprised," said Esme, her tone more accusatory than she'd intended. "I haven't heard from him either. He doesn't return calls. It's unprofessional."

"You don't understand," said Alba. "Suarez was arrested by the junta two weeks ago."

"The lawyer?" Esme's skin warmed. The junta targeted guerrillas, young radicals, Montoneros, members of the Ejército Revolucionario del Pueblo—the ERP—but the prospect of a lawyer being kidnapped intensified her terror. She tried desperately to mimic Alba, to steady her shaking hand to sip her tea.

Alba nodded slowly. "He's missing."

Reina dabbed at the corner of one eye beneath her glasses, then quietly described the incident as it had been relayed to her. It happened outside the ministry, with Suarez being forcefully ushered into the back of a Ford Falcon by the junta in broad daylight.

Esme's chest constricted. They might very well take her, too, especially if she kept this up with Alba. What would happen to Matías then?

"So, I can't file the writ." Esme whispered the words as she realized them.

"I'm sorry to tell you this," said Reina. "But no lawyer is going to help you. It's too risky. And even if they did, there wouldn't be much hope."

Esme hated Reina for saying what she knew was true.

"I can pay." Esme's voice sounded desperate to her own ears. "I have a little money saved up."

"Pshh." Reina shook her head. "How much do you think you would have to pay someone to take the risk of being kidnapped?"

"Quiet," said Alba. They sat in silence as the server refilled the water glasses.

"You can certainly try to find a lawyer to file, Esme," Alba said softly once the waiter had gone. "And maybe another judge would handle it differently. We each have to do what we think is best."

"No lawyer is going to help you," Reina repeated flatly.

"There's another woman I met," said Alba. "Her brother went missing. She used to work in a legal office, and she has a typewriter. She's going to type up a writ and try to file it on her own without help from a lawyer. Maybe she can help you too."

Esme glanced through the plate glass window at the junta on the street. These women were grasping at straws, but Esme didn't have a better option. Perhaps she wasn't so different from Alba after all.

"There must be a brave judge."

Reina let out a dubious sigh, trilling her lips.

Esme dropped her gaze to the napkin in her lap. "I asked my priest for help." When she looked up, Alba and Reina had locked eyes.

Alba leaned in. "I know a mother who was working with a group of nuns in a parish in the suburbs. The nuns were going to help petition on her behalf."

Esme lifted a hand to her mouth, then quickly dropped it. "And?"

"A group of their clergy members got into a car accident last month, including two of the nuns," said Alba. "They didn't survive."

Esme drew in a small breath.

"No one from the church is helping us either," said Reina. "It's far too risky."

"Well, we can't just do *nothing*," said Esme.

The server arrived to clear the table and all three women smiled politely. Alba perked up falsely, gestured for the bill.

"You were telling us about your holiday, Esme," said Alba loudly.

Outside, the junta loomed, their shadows darkening the tablecloth.

CHAPTER 4

A man shoved Lorena to the floor, where the raw wood drove splinters through her palms and bare thighs. Her hands were cuffed behind her. She moved her fingertips along the ground to orient herself. She was sitting on a plywood panel, based on the way it tilted and warped under her weight. They'd torn off her clothes and dressed her in something short and stiff, jute or burlap, the same material as the head covering she still wore. Her underpants, thankfully, remained on.

José moaned from somewhere nearby, and Lorena could sense other people moving around her. It was dark and humid. The sharp, rancid smell of vomit and bleach hung in the still air. An abrupt tug at her head covering restored her full vision. Suddenly José's naked body was upright before her, tied to a table as though on display. Rope bound his wrists and ankles tightly, cutting into his skin.

She lunged forward toward her husband, but when she thrust her body, she discovered that her cuffs were attached to the floor behind her. She pulled anyway, so hard that the metal dug into her wrists, scraping through her flesh.

Where the hell was she? The car ride hadn't been long enough to take them outside the city. She'd counted three flights of stairs when they brought her up here to this dank, open floor, lit only by moon-light that bled through a single barred window. It had to be three or four in the morning by now. Her eyes darted around the room, which was scattered with thin mattresses, metal beds, and, most dis-tressingly, dozens of other people. They were all blindfolded—some crouched, others lying down—and filthy, but alive. The junta wanted her to see this.

Awareness arrived then: This place had been here since the coup began, maybe longer. The possibility had been polluting the air around her for months, leaving a residue on her skin. This was the source of her inexplicable rage, the horror she'd conceived that only Claudio had recognized or acted against, the terror that subdued Esme and José into complacency. This was what everyone in Buenos Aires pretended didn't—*couldn't*—exist.

Yet here she was.

José's head lolled to one side. What had they done to him? She no-ticed a small box at the foot of the table: an electric transformer of some kind with wires springing out like curly hair. A small red bulb was lit up next to a switch and numbers on a voltage dial. To the right of the table, the man who had shoved her to the floor now held a long wand with a wire tail that led to the box. A second man, an officer, stepped past Lorena and approached him.

Lorena started to scream, but thick fingers pushed a wadded rag into her mouth, salty and dry, triggering her gag reflex. A face eclipsed her vision.

"Claudio Valdez," the officer said.

It was the man with lentil-colored eyes, the one who'd let her leave Matías with Esme.

"I'm taking that thing out of your mouth and we're going to have a little chat, *claro*?" he said. "And you're going to do all the talking. Don't stop until you've told me everything you know about Claudio Valdez."

He moved to adjust the dial, cranking the voltage.

Lorena shook her head in despair, but her tormentor took it as a re-fusal. He nodded to the other officer, who touched the bronze tip of the wand to José's bottom lip. José's face tightened, the veins and tendons in his neck jutting out like cords, and his body stiffened, petrified for the span of several seconds. Lorena's eyes blurred with tears. She grunted deeply through the rag, biting down, her saliva soaking through.

Lentil Eyes turned the dial down and abandoned the box to get close to her face again. Before he could fully approach, an officer whipped a blindfold around her head, jerking it back. He tied it so tightly that it creased, exposing a sliver of view beneath her left eye.

"I said, 'Claudio Valdez,'" Lentil Eyes repeated, calmly. "When was the last time you saw him?"

Lorena's mind flew back through time to her secretive encounters with Claudio, then immediately pushed every image of him from her thoughts, desperate to erase the evidence from her own memory.

"Who else worked on the paper?" asked Lentil Eyes. "Who went to the rabbit house, Lorena Ledesma? Who did you see there?"

Lorena resisted the futile impulse to sob. The "rabbit house" was an underground printing press run by the Montoneros out of a residential home in La Plata. The owners bred rabbits as a front, and the animals were everywhere, or so she'd heard from Claudio—she'd never been inside. If this officer knew it existed, the junta must have already shut it down. But it sounded like they didn't have Claudio. She tilted her head back and, through the slice of opening in her blindfold, saw the torturer with the prod move closer to José, touching its tip to José's earlobe. His body tensed; he screamed loudly.

She heard Lentil Eyes light a cigarette, then smelled its smoke. "You can tell me now or we can keep going like this all night." He pulled the rag from Lorena's mouth. "Who else was there?"

Her words came in quick gasps, before the electric prod could jolt back to life.

"I'll tell you anything you want to know. Please. Just leave him alone." She would lie. She was capable of that. She just needed to make them stop torturing José.

"Don't hurt her," José groaned, barely lucid. Lorena flushed with shame. What had she done to her sweet husband? *Come after me instead, you bastard*, she thought. *Put me on that table. I'm the guilty one.* But she kept her lips tight.

Lentil Eyes waited in mock anticipation. This was her punishment. God was punishing her for what she'd done. In response to her silence, the torturer moved the *picana* to José's ribcage without hesitation. José jolted, tensed, then screamed again. His voice was raw. When the officer dropped the prod to José's inner thigh, Lorena shrieked until her own vocal cords strained.

"Stop! *Stop!*"

Lentil Eyes shoved the rag back in her mouth. The crackling of electricity ceased. José went silent. The whole room was silent. How could so many people not make a single sound?

A hand yanked her blindfold down. José's body hung limp in full before her on the table. She prayed he was merely unconscious. The terrible face engulfed her view again.

"Start talking," said Lentil Eyes. "Claudio Valdez. Everything you know. Last chance, or I'll stop asking nicely."

Lorena met Claudio at a student rally in June of 1969. She was nineteen, and the whole world seemed on the cusp of an awakening. Protests were taking place throughout the country—the Cordobazo and Rosariazo had been the biggest uprisings Lorena had ever seen—and artists, intellectuals, academics, and even middle-class professionals were coming together to form the "new left." The students' movement merged with general strikes of autoworkers. Grown men like her father mobilized alongside Lorena and her classmates. They took to the streets in their coveralls to march against a government that had abandoned them, a ruling class that exploited them for a profit. Lorena was exhilarated. She wanted nothing more than to be a part of it.

"Take the sturdy one," Gustavo had said from the doorway of the garage as Lorena rummaged through his plywood barricades and rolled-up fabric banners punctured with wind vents. Her father pointed at the thicker of two folding wooden A-frames, and when Lorena picked it up, she knew she was taking up her father's fight, carrying a weight he could no longer bear.

Gustavo was barely fifty then, but his years of struggle were deep lines drawn into his face. Argentina's "revolution" a few years prior was supposed to be a new beginning for the workers who had revered Juan Perón—*Perónism without Perón*, they promised—but Gustavo had been wary, and his hesitation proved right. General Juan Carlos Onganía pandered to the labor unions, lip service to keep their resistance in check. Then he'd raised the retirement age, denied the right to strike, supported corporations, and implemented laws repressing anyone who didn't participate in his initiatives.

The people weren't standing for it any longer.

When Lorena kissed her father goodbye that day, his skin was flushed, his brow damp.

His heart is stressed, Esme fretted, but her mother always worried too much.

Lorena headed toward the park with the heavy A-frame under her arm, her bulky winter coat and woolen mittens protecting her from its splintering slats. In the cold air of the street, distant chants from the rally swelled, their power culminating. Her steps gained momentum as she burrowed her chin into the chunky scarf Esme had knitted for her.

At the edge of the park, José waited for Lorena in a collared shirt and wool sweater. They'd only been dating a few months after meeting in a sociology class. José was gentle, refined, and clearly smitten. He took the makeshift barricade from her arms and carried it through the crowd to the center of the park, where a group of classmates gathered. There, Ernesto Ramos, whom she'd known for years, stood talking to another student, scribbling in his flimsy notebook, presumably conducting an interview for the university publication he ran. Lorena watched as the interviewee took a pull from his cigarette and responded thoughtfully to Ernesto's questions. She hadn't seen him before. He was handsome with thick curls, and when he glanced over at her and began to approach, Lorena's heart lifted.

"*Che*," José said, reaching out a hand. "Claudio."

Claudio clapped José's shoulder in a friendly way. There was a fluidity to his body, a constant movement, like dancing. His attention moved swiftly past Lorena and to the A-frame under José's arm.

"That's brilliant. Put it right over there at the curb. The cops are already getting annoyed with us." His laughter hitched when Lorena caught his eye.

"This is Lore, my girlfriend," said José, using the term for the first time aloud. "She's the one who brought it."

Claudio opened his mouth, then closed it again. His dance stopped for a moment.

"Thanks for the help," Claudio said to her.

Lorena felt a surge of heat. She wanted to say more, to do more, but Ernesto joined them then and wolf-whistled at her playfully, instantly demoting her from fellow revolutionary to just another pretty girlfriend.

"*Boludo.*" She narrowed her eyes at Ernesto.

Claudio's laugh was infectious music.

"Come on," said José, pulling Lorena toward a nearby tipa tree and away from Claudio.

The rally was a memorial for a fifteen-year-old student killed by military police during the recent protests. Claudio took center stage, speaking boldly and leading the rallying cries.

¡Viva la patria! Claudio yelled, and the crowd responded in kind. *This is our moment of national liberation! We must take action!*

José leaned back against the tree trunk and opened his stance. Lorena nestled into the safety of his body, fitting nicely against his lean frame. From the space between his legs, she chanted back heartily. *¡Viva la patria!* When her emotion flared high, José put his arms around her waist carefully, as if she was made of glass. She settled into his touch.

Claudio preached, offering quotes from Che Guevara and other revolutionaries between waves of roaring cheers from the students. Officers lined the perimeter of the park. Claudio held up a photo of the boy who'd been killed.

Luis Norberto Blanco gave his life for our struggle, Claudio cried, *but it's better to die standing than to live life on our knees!* The students' voices exploded in response to his words. When Claudio raised his arms and shouted, the hem of his jacket lifted, revealing a slice of bare skin above his waistband that triggered an unexpected hunger in Lorena, despite José's hands on her own stomach. Claudio was a force. Chasing him would be like grasping a comet's blazing tail—equal parts futile and destructive—but Lorena wanted to nonetheless. He was the type of person who would change the world.

At the fringes of the crowd, a few men too old to be students whispered to one another. They were eyeing Claudio, the proficient young orator, evaluating his magnetism.

How often Lorena looked back on that moment, that fork in the road.

Within one short year of that day, the recruiters had claimed Claudio as a registered Montonero and the group was credited with kidnapping former president Aramburu, who'd led the coup against Perón. Soon after, Gustavo's heart expended its last beat. Lorena no longer searched the landscape of her future for possibility, but for the safe and comforting path provided by José—one which led her, with Esme's encouragement, to a sweet and uncomplicated life of relative safety and contentment. She suppressed thoughts about the chances she didn't take, adventures she'd bartered in exchange for the life she had. The past was behind her.

But then, in a single afternoon, she'd risked everything and everyone she loved. For one breath of ecstasy, Lorena had paid the highest price.

———— · ❖ · ————

It smelled of rain and wet cement. The roof leaked; the thin mattress absorbed the falling drops. Her ill-fitting clothes chafed her bare skin. It was sweltering hot during the day and damp at night. She remained blindfolded, barefoot, and, most of the time, cuffed to a bed frame.

She sensed the presence of the other prisoners, but they weren't permitted to talk. Occasionally they exchanged whispered grievances and small shows of solidarity. Sometimes, usually at night, the junta burst upstairs, rounded up a group of prisoners, and transferred them to other places. Another squad would bring in a new group, their boots firing like cannons. These transfer officers were from somewhere else, it seemed—unlike Lentil Eyes, a constant at the prison. He supervised trips to the basement, where Lorena and the others were made to sit on a cement bench just outside of the *parrilla*, the electric shock torture room. Lorena and José went in together and were asked repetitive questions to which neither had answers—*Who worked at the rabbit house? Where are the weapons? How many people were there? Names! Now! Everything you know!*—then dragged back upstairs, ulcerated, burning, inconceivably thirsty.

They were harder on José. When she wrenched her neck to peek under the slit in her blindfold, she saw him sitting on his bed in a pair of shorts she'd never seen before. He still wore one of his bedroom slippers from home. His head was sloppily shaved, pocked with fleabites. He rested it against the concrete wall. There was a small open cut on the inside of his ear.

Nights kept coming, followed by mornings. An indeterminable number of days passed. Lorena was hungry. Occasionally Lentil Eyes brought day-old bread on a tray and a small tin cup of water. Once, a chunk of stale pan dulce appeared. Christmas had come and gone, Lorena realized, holding the bread in her hands like a sacred gift. Where was Matías now? Was he afraid? Again and again, she replayed the moment she'd handed him to Esme and felt the same mix of relief and incapacitating regret. Her boy. Her baby. She hated herself.

During the next transfer, a group of new prisoners arrived. Lentil Eyes cuffed a woman next to Lorena on the same bed. Lorena could feel her small frame, the height of her shoulder, the long, soft curls that brushed against Lorena's bare arms. She thought of the girls she went to school with and missed those friendships terribly. She was suddenly so desperate for connection, so drawn to the warmth this woman's body emanated, that when night fell in earnest, Lorena dared to speak.

"What's your name?" Lorena asked.

Even if the junta had allowed them to talk, the prisoners had no reason to trust each other. There was no way to know that what they shared with another person wouldn't be used against them in the parrilla.

"Flavia," the woman whispered after a long silence.

Lorena told Flavia who she was and, during the black hours of night, under shallow breath, they shared their stories. In whispers, Flavia recounted her horrific circumstance. She had been pregnant with her second child when the junta arrested her and had just recently given birth. Her baby girl, Marcela, was delivered in the prison where she'd been kept after her arrest. There was a doctor there, Flavia said, who worked for the dictatorship. A few weeks after the baby was born, the junta drove Flavia and Marcela to Flavia's mother's house, where she'd been permitted to briefly see her four-year-old daughter. She'd left baby Marcela with her mother before the junta transferred her here.

"My husband is with the Montoneros. He'll leave the country with the girls if he must, but as long as they're safe, that's all that matters," repeated Flavia. "They'll be safe with my mother and my husband until this is over."

"Over?"

"The Montoneros are reassembling in Rome," Flavia whispered. "They're planning a counteroffensive."

Lorena drew in a slow breath. Was Claudio in Italy, plotting against this junta? If the Montoneros brought down the dictatorship, Lorena and José could be released. She would hold Matías in her arms again. *Please, God.*

"Just keep your head down," Flavia warned. "And pray none of the guards take an interest in you. There was this one woman in the last prison . . . " She was quiet for a long time. "God help her."

Lorena pressed her knees together.

In the morning, Lentil Eyes dropped a tray of bread and fruit next to Flavia's bed. They'd been feeding Flavia well, Lorena noticed—even letting her rest when the others were taken to the basement. Flavia chewed the food as Lentil Eyes lit a cigarette.

"You might be interested in knowing that your friend Ernesto Ramos is dead," he said to Lorena. He kicked the empty metal tray on the ground.

Lorena hadn't heard Ernesto's name since university. She wrapped her arms around her torso.

"There's no one left at the rabbit house to protect," he said. "You might as well save yourself by giving up their names."

I've never been to the rabbit house, Lorena thought, a refrain she'd uttered countless times aloud.

She braced for him to hit her, but he just flicked his cigarette and walked away. Flavia was a despondent presence on the next bed.

The temperature of the outside air through the barred window had dropped. The season was changing.

Later that evening when the boots returned, Flavia was taken away in a transfer. Lorena never saw her again.

CHAPTER 5

Light spread through the stained-glass skylights of Café Tortoni and fell across the linen tablecloth where the three mothers sat having lunch. Under the heavy gaze of surrounding officers, Esme glanced back and forth between the other women: Reina, in a floral blouse and her tinted glasses, and Alba, whose smile masked a deep weariness. Lorena had been missing for ninety-four days.

"I've invited two new friends to join us today," said Alba. "They have some unique problems with their . . . flowers. I thought we could offer advice."

Flowers. Pups. If they were nothing more than middle-aged women socializing over tea, they could continue the work they'd been doing for the past three months—meeting up in public, sharing information, secretly keeping one another abreast of their searches even in the presence of the junta.

Esme dabbed the corners of her mouth with a napkin, slightly irritated by the prospect of more mothers, more burdens. It was hard enough to investigate the disappearances they were already working on. Nonetheless, Alba had been Esme's greatest source of hope since Lorena and

José went missing. She'd helped with the applications for habeas corpus, plunking away on the typewriter her paralegal friend had lent them, and she'd gone with Esme to the ministry to file both of the writs—one for José, too, since his parents had both passed.

Esme had fallen into a tenuous routine with Matías, each minor adjustment a reluctant concession to Lorena's absence. She rarely went to her own apartment anymore and would let her lease lapse soon. Alba and Reina were her only reprieve from a world that seemed to over-power her sanity. She needed the hope Alba provided and the plans they stitched together, however fruitless. She needed someone else who un-derstood the unforgivable thoughts that tangled inside her mind: No one could disappear without a trace. Perhaps Lorena and José were guilty of something horrendous after all. Perhaps they'd run away. Esme's doubts weren't rational; she knew Lorena would never leave Matías. But as time passed without any explanation or clue as to Lorena's whereabouts, her cognition scattered like water, seeking answers at the edges of reason.

"No, no, no," Alba reminded her each time Esme called in a tearful panic. "This is exactly what they're trying to do to us. They're trying to make us crazy. People don't just disappear, Esme. The junta have your daughter. Our government is lying to you."

"But *where*? How could *everyone* be lying? What if she ran off with Claudio?"

"No," Alba sounded desperate, speaking as much to herself as to Esme. "Don't you dare forget what you saw happen that night. You must remember the truth, Esme. Your daughter was *taken*."

It wasn't easy to muster Alba's conviction, but Esme was grateful for her advocacy. There was no denying that they were in this together and that Alba was at the helm. Alba collected photos of all the detained children and kept them in a notebook with the contact information of anyone she met who had missing family members. There was real danger in Alba's records—a ready-made arrest list for the junta, if they ever found it—but Alba was so effective at circulating information within her network that Esme had given her a copy of Lorena and José's wed-ding photo to add, just in case.

"Here she is," Alba announced now as a fourth woman approached the table. "Señoras, this is Hilde."

Hilde stood at the tablecloth's edge, petite with short chestnut hair and shimmery eyelids. She wore a copper blouse and a scarf with large purple flowers, her pearl earrings tiny drops of milk against her skin.

"So nice to meet you," said Hilde flatly. Esme had the impression that it had taken a lot for Alba to talk Hilde into coming, and a pretense of moral sophistication thickened the air when Hilde sat down next to her.

Moments later, a second woman arrived. She fiddled with the knot at her chin, unfastening her pink headscarf.

"Rosa," said Alba. "So nice of you to come. Please, join us."

Rosa took a seat and fluffed her matted hair with one hand. She gave Alba an intense look, took one of the menus the waiter offered, and glanced around skittishly.

Outside the café, a distant screech of car tires was followed by the distinct pop of gunshots firing from a few blocks away. Rosa yelped, then covered her mouth. Soldiers rumbled past—the junta bolting down the street toward the gunfire—but the commotion quickly settled.

"God help us," said Rosa, making the sign of the cross.

Hilde removed a cigarette from a silver case engraved with butterflies, lit it, then motioned vaguely toward the door, the fighting, perhaps toward the whole country or even the entire world. "You think God has anything to do with this?"

"Hush," said Alba.

Esme took note of Hilde's floral scent beneath the menthol smoke and felt a distinct fondness toward her. She got the impression Hilde had traveled in from outside of the city, but she didn't ask.

A throng of junta soldiers barged into the restaurant then, basking in the afterglow of whatever had transpired on the street, filling the restaurant with sounds of their boots and banter. Stools scooted against the floor as the soldiers sidled up to the bar, one clapping another's back. Rosa looked petrified. Esme wondered how such a timid woman would be anything but a weight for them to carry.

"I'm having quiche," said Alba. She guided the conversation quietly, in code, as the women ordered lunch. Their voices fell to whispers.

Hilde was Chilean, Esme learned, but she'd worked as a midwife
in Argentina for most of her life. Her situation was indeed unique. Her
son, a member of the Montoneros, had been captured in broad daylight six months prior, and her daughter-in-law, Julia, had been arrested
the following day. Julia was five months pregnant at the time. Hilde's
grandchild would have been born by now.

"My 'pup' is expecting too," whispered Rosa, a retired librarian whose
daughter had gone missing along with her fiancé. "Ines was four months
along when they took her. She's seven months by now."

"They have to bring the babies back to you." Reina said in a hush
after the plates had been cleared. The five women were leaning in close
now as though mired in a bout of gossip.

"They won't," said Hilde.

"They must. You're their family. What use would they have for keeping little ones in custody?"

"It's inhumane," said Alba.

Hilde leaned back, lit another cigarette. "I can't get inside the hos-
pitals, but I've been to three shelters and two orphanages so far."

"On your own?" Esme asked.

Hilde shooed away a fly and exhaled.

Alba straightened in her chair, cleared her throat, and widened her
eyes at Rosa.

"I'm not sure if you're aware, but it's Rosa's birthday next week. A
friend of ours is throwing a little party for her. I hope you'll all join us.
It's on Sunday afternoon."

Rosa raised her eyebrows.

Alba was bold. This was the first time she'd suggested a larger gathering.

"All our friends will be there," said Alba, reaching for her purse and
removing a pen. She scribbled an address on the back of three cocktail
napkins and subtly passed them beneath the table to Reina, Hilde, and
Esme. A couple at the neighboring table got up to leave, the legs of their

bistro chairs bleating against the floor. A ring of condensation bled into the paper coaster under Esme's water glass.

"I'd love to come," said Reina, her expression vacant behind her tinted glasses. She looked at Rosa, who coughed nervously.

Esme stuck the napkin in her handbag.

"Happy birthday, dear."

———— · ❖ · ————

On Sunday afternoon, Esme held a bouquet of flowers as she approached the unfamiliar apartment building. She questioned whether she should have come at all, then questioned whether she should bring a gift. Neither mattered now. It was too late. She was here, and the babysitter could only watch Matías until five o'clock.

As she turned onto the block, two members of the junta patrolled the corner. Her heart raced.

"Identification," said one of the officers.

Esme shifted the flowers in her arm and reached into her purse, producing her identification card. The officer checked it, then stared at her. Esme could see the neat tracks left in his graying hair by the teeth of a fine comb. He smelled of musky cologne, tobacco, and limes.

"This isn't your neighborhood," he said. "Where are you off to?"

"Just going to see a friend. She lives right—" Esme's words lodged in her throat as she gestured toward the building. *Out for a long walk,* she should've said. Anything but indicating Alba's meeting place. She hadn't practiced.

"Bringing flowers." The second officer backhanded the blossoms. "Is it a special occasion?"

"A birthday," Esme mumbled.

"A party?"

"No," she replied, too quickly. "Just a visit, that's all."

The officer handed her the ID card. He narrowed his eyes at her. After a long pause, he motioned for her to proceed, though it felt more like a dare than permission. Esme advanced to the entrance, but before she could press the buzzer, a woman she'd never seen before unlatched the door and hurriedly waved her inside.

"We can't take the lift," the woman whispered. "The porter will be suspicious. There are too many of us. They'll report a gathering. Come this way. Follow me."

"The junta are right outside," said Esme, trailing the woman silently up flight after flight of stairs.

When they entered the sixth-floor apartment, Esme was winded and terrified. It was far more crowded than she'd expected from the quiet hallway. In the open kitchen, a pitcher of cream, a dish of sugar cubes, and a bowl of cookies sat on a plaid tablecloth. The woman who had brought Esme upstairs poured her a cup of strong coffee and handed it to her like an admission ticket. In the living room, nearly two dozen women perched on couches, stools, and armchairs with little plates of cookies dispersed among them. Photos of young men and women were laid out on the coffee table along with papers and documents. Some women were in low conversation with one another; others were tearful, speaking quietly with handkerchiefs in hand. Tissue boxes and teacups on saucers floated from hands to surfaces and back.

Esme glanced nervously at the door. Every billboard, news station, and campaign poster in the country reminded her of her obligation to denounce subversion, to be a good Argentine citizen, to squelch the slightest uprising. She couldn't justify being here if the authorities barged in.

"Ladies," Alba said in a hushed, urgent tone. "We have some news to share with you while we have the chance."

Esme stood next to a large vase on the floor near the entryway and gazed through the stalks of decorative wheat protruding from it, surveying the room. She spotted Hilde seated on the couch, twiddling her clear manicured fingernails. One of the other mothers handed Alba a paper, which Alba held up for all to see.

"This is an underground publication found in the bedroom of one of our missing daughters. She was taken last week by the junta while leaving Parque Lezama." The woman who'd handed Alba the paper dabbed at her leaking eyes with a tissue, but she looked more determined than bereaved. "It was printed four weeks ago," Alba went on, "and it describes hidden execution sites and secret detention centers throughout the city and country."

There was collective murmuring as Alba passed the paper around. When it came to her, Esme didn't take it, but she glanced at it over the shoulder of another woman seated on the couch to see its contents: Cadena Informativa. Agencia de Noticias Clandestinas. Indeed, there were articles about alleged prisons where missing people were being held, interspersed with notes: CONTINUE TO CIRCULATE THIS INFORMATION IN WHATEVER FORM YOU CAN. TERROR IS BASED ON A LACK OF COMMUNICATION. DISTRIBUTE THE TRUTH.

Esme envisioned Lorena sleeping in a prison all these months. Was she with José? If so, could he protect her? José was smart, but he was not a physically imposing man.

"I know you've all risked a lot to be here," said Alba, "but you're here because you're looking for answers—we all are—and we'll share anything useful that we know. In addition to this publication, we've received information from a young woman whose friend—we'll call her Lucia, for safety reasons—was recently arrested, detained for a short time, then released. During her brief imprisonment, Lucia claims to have seen Reina's son, Paulo, in a detention center. We know that he's being kept alive, but we don't know for how long."

Reina lifted a hand to her mouth. Esme felt a pang of hope for her friend, followed immediately by jealousy.

"We have other news," said Alba, motioning for Rosa to join her. Rosa approached with a piece of paper that Alba unfolded. "An anonymous source has identified prisoners matching the following descriptions, seen alive as recently as the past three weeks: a young girl, reddish curly hair, probably in her late teens; a young man, medium height, likely early twenties, scar on his right eyebrow; a couple: a woman with long dark hair in her midtwenties and a man also in his twenties, tall, thin, brown hair, likely detained together—"

"Lorena," Esme breathed. Alba finished reading the list, but Esme didn't hear another word. She caught Rosa's eye and ushered her over.

"Rosa," pleaded Esme. "I think that's my daughter and son-in-law. The couple on your list."

Rosa nodded, put her jittery hands on Esme's forearms. "Then maybe they're alive. That's good news, Esme."

A question perched on Esme's tongue, one she knew she couldn't ask. But Esme thought so fiercely of Lorena now that she couldn't help herself. "Rosa, how did you find this out? You have to tell me more."

Rosa went quiet. She looked like she might cry. "I can't."

"Please, Rosa," said Esme.

"No."

"For the love of God. I'm begging you. I have to know where Lorena is."

Rosa's face crumpled. She took two steps toward the wall and dropped her voice to a whisper Esme could scarcely decipher.

"There's a nurse," Rosa said at last. "She works in one of the prisons. My cousin went to school with her. But you mustn't tell anyone." Rosa looked around. "Please, it's too dangerous. She only agreed to look for my daughter, Ines, since she's pregnant. She hasn't seen her yet. We could lose all our information if we ask too much of her. Alba's the only other one who knows."

Alba was passing around papers. "These execution sites we've read about—if our children are among them, God forbid, we need to know. We are entitled to answers."

One of the women let out a sob. Another tut-tutted. More murmuring broke out.

"Ladies," hushed Reina. "Some of us have begun drafting petition letters to international human-rights organizations. I know many of you have traveled long distances to be here. Please, sign the petitions and take signature pages back to where you've come from. Ask other mothers to sign them, too, and bring them back when we meet next. But be careful with them, please. We don't want them confiscated. And we can't lose any of you."

Alba glanced at Esme. "Many of you have filed writs that have already been denied, and some of us are still waiting," she said. "We have very few options, and no one is foolish enough to take on this government alone. It doesn't matter now what your politics are. They've taken our children, and they won't tell us where they're being kept. These are our *children*. It's the most perverse crime imaginable. We are their mothers—we have a right to know where they are."

Some of the women nodded, dabbing wet eyes; others sat alone, looking enraged and solitary, uninterested in being consoled.

"I'm proposing we make ourselves seen," Alba went on. "People need to know that that they've taken away our family members. We need to make others see us so the truth can't be denied anymore. Our children haven't *disappeared*."

"We're going to be collecting money for the advertising fees to publish a list of the names of our missing children in the newspaper," said Reina. "Please give what you can. No one has to know where the money came from."

"They'll find out," said one of the mothers.

"Maybe it's time they do," said Alba. "Nobody should have to be invisible. We need to make ourselves seen by the president himself, if that's what it takes."

"What are you suggesting?"

"That we gather in front of the Casa Rosada until Videla sees us outside his door."

"In *public*?" said Rosa.

"Alba," protested Hilde. "Don't be ridiculous. What do you think will happen? They'll arrest us too."

"Then let them take me," said Alba. She put down the papers on an end table and faced Hilde head-on. Esme had never seen Alba so incensed, so raw. "Let them kill me if they're going to. What else do I have to lose, after all? They've taken my *son*."

Esme glanced at Rosa, who turned her head slowly to return Esme's cautionary look. She thought of Matías, home with the babysitter. Like Hilde and Rosa, Esme had more at risk than Alba or Reina did. They had grandchildren to consider.

"It will be peaceful," said Reina quietly. "A vigil for our missing children. Mothers asking for answers, nothing more."

"We'll go to the Plaza de Mayo holding photos of our children for all to see," said Alba. "We'll make them know our children's names. They won't be able to ignore us anymore."

A lump rose in Esme's throat. Based on the reactions in the room, Alba's plan seemed to be taking hold.

"We'll have to stay on the move," said one of the other mothers. "No standing still. We can't be seen as gathering publicly."

"And no husbands," said another. "The men will be antagonized by the guards. It's too much of a threat. We don't need more incidents. We need answers."

"How will we know when to meet?"

"And where? We can't just stand around."

Esme's stomach turned over with fear. She was being swept up in a wave, and although it terrified her, it seemed to be the only current with any momentum toward finding Lorena. She glanced out the window. Down on the street below, the officer who'd battered the flowers was pacing on the corner, holding his gun.

The women left the apartment one by one throughout the afternoon so as not to draw attention. As Esme walked home, her heart raced. Alba's idea was dangerous, but what other option did she have? Lorena was alive. Someone had seen her, despite what the police said. She had to question what the government was telling them, to publicly disbelieve the lies. All the mothers were asking for was truth. Would the junta arrest them for that? Would they classify Esme as a dissident, take her away from her grandson, just for wanting the truth?

She knew the answer, of course.

As she walked up the front path to the house, Esme had a realization that came as a relief in some way. She'd asked it of herself for years, as perhaps all mothers do: Was she willing to die for Lorena?

The answer came simply: yes.

"'Buela," Matías cooed when she took him from the neighbor girl's arms. When she held him, he clung to her tightly, as though they were anchoring each other to the spinning earth.

"My sweet boy." She kissed his hair. He was Lorena's son, but he also had much of José in him, too—his gentleness, his shy smile. Matías was the best of both of his parents, and Esme's love for him made the simple answers more complicated. She was willing to risk her own safety, but if something happened to her, there would be no one to look after her grandson. She was willing to die for her daughter, but she was equally compelled to live for Matías.

———— · ✤ · ————

After mass on Sunday morning, Esme approached her priest again.

"Padre, I'm not sure if you remember me," she said, though she knew full well he did. He made a point of avoiding eye contact. "I'm still searching for my Lorena. I've filed a writ of habeas corpus with the Ministry of the Interior. It's still pending, but I have a copy of the filing here. I have certainty that Lorena is alive, in custody. I've written a letter to the Vatican, asking his holiness to intercede. Although I haven't heard back yet, it would help, surely, if you would be willing to write a letter of support on behalf of the Church—"

The priest turned to face her and, to his credit, looked her in the eyes. Another priest had been killed outside of the city recently for far less than what Esme was asking of this man now. They both knew he wouldn't act. His only concern—like every other citizen—was protecting his own corporal humanity.

"I'm sorry, señora," he said formally. "Your daughter's fate is in God's hands. May peace and God's love be with you through this trial." He made the sign of the cross in the air in front of her and turned away.

It was what she'd expected. Esme thought of Alba's words. *People don't just disappear. Our government is lying to you.* Her church and her country were interchangeable now. Everyone was ridden with fear, content to hide safely within their own complicity. Everyone conceded to the lie.

But Esme's faith was strong. She knew God. This one cowardly priest was hardly God.

"I'll pray for you," she murmured to his back, and promised to say an act of contrition later for the utterances that followed.

Three weeks after Easter, when Esme went back to the ministry to check on the status of the writs, both had been denied.

There was no next step.

Esme knelt on the kitchen floor with her rosary and cried quietly into the seat of a chair. Even when Matías toddled in and touched her shoulder, Esme didn't look up. It was maddening. Lorena was out there somewhere, alive, but Esme couldn't reach her, couldn't touch her. She felt utterly hopeless. There was nothing left to do.

The first time the phone rang, Esme ignored it, but the second time, when she answered, Reina's voice came through the receiver like a prophecy fulfilled.

"We're going to the Plaza tomorrow for the vigil. If you decide to come, bring a little nail, like the ones Christ suffered, so we'll recognize one another. The others will do the same. Come at exactly half past three. We'll walk around the pyramid."

Lorena was locked away in a prison somewhere. Esme had to call out for her, to cry out into the world until Lorena heard her voice. She was Lorena's mother. This was her job.

Esme collected herself, tended to Matías, and kissed him apologetically.

In Lorena's bedroom, Esme found a photo of her daughter and taped it to a placard. She took string, threaded it through each corner and made a loop so that she could wear it around her neck. Her hands shook, so she wrote Lorena's name slowly. LORENA ARIAS LEDESMA. Writing the letters felt like pushing a boulder. She formed the words carefully: *Where is my daughter?*

Matías came into the room to see what she was doing. He picked up an extra piece of string and dragged it gently across the bedspread.

"Mamá," he said when he saw the picture.

Esme pulled her lips in to hold back tears, then took a photo of José and made a second card.

——— · ✥ · ———

On Thursday afternoon, she called the babysitter again, torn by guilt, desperation, fear. If she went to the plaza and was arrested, Matías would be left with no one to care for him. If she didn't go, if she quietly accepted Lorena's fate without doing anything, she couldn't live with herself. Every day she let pass was another layer of cement on the truth. She had to call out Lorena's name.

In the garage, Esme found a plastic jar of nails and took one out. A flake of rust stuck to her palm.

The cold afternoon sky stretched out above the Casa Rosada. Esme lifted her coat collar as she headed toward the Metropolitan Cathedral, huddling up against the chill. She sat on a bench, holding her nail in her lap between two fingertips, the photos hanging over her winter coat on a string around her neck. She waited. The junta surrounded the plaza. On a nearby bench, another woman sat with a nail taped to her lapel. Esme didn't remember seeing the woman at the gathering, but they locked eyes now.

Before long, Alba arrived. She began walking first, a good distance away from Esme, holding a photo of Ernesto at her chest. She had written his full name and the date he disappeared. *Where is my son? Where is ERNESTO?*

Esme got up and started to walk near Alba, but not too close. They'd circled three times when an officer noticed them and approached. He held a gun across his chest. He walked over to Alba, touched the hem of her coat with the barrel of his gun.

"Hey," he said. "What the hell are you doing?"

Alba kept walking, chin up, circling the pyramid. She said nothing.

"Crazy bat," he said.

It was good that the husbands stayed home.

"Look at these hags," one officer said mockingly to another.

The mothers didn't say a word.

Esme counted the days she'd spent without Lorena as she walked. It distracted her, keeping the fear at bay. *One, two . . . fifty-three, fifty-four . . . one hundred seven, one hundred eight . . .*

Reina arrived and started walking with them. Hilde came too. Rosa wasn't there, but Esme wasn't surprised.

They paired off as they circled the pyramid—about a dozen women in all—and kept their heads up, eyes straight, walking silently with pictures of their missing children.

"Go home, you pinko crones." The junta's laughter had a violent undertone. When the mothers still didn't respond to the insults, an officer approached Alba again. This time, he clutched the sleeve of her coat.

"We're serious," he said. "Get out of here."

Alba tried to keep walking, but the officer held tight, pulling on her sleeve until he'd torn the fabric. Alba stumbled backward. When she regained her footing, she looked him dead in the eye, incensed.

"We'll go home when you tell us what you've done with our children."

The officer shoved Alba into Esme and lifted his gun. Esme steadied her friend, then immediately beckoned Alba in the opposite direction.

The mothers began to disperse. By the time Hilde caught up with Esme and Alba at the bus stop, Alba was more energized than ever. They'd walked for nearly twenty minutes before the junta chased them off. The officers had noticed them, which meant that maybe someone in the Casa Rosada had noticed too. If they kept at it, they might finally get some answers.

Esme headed home, relieved to be alive. She was certain that Alba would keep organizing the vigils until they got a response from the government. Perhaps the response would be the paramilitary at Esme's door tonight. She didn't know. She just had to keep going.

CHAPTER 6

The air had grown colder. Lorena had been missing for two hundred and forty-eight days. Matías had turned three and didn't say "Mamá" as often. He learned more words, new words, and referred to himself in third person. He knew all his colors; he liked to finger paint. His soft hair was badly in need of a trim. All these things Lorena should have experienced.

Every Thursday afternoon, Esme met Alba and the mothers in front of the Casa Rosada. People had begun talking about them—the locas de la Plaza de Mayo, the crazy women. Perhaps they were crazy, but more of them emerged each week with photos of their missing children. Everyone was distracted by football; the city was crawling with international journalists and correspondents as the country prepared to host the World Cup. Even the air particles seemed to be rooting for Argentina, threatening to carry away the collective memory of the *desaparecidos* like a faded scent on the wind.

The junta continued to tolerate their vigils, dismissing them as foolish; the women were too powerless to warrant a legitimate reaction.

"We're going to start wearing pañuelos when we walk," said Alba, fastening the corners of a white kerchief under her chin. "Like this."

"They look like baby nappies," said Reina.

"We need to be seen," Alba insisted. "We need to make people think about what's been taken from us so they might finally question the truth. We need to get their attention."

"The junta are relying on people to stay quiet and scared," said Reina. "If no one speaks up, they win."

"'*First they came for the Socialists*,'" Rosa recited.

"Exactly."

On their first Thursday wearing white scarves, Rosa showed up. She carried a poster with a photo of Ines. Beneath her daughter's name, she'd written: *Four months pregnant when she went missing. Baby was due in May 1977. WHERE IS MY GRANDCHILD?* Esme was relieved, invigorated, and terrified by how many other women were walking. The white scarves seemed to amplify them.

The officers lingered nearby, bored and preoccupied. As she circled the pyramid, Esme moved closer to Alba, the sleeve of her wool coat brushing against the edge of Alba's WHERE IS ERNESTO? sign.

Esme thought of Lorena now and felt stronger than she had before. They had organized the group well today. Their white scarves mattered. Perhaps someone in the Casa Rosada would see them and risk sharing some piece of information as to the whereabouts of those who had disappeared. Even if it was just to placate the crazy mothers.

On their fifth lap around the plaza, the click of a camera shutter caused Esme to turn her head. She caught sight of a man in a brown leather jacket crouching several yards behind two of the officers, his lens aimed directly at Esme and Alba. Esme's heart raced. She envisioned photos, headlines—their children's faces, published for all to see—and trembled with hope and dread.

One of the young officers spun around.

"Get the hell out of here," he called, lifting his rifle to chase the photographer off.

Esme glanced across the circle. Twenty feet away, Hilde and Rosa hadn't seen the commotion. The soldier turned to consult with one of his colleagues, and they both glanced up at the Casa Rosada, then back at the mothers. When a senior officer took a step toward Alba, Esme knew something was about to go terribly wrong.

"Come with me," he said, wrangling Alba by the upper arm.

"Get your hands off me," barked Alba, brave as ever.

"You're making a scene out here. This display stops now."

"Then tell me where you've taken my son. Tell us where our children are."

"Let's go," said the officer, shoving Alba toward the perimeter of the square, where a long military bus was parked. At once, a dozen other officers broke up the circle, rounding the women up one by one.

"If you like attention so much," said an officer, grabbing Esme by the forearm and jostling her toward the parked military bus, "you'll get plenty of it down at the *comisaria*. You can all come in for questioning."

Esme turned to look back over her shoulder, panicked. She caught sight of Rosa through the crowd as she was wrangled by an officer. Esme's chest constricted. The officer shoved her behind Alba onto the cold bus and into a shabby leather seat near the back. All Esme could think of was Matías, home with the babysitter, his little fingers maneuvering the pages of his favorite book. *I won't be any later than five o'clock*, Esme had told the girl. Her eyes filled with tears of anger. What had she done?

Alba's body filled the space in the bus seat beside her. The card stock strung around Esme's neck had bent, creasing the photos of Lorena and José. Through the cloudy bus window, Alba's *WHERE IS ERNESTO?* sign lay face up on the concrete.

Esme watched in horror as the rest of the mothers were forced onto the bus—Reina, Rosa, Hilde, and nearly a dozen others. Alba sat with both hands between her knees and elbowed Esme once, hard. Esme's fear turned acrid; she was suddenly furious with Alba. This was all her fault. How stupid she'd been to get them all involved in this to begin with.

"Help me," Alba whispered.

Esme watched Alba slide the pocket notebook from her purse, its pages filled with photos of the missing, names of dozens of other family members scattered across the city. God only knew what other information Alba had in there—attendees of "parties," petitions, letters,

informants. Alba was a fool to have brought it with her. All their organizing, all their work would be handed over to the junta like a gift the
moment they disembarked from the bus.

The bus door creaked shut. The young officer walked the aisle threat-
eningly, then turned to face forward, hovering two seats from the back,
just in front of Esme and Alba. They were close enough to see the hairs
along the back of his neck. Cold air streamed in through the top of the
bus windows, which were hinged open.

Under the growl of the engine, Alba peeled a page from her notebook
and began tearing it up into tiny pieces. She nudged Esme desperately,
passing her a second page. Esme took it, shredding it silently but frantically between her fingers. As the bus rumbled toward San Cristóbal, Alba's
hands moved swiftly between their laps. Another page, then another. The
photos, the notes, all the contact information Alba had so carefully collected
were turned to scraps between their fingers. But there was no way to reach
the open windows to discard the pieces without the officer seeing them.

By the time the bus pulled up in front of the federal police station,
all that remained of Alba's precious notebook was a coil binding and a
few empty pages between cardboard covers. They both clutched piles of
confetti. When they stood, Esme dropped half a fistful and stared down
as the bits of paper turned brown and wet between the rubber grooves
of the floor mat. She stepped over them. Alba left the bus ahead of her,
and Esme kept her eyes forward, conscious of the trail of white scraps
her friend left on the street behind the officer, just out of his view.

Inside the police station, the detained women filled the hallway.
Esme could hear Hilde and Rosa down the hall asking the junta if they
could call their husbands. Sending these crazy women home to their
husbands seemed to resonate with the guards, but Esme couldn't call
Gustavo, and Alba never made mention of her husband.

A guard guided Alba and Esme to a holding cell with a group of
others. He locked the barred door and turned his back.

"I've got to get home to my grandson," Esme whispered to Alba.

"Keep your mouth shut," said the guard. "You should've thought
about that before you decided to make a spectacle of yourself."

Alba sat down on a wall-mounted bench, her face stone. Esme remembered her expression that afternoon in the apartment: *Let them take me.*

One by one, slowly, Esme watched through the bars of the holding cell as the women in the hall were pulled aside and questioned, searched, made to complete forms on clipboards, show identification, provide personal information, and attest to the names of the others. The wall-mounted clock ticked forward from four thirty to five, five thirty to six.

Esme started to weep quietly, enraged with herself. At ten minutes to seven, the guard finally pulled Esme out of the cell and patted her down, asked her questions, made her fill out paperwork.

"Are you completely unaware of our current laws?" he asked finally. "You want to explain your involvement in these theatrics?"

Esme's anger surged. *Tell me where Lorena is, you bastard.* She swallowed the words like stones. "I need to get home to my grandson."

"Grandson?" The officer brightened. "Does he live here?" The tip of his pencil touched the line where Esme had written Lorena's address. "Maybe we should bring him in for questioning too."

Esme stared straight at him. She wanted to smack his smug face.

"Get back in the cell," he said. "You should be ashamed of yourself, parading around like that."

Please, God. Esme's heart pounded. What if they did go to the house? What if they took Matías? He was just a little boy. Her eyes returned to the clock. Seven fifteen, then seven thirty. Matías would need dinner. A bath. His bedtime story.

At eight fifteen, the interviewing officer came to the holding cell with his coat on, ready to go home for the day. He had a safe home somewhere, Esme guessed, where his family and children were waiting for him each evening. She was just another task on his daily list. He was going to leave her here.

"That's it for tonight," he told the guard. "We'll finish questioning in the morning. If you've already been questioned, you can go, but think twice before you pull a stunt like this again."

Esme's heart raced as the guard unlocked the cell door.

"The rest of you, get comfortable. You're sleeping here tonight, and it's going to be a long one—the heat is on the fritz."

She looked back at Alba, who was sitting on the bench, her face drawn.

"Go," said Alba.

———— · ❖ · ————

By the time Esme caught the last bus home and arrived at the house, it was after nine o'clock. The windows were dark. When she unlocked the door, all the lights were off. There was no one inside.

She turned on the lamps in every room, no longer able to restrain her sobs. What a foolish woman she was—a terrible mother, a terrible grandmother. She couldn't even ask God to forgive her now. Matías was an innocent boy. Her job was to protect him for Lorena, and she'd failed. She called his name, but her voice fell flat against the silence.

Esme ran out of the house, back down the front walkway, and along the sidewalk to the neighbor's door. It was past curfew, but Esme didn't care. She lifted the knocker several times, crying openly now.

When the bolt of the lock unhitched from inside, the babysitter's mother appeared in the doorframe in a velour robe. She assessed Esme with her arms crossed, then shook her head in disdain. She turned back toward the dim light inside and left the door open for Esme to follow.

There, asleep on the couch in the living room, was Matías.

"You've got some nerve," the woman said. "My daughter's still in school. She has homework to do in the evenings. She's a responsible girl. A good girl."

"I'm sorry," said Esme, already on her knees beside the couch, collecting Matías in her arms, kissing his temple.

"We won't be put in this situation again," the woman went on. "We're not like you. Don't come back here."

Esme gathered Matías up, the full weight of him in her arms.

If they took your daughter away from you, she thought, *you might be more like me than you think.*

"I'm sorry," she repeated, and carried Matías quietly home.

She wouldn't do it again. Esme promised herself now: no more meetings, no more vigils, no more petitions, no other mothers. That was it. She was done. She had a second chance, and she would never leave Matías again. Ever.

———— · ❖ · ————

Rosa called on Sunday asking Esme to meet her at Café Tortoni, her tone urgent.

"I have news, Esme. It's about Lorena. Bring Matías if you need to. We'll invite Hilde to watch him. But you have to come today." Rosa's voice quivered. "We have to go somewhere together, you and me. We won't have this chance again."

Esme bundled Matías in the stroller and made her way to Café Tortoni. She took a seat at the table next to Rosa, who was toying with the gold crucifix around her neck. Hilde stubbed out her cigarette and leaned over to entertain Matías with her bracelet. Esme had the urge to run home with Matías and lock the door behind her.

"What is it?" Esme whispered hastily to Rosa once they'd placed their order.

Rosa shook her head. She was afraid to talk in public; they were all under scrutiny. Alba had been released the day after the round up, but only after nearly catching pneumonia from sleeping in that cell. Beneath the table now, Rosa passed a small slip of paper to Esme. She unfolded it with her thumbnail. On the paper were a few scribbled words; it looked as though it had been torn from a longer list of names someone had written in haste.

Lorena Ledesma. Seen alive in prison, early June.

Esme's eyes flooded with hope as she crumpled the paper. She stared down at her saucer, and her muscles went slack.

"I'll have the special," Hilde said to the server. "What will you have, Esme?"

"The same," Esme choked.

"Hilde, why don't you take Matías for a walk in the plaza after lunch?" said Rosa. "Esme and I are going to the library."

Esme looked up at Rosa. She didn't want to leave Matías, even with Hilde, but she sensed Rosa's urgency. There was more to know.

"There's a book I wanted to find," Rosa went on. "It's that one we talked about, Esme, remember? That one about the nurse?"

Esme glanced over at Hilde, who lit another cigarette and nodded.

"I can't remember the title, but I thought you could help me find it."

Once they'd paid the check, Esme kissed Matías and made Hilde swear on her own grandchild that she'd be careful with him. As they made their way to the library, Esme linked her arm through Rosa's and whispered anxiously.

"Will the nurse be there?"

Rosa nodded. "My cousin Enrique arranged it."

"Was she the one who saw Lorena? How do you know she'll talk?"

"Shh. Her bread's been buttered. We just have to be careful."

Esme dug out her old library card from her purse. Inside the building, sections on politics and philosophy had been blocked off by the junta, the shelves cleared. Esme took a seat next to Rosa at one end of a large leather-top writing table in the common area. She hitched one ankle over the other and leafed through a periodical. Rosa found a government-sanctioned classic novel and pretended to read innocuously.

Within the hour, a stocky woman approached the other end of the table with a reference book in her arms. Her straight black hair was cut bluntly in a bob, and her glasses were so thick they distorted her eyes.

Esme looked up. Rosa's eyes widened, and she gave Esme a slight nod.

"I'd like to sit here," the nurse said to Rosa, "but this table is a bit crowded."

Rosa looked at the five empty seats, then at Esme, then back up at the nurse pleadingly.

"She's a friend," said Rosa.

Esme let her eyes drop to an article in the periodical, running them over the same words again and again, trying to become minuscule, invisible enough for the nurse to let her stay. At last, the nurse sighed and sat down on the same side of the table as Esme.

"I was hoping one of you could help me. I have trouble reading this small print." She opened the reference book and flipped to a certain page. It was an encyclopedia of plant life.

Esme scooted her chair closer to the nurse. Rosa shifted to the seat across from them, settling in with her novel again.

"I won't be here long," the nurse whispered. "I've always been fond of Enrique, but we only discussed Ines, no one else. I'm just doing this once."

An armed guard at the corner of the room glanced over at them, then pivoted his head, his gaze passing over what he saw: a few uninteresting women posing no visible threat.

The nurse's index finger chased the lines across the page as though she were reading silently to herself, but instead she began to speak in a low, flat voice.

"I don't know what part you want to hear," she droned. "But they keep them on the top floor of the building, *la capucha*, and it's all very orderly, efficient. If you watch long enough, you can see the junta carrying supplies in and out in broad daylight. It's only invisible because no one chooses to notice it. But it's all there. It's all true."

It's all true. Those words alone were enough to empty the air from Esme's lungs.

The nurse's finger continued to move steadily over the words on the page. Esme looked on, mumbling a word here and there when the nurse prompted her for "help." *Moss. Spores. Vascular Fern. Cultivar.* She noticed the preposterous thickness of the nurse's glasses. A disguise, Esme realized.

A librarian wheeling a cart of books stopped nearby to return one to a shelf. The three women fell quiet for a long moment, as though Videla himself were standing over their shoulders.

"This is such an interesting story," whispered Rosa, holding up the novel.

The librarian turned around. "We've got several others by the same author," she said, pointing to a back section on the far side of the room.

"Thank you," Rosa said with a smile. "I'll have a look."

When the librarian rolled the cart away, Rosa didn't break character. "I won't spoil the ending for you," she said to the nurse, "unless you've already read this one. Do you remember? Something happened to the woman—" Rosa's whisper softened until it was nearly imperceptible. "Lorena Ledesma. Back in June?"

The nurse raised her eyes from the book to Esme.

"You're her mother?"

Esme nodded.

"I remember that one," she murmured.

The way she said it prompted Rosa to lock eyes with Esme in alarm.

"The baby had a birthmark on her right thigh."

Esme's throat tightened. "Baby?"

The nurse looked warily up at Rosa, whose eyes were wide.

"They're running their own *Sarda*," said the nurse. It was Buenos Aires's best maternity hospital. "That's how they see it, at least. The spoils of war."

Esme tremored, hunching forward in her chair. If it weren't for her will not to be seen by the officers, she might've collapsed on the table.

"Lorena wasn't pregnant," Esme uttered under her breath.

The nurse looked dumbfounded by her ignorance, then gave a shallow nod. "She named the baby Ana."

"That's impossible," said Esme. "It couldn't have been her."

The nurse pointed to a paragraph about botanicals and nodded resolutely.

Esme rocked back and forth in her seat a little, clasping her hands so tightly she thought her bones might break. Her head was spinning. She wanted to jump up from her chair and shake the woman, scream every question in her mind, but if she so much as stood up, the officer in the corner might look her way or approach. She kneaded her hands in her lap with great force.

"She was pregnant?" Esme breathed.

"Your daughter told me her name. That's how I remember her."

Esme's jaw clenched. "Where is Lorena? What happened to her?"

The nurse lifted her finger from the page as though she'd suddenly remembered something useful. "She said she wanted the baby returned to you." Her mouth tightened. "I didn't see her again after the birth, but there was a doctor at Campo de Mayo who made arrangements for the babies through the church."

The novel wilted in Rosa's hand. "The church?"

Esme's mouth had fallen open now. She couldn't move.

"I've got to go," said the nurse, suddenly shutting the botanicals book and sliding it to the center of the table. She moved to stand up, then hesitated and looked straight at Rosa. "I wanted to be a caregiver. Ask Enrique. I never thought I'd be filling syringes with sodium pentothal. But Hell is full of people with good intentions, I suppose."

As the nurse walked away, her muted footfalls faded across the thin carpet until the library door groaned shut behind her.

Esme bowed her head. Tears filled her eyes. Rosa hooked a hand under her arm.

"Let's go."

The tears began to fall down Esme's cheeks and neck, saturating her eyelet collar. She couldn't stop envisioning Lorena in prison, pregnant, and she couldn't stop hearing the nurse's words: *She wanted the baby returned to you.*

Rosa bracketed Esme's shoulders, pulling her upright. "Get up."

"I need some air," whispered Esme.

"There's air all around you," Rosa hissed. "Stand up. You have to be strong."

"Where is she, Rosa? Where's the baby? What did they *do* to her?"

Rosa shook her head, propping Esme upright. "You can't fall apart, Esme. Not here. Not yet."

——— · ⚜ · ———

When Esme finally got home, she pulled Matías into a chair and cuddled him to comfort herself until he no longer wanted to be held. He squirmed out of her arms and pointed to a photo of his parents on the end table.

Esme picked up the frame.

"Do you know who this is?" she asked, holding it in front of him.

Matías hesitated. Esme's eyes welled. She prayed he'd answer. That too much time hadn't passed.

"Mamá," he said. "Papá."

Esme let out a single sob that came from the depth of her heart, then sniffed deeply, gathering herself. She hugged him tight.

"Yes, that's right, my love. That's your mamá, María-Lorena. And your papá, José. I'm going to tell you the story of how they first met. And then I'm going to tell you a story about your mother when she was a little girl. And then we'll draw some pictures of them to help us remember."

Matías was delighted.

"And guess what else, Matías?"

He looked up at Esme in anticipation.

"You have a baby sister. Her name is Ana. And we're going to find her. That will be our adventure. What do you think about that?"

His eyes seemed to understand everything.

"Matías find," he said.

"That's right, my love. Matías will find his baby sister."

PART II

PART II

CHAPTER 7

JUNE 2005

On a shaded bench in Union Square, Rachel focused on the ink trailing from her pen's tip as it bled into the textured paper, outlining the sky-line. Along the avenues, buildings saluted the afternoon sun. Off-duty taxis filled clogged streets with horn blares. Summer was beginning to expand through the city, pushing down onto rooftops into cross-street crevices. Floor-to-ceiling bistro windows bloomed open in response, their tables brimming with colorfully dressed patrons. The air hung still and hot as bus exhaust.

Rachel pressed harder with her pen, anchoring herself to the moment. She'd been trying to regain her footing since receiving the phone call from Dr. Marisol Rey the previous evening. She replayed the conversa-tion in her mind, sorting out questions she was prepared to ask: *How did you get my contact information? Do you know my birth mother? Do you know where my biological family is now?* She would be direct, reveal-ing none of the fundamental anxieties accompanying these inquiries, the prospect of learning precisely who abandoned her. She'd conducted an online search for "Dr. Marisol Rey" after the party and navigated a few profiles in Spanish until she reached a single thumbnail photo: a woman in her thirties, full lips and a billow of soft, dark curls—only a couple of years older than her, far too young to be her birth mother—smiling above a brief biography. Dr. Marisol Rey held a PhD in Latin American Studies and worked as an adjunct professor for an international university in Miami.

Rachel set down her sketchbook. Her father would not approve of her being here. But it was broad daylight. She didn't have much money on her. From her bag, she exhumed her miniature Magic 8 Ball key chain—a birthday gift from her roommate—and shook it, the blue liquid revealing a proclamation: YOU MAY RELY ON IT.

Does this woman really have answers?

A triangle emerged through blue liquid: ASK AGAIN LATER.

She shook it again.

BETTER NOT TELL YOU NOW.

Beneath the scaffolding on Fifth Avenue, Mari's face, which perfectly matched the photo online, emerged from the shadows. She wore a cotton skirt and sleeveless button-up, her thumbs hooked through the straps of a drawstring backpack. Rachel shook the key chain at length one more time and glanced down as the response surfaced: IT IS DECIDEDLY SO.

She threw the key chain back in her bag.

"Rachel?" Mari's espadrilles picked up pace, one hand splayed across her chest as she approached. She carried a pleasant, fruity scent.

Rachel stood up. "Dr. Rey."

"Oh my God, I'm—oh, I'm sorry." Mari extended her hand, which was warm and soft when Rachel took it. Mari's eyes brimmed with tears. "I wasn't sure you'd come," she said. "Here, let's sit. Please. And call me Mari. I'm just Mari to you."

Rachel cleared her throat. They both sat down. Mari set a plastic bag on the bench beside her, crumpling its "I ♥ NY" insignia. A nectarine tumbled out.

"I'm so happy you came," Mari repeated. Rachel caught the stray fruit as it rolled toward her on the bench, then passed it back to Mari.

"Thanks," said Mari. "I just love farmers' markets. And everything is so ripe right now." She scanned the produce stands, the artisans, the farmers from New Jersey and upstate moving crates of fresh greens from the back of trucks. The sun caught her curls and the curve of her cheek as her gaze landed on a stack of ripe tomatoes nearby. "Look how fresh those are! I wish I could grow tomatoes that beautiful."

Rachel shifted her weight, arranged her hands in her lap. "My mom has a garden," she offered. The words *my mom* echoed, but Mari didn't flinch.

"I love that," Mari said encouragingly. "We had a few fruit trees growing up in Florida, but that's about as close as I've gotten to having one myself."

"But you still live there?"

Mari nodded. "Since I was four years old. I go back and forth to Buenos Aires for work now. My sister lives in Argentina. Have you been?"

Rachel shook her head. "I did a semester in Spain."

"*Qué lindo.*" Mari pointed to the sketchbook. "You draw?"

Rachel slipped the book into her bag, her shoulders high and tight. "Nothing serious. What brings you to New York?"

"My work." Mari slid her arms from the straps of her backpack and pulled open the drawstring. "And you. You're kind of a big deal to us."

Rachel squinted. What contact form had she filled out that might have landed her on Mari's radar?

"What is it that you want to tell me?" Rachel asked.

Mari reached into her bag and unwound the thin leather strap of an overstuffed Filofax planner. She leafed through its loose pages to extract a plain envelope. From it, she slid a stack of small documents—postcards, several photos—and handed Rachel a three-by-five color print.

"I'll get straight to the point," Mari said. "Here."

In the photo, Mari stood in a small yard flanked by palm trees. She wore sunglasses and a ponytail, her arms latched affectionately around the waist of a young man in a blue-and-white-striped polo shirt. The stranger's face stirred something unexpected in Rachel, a heightened awareness at a cellular level. He looked to be in his early thirties, a lock of brunette hair flopped partially over one eye. She felt a prickle of recognition.

"I think I've seen this guy before."

"He looks familiar?"

"I don't know—maybe. Who is he? Why are you showing me this?"

Mari smiled. "His name is Mat Ledesma. He's very dear to me, and he's been looking for you for a long time."

They sat in silence for a few tense beats.

"Mat and I think he's your brother," Mari said.

Rachel stared at the photo. Deep in her core, a tingling sensation began spreading out through her limbs. Mat smiled up at her from the paper. Did they look alike? Rachel quickly handed the photo back, forcing distance between herself and the stranger it depicted. The questions she'd planned to ask seemed suddenly irrelevant, embarrassing. She'd been expecting information about her adoption, not something this imminent. Not a *brother*.

"I don't understand. How did you find me?"

Mari spoke slowly, doling out her words as though from a dropper. "Mat's mother was kidnapped from their home in Argentina when he was two years old."

"God, that's horrible," said Rachel.

Mari nodded. "And we believe she gave birth to a baby girl in June of 1977."

"You think that was *me*?"

"We have reason to believe that may be the case, yes."

Rachel turned her head away and smiled nervously. "Argentina? You have the wrong person. I was adopted in Virginia."

"I know," said Mari. "You were abandoned at the Joy & Light Family Center, which is where your adoption was processed—isn't that right?"

A sinking sensation entered Rachel's sternum, like barometric pressure dropping before a storm. "How do you know that?"

"Mat's been looking for you for as long as he can remember. We've been trying to find out as much as we can about the circumstances of your birth. He really wants to meet you." Mari's hand hovered in the air just above Rachel's forearm. Her tone was gentle, somber. "Can I ask, how much do you actually *know* about your abandonment?"

Rachel met her gaze directly. For a long moment, the two women assessed one another. Mari's brown eyes were kind. Rachel's instinct was to trust her, but her instincts could be wrong—her father warned her about this constantly. Mari knew things that Rachel didn't, which meant she had a certain power over her. Rachel had to be careful.

"The person who abandoned me didn't want to be found," said Rachel. This was true, as far as she knew. It had been her aunt Daphne—her father's sister-in-law, a longtime social worker at Joy & Light, about twenty miles northwest of Howell Grove—who'd found Rachel on the porch that summer morning. She was only a few weeks old, left outside in a baby carrier covered with a little blanket and wearing a clean diaper. The pediatrician from the department of health and human services determined that Rachel had been born prematurely, but was otherwise healthy—recently fed, no traces of prenatal drug exposure. Years later, when her dad hired a private investigator at Rachel's request, they'd found no hospital records of live births in the surrounding counties, no pregnant women who'd carried to term under a doctor's care within three hundred miles of the shelter. No one anywhere who could've possibly been her birth mother.

But this was the first time anyone had mentioned Argentina.

"Was there anything left behind with you when you were found?" asked Mari. "A blanket, maybe?"

Rachel steeled herself, trying not to react.

"Here," Mari said quickly, removing another wallet-sized photograph from the pile. It had a white scalloped border that hearkened back to another era. Rachel's hand trembled slightly when she took it. A peculiar version of her own face stared up at her: a cautious smile with dark hair pinned loosely at the temples, calm eyes smiling beneath thick lashes. The set of the eyes, the arch of the hairline—they were just like Rachel's. Blood pumped in her ears. The woman in the picture watched patiently, waiting. Rachel flipped the photograph over. On the back, in cursive pen, a faded caption read: *Lore, 1975*.

"This is Mat's mother," said Mari. "Lorena Ledesma."

The churning in Rachel's core flooded her with a storm of vulnerability that terrified her. She studied Lorena's face and felt drawn toward something she knew but didn't yet understand.

"Is she alive?"

"She's a desaparecida," said Mari. "One of thousands who went missing and has never been found."

Rachel covered her forehead with her palm and let out a single, sharp laugh. "Is this a joke?"

Mari looked at Rachel as though she were a child—precious, impressionable, naive. "I'm not sure how much you know about this, but when we were young, there was a dictatorship in Argentina. The government ran a 'process' to eradicate subversion. Thirty thousand people disappeared, many of them innocent—and Lorena Ledesma was among them. The psychology behind it was very effective at creating a state of terror—the families had no answers and no closure." Mari handed her an image of a crowd of women standing in the street with anguished expressions wearing white kerchiefs tied around their heads. They held photos of young men and women around Rachel's age. "There was a group of mothers who stood up against the regime to break the silence. Some of their children were pregnant women, like Lorena, and about five hundred babies were born inside prisons or kidnapped along with their parents. The government believed that subversive parents would raise rebel children, so the babies were given up for adoption, often to families and friends of the military. The children were raised without any knowledge of their birth family."

Mari handed over another piece of cardstock about the size of a postcard. It was a black-and-white flier, a grainy image of a human palm splayed open and blanched as though someone had photocopied it. Each fingertip was wrapped in a piece of white cloth and held in place by a spiral of wire. On each piece of cloth was the oily image of a fingerprint. A small line of words marked the heel of the palm: *La identidad no se impone.*

"This was one of the campaigns," said Mari. "And here's another—"

She passed Rachel a second card, this one a colorful image of a little boy curled up and hugging his knees. Below him were the English words: *My grandmother is looking for me. Will you tell her where I am?*

"The Abuelas de Plaza de Mayo have found seventy-four of their missing grandchildren so far," said Mari. "Lorena's mother, Esme, is still searching as we speak. But they're getting older, and time is running out. There are still hundreds of missing grandchildren yet to be located. I work for their identity archive. Our job is to keep the memories of the desaparecidos alive so that their children will have a family heritage to discover even after the Abuelas are gone."

"And the people who disappeared—?"

"Many were killed by the junta, but many were never found. They were officially considered 'absent forever.'"

Rachel shivered. "How did you find me?"

"Last month the Argentine Supreme Court ruled some of the long-standing amnesty laws unconstitutional." Mari collected the fliers. "In preparation for repeals, they reopened cases against members of the military. A woman reached out to the Abuelas' office with a testimony that she'd been keeping to herself for decades. From her story, we learned that a US soldier may have been involved in transporting a child of desaparecidos from Argentina to the United States around the time you were born." Mari paused, something complex and uncertain flashed across her eyes. "It's only a secondhand account, but there were very few US military officers in South America at that time."

Rachel took a breath. The air smelled sweet and filthy—glazed nuts roasting in a nearby street cart. She lifted her head up toward a snarl of twiggy branches against the blue afternoon sky.

"Did your adoptive father ever tell you that he was stationed in Argentina?"

A floating sensation passed over Rachel. She envisioned her dad in the expansive backyard of her childhood home moving bags of soil to the greenhouse for her mom, whose florist business supplemented his military pension.

Thanks for the card, Dad, she'd said when they spoke on the phone the day before.

His breath had been labored through the receiver. *Oh, right. You can thank your mother. Happy birthday, kiddo. Stay safe up there.*

An unexpected memory surfaced: crisp autumn leaves in flaming shades of rust and saffron. Rachel must have been nine or ten when her father raked them into careful paths, designing a custom maze that covered the entire yard. He must have been between deployments then. Vietnam, Honduras, the Persian Gulf. Maybe South America too—she didn't know where he'd been, specifically. Whole swaths of her childhood were clustered into a collective chapter of his absences before the retirement party they threw for him when he returned from Desert Storm. His military career wasn't something she was encouraged to ask about.

"You think my dad has something to do with this."

Mari tilted her head, rendering Rachel a child again. "We believe the officer in the witness's testimony is your adoptive father, yes—Jonathan Sprague. Although we're not accusing anyone of anything yet."

A tightness grasped Rachel's chest. The possibility of her father hiding such a colossal secret for so many years was ridiculous. What would he say if he even heard such an accusation? *Convenient.* That's what he would say, with a chip on his shoulder. *Seems pretty convenient that a soldier who* happened *to be in the country and* happens *to have an adopted daughter would get accused of trafficking a baby.*

She inhaled another lungful of hot city air.

"You believe it's him just because he may have been in Argentina?"

There was a subtle shift in Mari's bearing. "Appropriating a child is a serious crime," she said. "There are international treaties that prohibit it."

"Do you have any proof?"

Mari straightened the stack of photos and fliers, attempting to put them back in the envelope. "There were only two babies born in prisons that June," she said. "From the photo of Lorena, I think you can see why we think that the baby in the witness's testimony is you."

"But you don't have any proof."

A sharp smell cut the air between them as a homeless man picked through the garbage pail next to Mari. She held out her bag of vegetables and fruit.

"Here you go," Mari said.

The man took the bag, nodding.

Rachel's insides twisted like a weathervane pointing to both pain and hope.

Mari pulled a long brochure from her backpack and handed it to Rachel.

"You're the proof, Rachel. That's why I'm here."

Rachel scanned the list of Manhattan addresses on the glossy paper: a list of clinics throughout the city.

"There's a very simple way to find out the truth. You don't need anyone's permission to take a DNA test. Your adoptive parents don't even have to know."

Rachel reached for her Magic 8 Ball key chain, fiddling nervously with her free hand.

Mari lowered her voice. "It seems like you have a pretty good life here. If that's the case, I'm happy for you. I don't know what you've been told all these years about who you are, but I believe that you're Lorena's daughter—Mat's sister—and that your grandmother and brother have been searching for you your entire life. Mat is prepared to come to New York at a moment's notice to meet you if you're willing. And no matter how good you have it now, I can't imagine you don't want to know where you really came from. Take some time to think about it. Take as much time as you need. It's a lot to process, I know, but it's completely up to you." She handed the envelope to Rachel. "Here, keep these. My card is inside. Call any time you're ready to learn more, day or night. I'll be here."

Rachel stared at the envelope in her hand. She opened her mouth, then closed it again as Mari walked away. Her body felt numb.

She didn't have to tell anyone. If Mari was completely wrong, no one would ever have to know she'd even entertained it. How could she walk away from the possibility of finding out more?

Rachel dropped her eyes to the ground and pushed an advertisement for psychic readings over the gritty pavement with the toe of her ballet flat. On the key chain, she shook the tiny oracle.

Is Mat my brother?

CANNOT PREDICT NOW.

Am I from Argentina?

REPLY HAZY, TRY AGAIN.

She opened the envelope flap with her index finger. The photo of Lorena Ledesma was face up on top of the pile.

Rachel stared at the photo.

Is this a picture of my birth mother?

WITHOUT A DOUBT.

A thousand questions poured forth in her mind, but the most fundamental was something that only her parents could answer.

CHAPTER 8

Jonathan buried his hands in his pockets and drew up his shoulders as he crossed Avenida del Libertador. A cold wind snapped against his uniform jacket. He was on his second tour in the Southern Command—a light mission of efficiency advising for Operation Condor, the US-backed coordination of intelligence among South American nations—and the Argentine armed forces had begun to get a handle on guerrilla activity since his last visit. But as he entered the plaza, a prickle ran down his spine. He swiveled, prepared for an exploding car bomb or Molotov cocktail.

"¡Vamos, vamos, Argentina!" Two ragged kids sang a soccer chant, laughing as they pelted paper bang-snaps on the pavement.

"Hey," Jonathan snatched one of the youngsters by his bicep. "Behave yourselves." He thrust the kid toward a nearby Argentine military officer, but the boy fled, detonating his last fistful of poppers on the sidewalk with a sharp smatter of blasts.

Jonathan froze. In a flash, he was back in a rice field in Vietnam in the pouring rain, enemy fire crackling in the distance and seven miles of wet grass to go before his men—ridden with gangrene and dysentery—could pitch tents on anything resembling dry land.

He lifted one of his waterlogged boots and backpedaled, gaining his bearings a moment too late. He crashed into a woman on the street, who stumbled across the sidewalk and fell to the ground. Mortified, Jonathan approached her to help her up. She had a fully made-up face, fresh haircut, and a high-quality wool coat that reached her narrow ankles. The glint of a designer watch peeked out from its sleeve. She inspected the heel of her shoe, then swung her thick hair over her shoulder and looked up at him with chestnut-colored eyes that were narrowly set.

"*¿Estás bien?*" she asked.

"I'm the one who should be asking you that," he replied in Spanish.

"I'm fine. It's just my shoe." She worked futilely to reposition the partially detached heel of her pump. "I won't be able to walk on it now."

"Where are you headed?"

"There." She motioned toward a bistro with muted interior lighting at the edge of the plaza.

He offered his arm and she took it, leaning her weight on him as she hobbled toward the entrance of the restaurant.

"I'm Helena," she said.

"Jonathan," he replied as they entered the bistro. "I'm very sorry about that."

"It's fine." She shimmied onto a barstool and looked around, her expression an open door.

"Are you waiting for someone?" he asked.

"Some of my friends. We're meeting here for drinks."

"I can stay until they arrive."

Helena glanced at the ring on his left hand and slipped off her coat. "I suppose it's the least you can do."

Jonathan perched on the barstool next to her as she ordered a drink.

"You seem sad," she said.

"Beg your pardon?" Her attention quenched something parched within him. An unexpected wave of self-pity crashed down. Before she could reply, a group of Argentine soldiers lumbered into the restaurant and sidled up to the bar next to them. To Jonathan's surprise, Helena slid from her stool to greet them.

"I've been waiting for you," she reprimanded the commanding officer, who looked to be in his midforties. "This nice *yanqui* kept me company while you all were out keeping the peace. Where's Camila?"

"I'm right here." A fashionable young woman in a fur coat trailed after the men, kissing Helena's cheek as the bartender took a round of drink orders. "Who's this handsome Americano?"

"The one who ruined my favorite pump?" said Helena. She introduced Jonathan to her friend, then to each of the other officers, and finally tipped her head to briefly rest it on the shoulder of the officers' commander. "And this is my cousin, Ricardo."

Ricardo shook Jonathan's hand. "*Mucho gusto.*"

Jonathan suddenly didn't want to leave. He wanted the warmth of the camaraderie he lacked with American colleagues from his own intelligence unit, most of whom had slowly left the country as Congress drew down foreign missions in the wake of Vietnam. He watched Helena now, who pruned the cellophane flags on the toothpick from her drink, twirling it between her fingers, and he wanted to be near her the way he'd once wanted to be near Vivian, before her depression had consumed her. Before she'd stopped touching him, before their marriage had become nothing more than an obsession with the absence of a child.

Ricardo sized Jonathan up, then glanced back and forth between him and Helena. He took the barstool beside Jonathan, clapped him on the back, and turned to the bartender. "A drink for her gringo friend." Then, in perfect English, he said to Jonathan, "You look like you need one, amigo. What will you have?"

Jonathan thanked him and ordered a drink, reverting to Spanish. The other men's glances were subtle, but they were paying close attention to their commander's interactions. A somber dinner crowd began filing in, and the other officers scattered to find tables, leaving Jonathan and Ricardo alone with Helena and Camila. The women excused themselves to the restroom.

"So what are you doing here, then?" Ricardo asked, sipping the whiskey the bartender set down in front of him.

Jonathan wasn't sure whether he meant in the bar or in Argentina, so he gave Ricardo a brief explanation of his assignment at the embassy: the paper-pushing he did with Fort Leavenworth to enroll Argentine service members into US military schools—mostly fixing the damn fax machine—and the security program he helped administer to ensure that the US assistance provided for Operation Condor was carried out defensibly.

"It's a shame Perón left them all so ungovernable," said Ricardo. "You must be counting down the days to get back home to your wife and kids."

Jonathan rested the edge of the beer bottle on his lips and tipped it toward the ceiling. It was a solitary mission, but nowhere near as challenging as returning home to Vivian. Her spiraling grief over these past few years had inflicted him with the permanent burden of suppressing his own.

"You're married, aren't you?" asked Ricardo.

"Yes." Jonathan looked down at the bar. "No kids yet, though. We're—my wife and I are going to adopt."

"How very benevolent of you." Ricardo leaned in. Jonathan was relieved when Helena emerged from the restroom in one stocking foot.

"Camila's his secretary," said Helena, once she'd settled onto the barstool.

"It's no business of mine," Jonathan replied.

"Your Spanish is very good. Where did you learn?"

"In Texas. When I was kid."

Sé bueno, his Oaxacan babysitter would warn him and his brother, Greg, when their parents were gone for weeks at a time on Baptist mission trips. Jonathan did try to be good. When he enlisted out of high school and left home for advanced infantry training and airborne school at Fort Bragg, he tried. All the months through special operations training, when he polished the Spanish he'd learned as a child, he tried. And the summer he met Vivian at the church fair, when he was a second lieutenant and she was a pretty girl from Virginia in a cotton blouse tied chastely around her torso, eager to do the things that shouldn't be done outside of the sacrament of marriage, he tried.

He took a sip of his beer. Even now, still, he tried to be a good man, though he feared he'd never achieve it.

Once they'd finished their drinks, Ricardo gave Jonathan his card. He patted him on the back again with his left hand, offering his right. "Nice meeting you, soldier," he said. "Come by and see me sometime soon. I'll take you to lunch."

Helena looked at Jonathan expectantly. He helped her with her coat in an odd gesture that fell somewhere between chivalry and charity. The fur collar brushed against her soft white neck as she slipped her arms through.

"See you soon, Captain," said Helena.

———— · ⬥ · ————

The pebbled driveway crunched beneath the jeep's tires as the vehicle slowed and came to a stop. Behind the wrought iron gate, a manicured lawn fringed the white columns of the prestigious *Escuela*—the Navy's school of mechanics. Jonathan waited in the passenger seat as the boyish Argentine private got out from behind the wheel and approached an officer on the other side of the fence to open the gate. The private parked the jeep in the back of the building, escorted Jonathan inside, and waited as he signed the register. When Jonathan's Argentine counterpart appeared, the man's face brightened with recognition.

"Yanquis," the tall officer chuckled, clapping Jonathan's shoulder as they shook hands. It was Adolfo, one of Ricardo's men—Helena had introduced them in the restaurant back when Jonathan first arrived. "Mucho gusto. What, are you making the rounds here? With a driver? Lucky you." He glanced at the private, who'd been assigned to Jonathan through the defense attaché office. "Are you auditioning to be his personal assistant?"

The private reddened. Jonathan smirked.

"Good to see you, Lieutenant," said Jonathan. "Just a couple of site visits today. A quick stop here first, then over to Olimpo this afternoon."

"Then a pile of paperwork, I bet," said Adolfo. "Come, sit. Have a quick coffee."

He led Jonathan across the mosaic-tiled lobby to the officers' lounge, leaving the private lingering in the entryway, and handed his FMK-3 to his aid. At a leather-top writing table with two guest chairs, Adolfo settled in across from Jonathan and hitched one ankle over the opposite knee. He ran his slim index finger across his forehead, sweeping aside hair that looked slightly overdue for a trim. He pulled a soft pack of cigarettes from his breast pocket and raised it, both an offering and a request for permission. Jonathan shook his head but gestured for him to proceed.

"How's everything going here?" asked Jonathan.

Adolfo shrugged, lighting his cigarette. "What can I say? We're doing what we can. Much more with the media now. That's going well. And SIDE has had some nice successes." The Secretaría de Inteligéncia del Estado, Argentina's secret police, had been working with Chile and Uruguay to target socialist politicians, reporters, and other high-profile enemies throughout the southern cone. "But we're still fighting off Marxists every day. Chasing terrorists into exile if we can't catch them."

A young woman set two espressos down in front of them. Adolfo dropped a sugar cube into his cup. Jonathan lifted his and took a sip.

A group of troops entered the building, filling the lobby with the sounds of their boots and loud banter. Adolfo straightened, peering at the soldiers as they headed up the stairway on the far side of the building.

"What's upstairs?" asked Jonathan.

Adolfo settled back in his chair and took a drag. "*La capucha.* Our biggest holding cell."

Once they'd finished their coffees, Adolfo stood up. "We've got some small munitions that need to be transported to the federal police building. I'm sure your assistant won't mind helping."

Jonathan shook his hand, thanked him, and said goodbye.

Outside, the private lifted four milk crates of leather restraints and batteries and loaded them into the back of the jeep. At their destination, an officer waited on the street to direct the jeep into the Olimpo garage, the federal police department's automotive depot. As the private set down the crates on the concrete floor inside, Jonathan looked around at the parked military vehicles, inoperative tramcars, and pallets of auto-maintenance supplies. It was quiet, near empty. The officer escorted them up the ramp to the first floor, where a small metal table sat outside a series of closed doors.

"We have six guards assigned to two shifts, each with shift supervisors," he said. "Space for twenty or thirty prisoners, maybe more. We just had a transfer, so the numbers are down."

Jonathan's eyes passed over the concrete wall of doors.

"We've seen the dregs, lately," he went on. "Maybe that's a good thing, I don't know. We had one in here the other day—ERP, I think—and he was like this." The officer sliced the side of his flattened hand across his own kneecaps. "No legs. I'm not even kidding you. Still out there trying to start a revolution."

Jonathan waited out the anticipation of laughter.

"And another one—weapons smuggler, I think. We feed them well before they're transferred. Less questions that way. They're treated like royalty, considering they're terrorists. They should get what they deserve. Instead they get us, the lucky bastards. Last week they had fig jam. It's a blasted five-star hotel."

Jonathan chuckled as the officer motioned toward the interrogation room. He took note of the *picana electrica*, standard voltage, and inspected a box of sodium pentothal vials.

The sky was turning pink when the private dropped Jonathan off near the embassy. From his residence, he called Ricardo's office.

"Captain," Camila sung through the receiver once Jonathan had introduced himself. "You're lucky you caught us. He's just getting ready to leave for the day. Helena told me about the new shoes you bought her. How was your dinner last week?"

Jonathan cleared his throat. "I'm just calling to make an appointment with Ricardo."

"Well, then." There was a flipping of pages. "He's free next Tuesday after lunch."

Jonathan rolled a ballpoint pen across a notepad on the nightstand. "Nothing sooner?"

"He's headed out for the day now. If you don't want to wait, why don't you meet him at the bistro in twenty minutes?"

"That's great. Thank you, Camila." He hung up and put on his coat.

He made his way to the restaurant near the plaza on foot. Ricardo was already at the bar, seated in front of a full glass of whiskey. He greeted Jonathan, then motioned to the bartender to bring a second one. Jonathan didn't object.

"How's everything with you?" he asked once he'd settled on the stool beside Ricardo.

"Eh. Another day. We made some arrests across town." Ricardo sighed. "A few of them resisted. It didn't end well."

The liquor was bitter on his tongue. "Sorry to hear it."

They both sipped in silence for a few moments.

"I have a nephew," Ricardo said finally. "Pedro. My brother's kid. He's interested in the exchange program at the Command and General Staff School in the States. He's a good candidate. You handle those enrollments, no?"

Jonathan straightened on the stool, then turned his head and looked directly into Ricardo's eyes. Suddenly they were teammates exchanging batons, assessing each other's capacity to carry weight.

"I do," said Jonathan.

Ricardo turned toward the colorful row of liquor bottles behind the bar. "He's interested in advanced military studies. Command and leadership specifically. He wants to be a general someday."

"Big ambitions."

"I wonder, do you think that could happen for him?"

Jonathan took a second sip of whiskey. It tasted much better than the first. There were still vacancies to be filled in Fort Leavenworth and the nephew of a high-ranking officer seemed as promising an applicant as any for the international program.

"If he's a good candidate," Jonathan said truthfully, "then I don't see why not."

Ricardo nodded. "I appreciate that, Captain. It's good to keep young people in this country on the right track. Half of them don't understand the meaning of patriotism."

"You're not alone there. Back home we just pardoned a hundred thousand draft-evaders."

Ricardo glanced over at Jonathan and lifted his glass. "Well, here's to those of us who still show up to the fight."

Jonathan clinked his whiskey glass against Ricardo's.

CHAPTER 9

Rachel swiveled her head nostalgically as she drove past St. Vincent's church in Howell Grove. As a child, she'd envisioned the dead lined up like busts of classical musicians along the rafters of the chancel—a heaven of sorts, a storage place for ghosts. For as long as she could remember, she had understood God. God existed in the strangest of places—in the scent of her mother's hydrangeas; under the delicate toes of the Virgin Mary crushing a concrete serpent outside the rectory; in the warm light of other people's windows. On the face of a saxophone player at a subway stop on the six train once. Most of all, in the scent of her sacred blanket, where she could bury her face and breathe in pure holiness whenever she needed it. Her religion—those angelic parents from her childhood bedtime stories—were always there, elusive and loving. She feared they might disappear if she found out who they really were.

She parked the rental car in the gravel driveway of the ranch house where she'd grown up. Here, on the two-acre plot of land abutting the woods at the bottom of a small hill, the presence of her rival twin—the blond ghost—was stronger than ever.

Rachel turned the engine off and stared through the windshield at the blackness of her backyard. In the distance, early fireworks popped like luminescent dandelions gone to seed. How easy it would be to take the envelope Mari had given her and throw it away like it had all been a mistake.

She gathered her bags, the slam of the car door piercing the spacious dark.

Inside the three-bedroom house, a nostalgic waft of graham cracker pie crust and Murphy's oil soap enveloped her. By the light of a table lamp, faded prints on worn fabric softened the wood-paneled living room. The floral upholstery of the couch, the eyelet valances. A fifty-five-gallon freshwater fish tank against the living room wall was the only change since Rachel had moved out.

"You made it," her mom whispered from the hallway in her robe. Rachel hugged her tall, bony frame against her own curves. "How was your trip?"

"It's good to get out of the city for the Fourth," said Rachel, but the real reason for her visit felt heavy in her bag.

Her mom's eyes followed Rachel's to the fish tank.

"The doc at the VA says it's good for him. Relaxes him, I guess. He's got too much time to think lately."

"He's the only retiree in the house now." Rachel set her bag on the armchair. She glanced over her mother's shoulder at the kitchen table, where a small birdcage was half-filled with peonies and a row of single calla lilies stood in test tubes. "Are you still doing arrangements for the church?"

Her mom shrugged. "I'm experimenting. I did the high school prom last month."

"That's great," said Rachel. She needed the encouragement.

"But your dad's still doing a few security jobs here and there, so we both keep busy." She adjusted the sash to her robe. "All right. I'll let you get settled in."

Rachel tiptoed to her childhood bedroom, struck by a sudden pang of guilt. The envelope seemed like a betrayal. She shut the pinstriped curtains, tossed her bag on the bed, and unzipped it. She took the envelope out and buried it under the eyelet runner on the dresser, then moved away, as though its tragedy were contagious.

All around were relics of her youth—photos in frames, a bronzed baby shoe, stuffed animals on her quilted bedspread. Her mom had placed a scented candle and a single hydrangea in a bud vase on the end table. Rachel shut the bedroom door and flicked the lock on the knob. She gathered up her long hair with both hands and twisted it on top of her head. The past was nearly visible here, as though the place itself had been scarred by time. She'd been right here with the blond ghost on a sunny afternoon years ago when her future was still a blank canvas, when she called out her plans to her parents, vulnerable and defensive about how they might echo back to her. She would move to a big city, she told them, and study something important: economics or art or political science. She was going to change the world.

She could still see the landscape of her teenage room—the black-and-white perfume ads, the canister of wide-toothed combs with spray nozzle handles, purple bottles of hair mousse, a tin of strawberry candies. Her bookshelf, where a half-dozen handheld American flags were propped in a mason jar—a residual collection from when she'd mobilized her soccer team at school. They'd made *God Bless Our Troops* banners for every game and launched a yellow ribbon campaign that infiltrated her entire middle school while her dad was in Kuwait. Her mom was taking courses at the community college then, and she perpetually left a book lying around the house with a highlighter stuffed between its pages: *You Can Start Your Own Business.*

"You'll need to decide how to make a living," her father said. The skepticism in his voice stung. "What do you think you're going to do?"

"I don't know. I haven't decided yet." She'd looked up at them. "I could start my own business."

"Doing what?"

"How am I supposed to know?" she'd flustered. "I don't even know where I came from."

Her parents had glanced at each other.

"I want to find my birth parents before I graduate from high school."

Her dad tilted his head.

"If that's what you want," he said without hesitation, "we'll help you."

When she wrapped her arms around his neck, he smelled of Irish Spring soap.

Rachel reached over to the end table now and touched the hydrangea her mom had left for her. She turned her face into the pillow and caught notes of detergent and a slight mustiness from the cellar laundry.

First thing when she woke up, she would tell them everything Mari had said. They were her parents. They always knew what to do.

———— · ❖ · ————

In the morning, the corner of the envelope peeked at her. She slid it out from under the runner, stuffed it in the pocket of her robe, and headed to the living room, where her dad was reading the newspaper in an easy chair. Thin cotton curtains bounced against the wire screen of the kitchen windows. Sunlight and the aroma of warm pancakes filled the room.

"Morning, kiddo," he said. "Good to have you home."

Her mom stood in front of the griddle, where batter was bubbling in neat pools. Rachel glanced through the cellophane at the homemade cake covered in whipped cream and berries on the counter. The spiral-bound church calendar on the wall showcased the Smoky Mountains above empty white boxes of days.

Rachel reached for the coffeepot, pecking her mother's cheek. "This house is like a time warp."

Her dad chuckled. His newspaper crinkled loudly as he set aside the business section.

"What's happening in the world?" her mother asked.

"London bombings," he said. "They still don't know who did it."

She flipped a pancake. "Can we have breakfast before we talk about terrorism?" She cleared her throat. "Who wants pancakes? Do you want pancakes, Jon?"

"No."

She shifted her gaze out the window to the back porch and clenched her jaw. Rachel pushed the screen door open and escaped into one of the Adirondack chairs with her coffee mug. As she pulled her knees to her chest, the weight of the envelope in her robe pocket caused it to fall open, exposing her upper thigh.

Her mom flung the door open with her hip, balancing a plate of syrup-drizzled pancakes in each hand. A fork tottered on the one she presented to Rachel. Her father filled the doorway, and he meandered outside in his slippers, settled into a chair across from them, and unfolded his paper again. As Rachel bit into a warm pancake, a squirrel darted across the ryegrass lawn. Her dad looked up from his paper, then at Rachel.

"You been using that chain lock on your apartment door?"

"Sometimes." She sounded like a child.

"You should use it, honey," said her mother.

Rachel suppressed a rising petulance. She would do what she came to do. She would broach the topic, however inelegantly.

"Dad?" she asked. "What do you know about Argentina?"

Her mother stopped chewing and looked up. Her fork clinked against her plate.

He tittered. "What kind of question is that?"

"I'm just curious. Do you know anything about it?"

"I know a lot of things about a lot of things. Like how many people would be happy to take advantage of a foolish young woman who leaves her door unlocked."

"I don't leave it *unlocked*." Rachel sat up straighter, baited. "Have you ever been to Argentina?"

He lifted his paper and sat back, then turned a single crackling page, face hidden. "I was based there once."

"Twice," said her mother.

He peered at her from behind the paper with a mix of curiosity and disgust.

"What?" her mom said, stabbing a piece of pancake and plowing it through the syrup on her plate. "You did two tours in one year. How could I forget that? You were off protecting the Free World while I was here alone."

They glared at each other.

"It wasn't an easy time for me," she said.

"Was it during the war?" asked Rachel.

"No, after Vietnam," he said. "But still ancient history now."

"Not Vietnam. I meant the war in Argentina. The Dirty War." The breeze stilled. "The one where people disappeared."

"I'm aware of what the Dirty War was," he said with mild condescension.

"Well, was that when you were there?" Rachel perched on the edge of the chair, her back erect.

He bent a corner of his newspaper down with one finger to meet her eyes. "I was stationed there, yes."

"Where did you live?"

"At the embassy. Both tours."

"Why were you there?"

"I was advising on a mission."

"What kind of mission?"

"A mission. It was called Operation Condor. Why are you asking about this?"

"I just wondered if you knew what happened there. What they did, I mean."

Her dad lowered the newspaper to his lap, then folded it up and removed his glasses. His eyes locked with Rachel's. "What *who* did?"

"The military." She suddenly felt nervous. "The government."

He pinched the bridge of his nose and let out a sigh. "You're really interested in this all of a sudden."

"I just want to know."

"Listen, kiddo, I don't expect you to understand, but it was a complicated time. You've never seen what chaos looks like up close." He forced a chuckle. "You want to tell me why you're asking about this?"

Rachel set her plate on the side table between her and her mom, reached into the pocket of her robe, and pulled out the envelope. She handed the entire thing to him and watched as pale creases formed at the corners of his eyes. He opened it, took out one of the fliers and examined it, then turned it over to its blank side.

Her mom placed her fork on the empty plate in her lap and leaned forward. "What is it?"

"Where did you get this?" he said. He waved the flier of the hand between his thumb and forefinger, the card stock warbling in the summer air. Rachel pulled her arms inside the sleeves of her robe and crossed them, hands locked between her knees. The syrup had a bitter aftertaste.

Her mother glared at him. "What is it, Jon?"

He rose from his chair to hand the flier to his wife. As he did, the newspaper slid from his lap. He jerked to catch it, still holding the envelope in his other hand. He slapped the paper against his thigh to keep it from falling. Two photos slipped out of the envelope and swung in the air like falling leaves. Rachel lunged to rescue the picture of Lorena from the dewy deck floor, but the other photo landed face up on the teak boards. The three of them stared down at Mat and Mari, smiling up from a backdrop of palm fronds.

Her mother picked the photo up and gently placed it on her knee. "Who's this?" she asked.

"Her name is Mari—Dr. Marisol Rey. And the boy's name is Mat. He's from Argentina." Rachel glanced up at her dad, but he'd turned his back to them and was gazing out across the backyard. "He's looking for his sister."

Her mom set her plate at her feet and scrutinized the photo.

"She's a professor. She works for"—Rachel nodded toward the flyer still in her father's hand—"that group. The Abuelas. She reached out to me last week about my adoption."

"Why didn't you tell us?" her mother asked.

"I'm telling you now. That's why I'm here."

Her dad strode the few steps toward her mom and dropped the flier in her lap, then paced away again. He rolled up the newspaper and twisted its thickness.

"What does it say?" her mom asked, pointing to the words on the flier.

"It's like, 'Identity doesn't impose itself,'" said Rachel.

Her dad dragged one hand down his face and turned back around to face them. His neck was flushed and blotchy, the way it looked after he'd spent an afternoon chopping logs for the woodpile.

"They think I'm one of the children who disappeared."

He pointed the rolled-up newspaper at the flyer in his wife's lap.

"That's propaganda," he said.

"They don't know for sure that I'm the right person." Rachel's voice hovered evenly. "It could be a mistake. Someone told her that an American officer took a baby to the United States."

He laughed and shook his head.

Rachel handed her mom the photo of Lorena. She examined it for a moment, then drew in a sharp breath. Her fingertips rose to her lips.

"That's Mat's mother," said Rachel. "Her name was Lorena."

"Helena?" she asked.

"Viv," said her father. "For Christ's sake."

"*Lor*ena," repeated Rachel. "Lorena Ledesma."

Her mom's eyes were wide, still fixed on the photo. "She looks like you," she whispered, flipping it over to inspect the back. A blue jay shrieked in the distance.

"It could be altered," said her dad.

"No, no. It's too old." Her mom held the picture toward him, but he didn't move.

"Dad, are you mad at me?"

"What?" He scooted the deck chair closer to Rachel and sat, resting his elbows on his knees. He stared at the teak deck boards as he spoke. "No, kiddo. No, of course not. I get why you would ask me this; I do. It's only natural. Listen, I'm talking to you as an adult now, okay?"

"Okay." Rachel hugged her knees, undermined by her pajamas, by the plate of pancakes, by the teenage angst that she still allowed to seep into her interactions with her parents.

He raised an eyebrow. "You were found on a porch in Howell County. I have no idea who in their right mind would've left an innocent baby like that, but your aunt Daphne would swear on a stack of bibles that you couldn't have come from Argentina any more than you could've come from the moon. We don't know who left you there, but it's not for lack of trying to find out. And you're a smart girl. Think about it." He gestured toward the picture of Mat. "I'm sure whatever story this woman is telling you about this young man is a tragedy, but what went on in his life doesn't have anything to do with you. It's understandable that they're chasing down any scrap of hope they can find—and it happened to lead them to you. Apparently I put you in this situation by being in the wrong place at the wrong time—by doing my job. Protecting my country and theirs, for God's sake." He lowered his voice. "Your mother and I took all the right steps. I've never broken the law in my life."

"No one's talking about the law," said her mom. "Let's just stay calm, Jon." She examined her husband with familiar concern. Rachel felt the blond ghost's disdain seep in. *Don't startle your dad, honey,* her mom would warn after Rachel made the mistake of sneaking up behind his recliner and covering his eyes with her tiny hands during an episode of M*A*S*H. Rachel had seen his pain up close. A career's worth of pulling a trigger had traumatized him, and he dulled the ache with whiskey and silence and categorical presumptions about the people his bullets had pierced: they were enemies, criminals, terrorists—not people like *us.* Even Rachel indulged his words, these mercies that helped him erase whatever it was he'd done.

"I just don't want you to get your hopes up thinking this might be something it's not," he said. "You've always been a little naive that way. You believe things too easily. I don't want to see you get your heart broken."

He was trying to protect her, but she was queasy with the urge to soothe him instead. She rubbed her bad knee, recalled the day she'd looked up at him in pain from where she lay injured on the soccer field. His face had searched hers then, as it did now, with concern and something else: an eagerness, a desire for kinship—*It hurts, doesn't it?* A hot current of indignation ran through her body.

"Do you think this woman Mari is lying? Or that it's just a coincidence?"

"I think it's a mistake." His tone was low. "I don't see why she would lie."

Rachel felt a sudden stab of regret for bringing Mari into what seemed a very private family matter—but then she wasn't entirely sure why it felt so private. It was *her* adoption.

"Think it through, Rach. These people think you're the child of a political prisoner." His eyes were sad but sincere. "It's impossible."

It was comforting, this certainty, the force of his authority that coalesced around his words. But when the sunlight fell over him, something shifted, subtle as a thin layer of dust or a change in the texture of his skin. There had been a rift growing between them since the Twin Towers fell, since his irritating enthusiasm for the Iraq War began to grow in direct proportion to the protests against it. Faint questions had begun to enter her mind each time he spoke. Doubts. Tiny little doubts.

But this was the first time in her life that she truly didn't believe her father.

The photo in her mother's hand had its own center of gravity. It was a magnetic force distorting Rachel's sense of certainty even further.

"Your mom and I raised you in the best way we knew how." He kneaded his jaw with one hand. "We've always wanted the best for you. We have nothing to hide."

There was an unspoken accusation from the blond ghost: *ingrate.*

"I know," Rachel said. "I just wanted to ask."

In the silence that followed, the air thickened. She could stay safe here, within the walls erected by her father, decorated by her mother. These walls protected her—they always had. But there was a hairline crack in them now. The truth was slippery, potentially irreconcilable. Taking a DNA test could mean trading her angel-ghost parents for real people made of flesh and bones—but it could also mean forsaking her trust in the only real parents she'd ever known.

"For what it's worth," he said, "I was in Fort Bragg the morning Daphne found you. I wasn't even home from assignment yet."

"That's true," said her mom. She peeled her focus from the photo of Lorena and looked at Rachel. Her eyes were imploring. *Please stop doing this.* Rachel felt crushed.

Her dad stood up abruptly. "They've just got the wrong person, that's all." He directed his words toward her mother. "It's just like you said. There's no need to get all worked up about it." He took the photos and the flier back from his wife and pushed them into the envelope, then turned to Rachel. "This lady who's been harassing you—you have her information?"

"Her card's in there," said Rachel. "But she wasn't harassing me." She glanced at her mom for support, but she just stood up, collected the breakfast plates, and brought them into the kitchen. Through the screen, Rachel heard them clatter in the sink as she turned on the water. He followed her into the house, the matter resolved.

Rachel watched through the screen as her dad sat down in the easy chair and stared silently at the fish tank. After several minutes, he got up and disappeared down the hall toward his den. Moments later, a car door slammed out front.

In the kitchen, her mom rinsed out the coffeepot.

"Where'd Dad go?"

"To the VFW." She gestured to the kitchen table, where she'd thrust a clump of wildflowers down the throat of an empty wine jug. A folder lay open. "He left those out for you."

Rachel's adoption forms—the abandonment notices, the statutory postings with no responses, the default termination of parental rights—spread out before her. She skimmed them: . . . *constituted by the failure to provide food, clothing, medical care* . . . There was a Department of Health and Human Services record, intake papers completed by Daphne on the day of Rachel's abandonment, and an inconclusive investigative report printed on security firm letterhead—*Secure World*—from 1993. She'd seen all of it before.

He'd left Mari's envelope next to the folder. Only the business card was missing. Rachel picked it up and brought it to her bedroom. She zipped it up in her overnight bag.

When she returned to the kitchen, her mother glanced up from the sink, then dried her hands on a dish towel.

"You want to come out to the greenhouse with me?"

Rachel nodded. She followed her mom down the porch steps and across patches of sun-dried dirt to the greenhouse, which stretched nearly thirty feet in length and was fogged with condensation. Her mother's T-shirt draped across her bony shoulder blades, and her white pedal pushers clung to her calves as she approached one of the long rows of wooden planting boxes inside.

Inside, the smell of wet soil was reminiscent of childhood harvests—fresh peas, string beans, carrots, watermelon, squash. Pumpkins scattered on the ground. Rachel wanted her mom to know she remembered these things now. She leaned back against the cabinet her dad built years ago and breathed in the dewy air, waiting for her mom to say whatever she came out here to say.

"The young man in that photo," her mom said at last, moving to the tomato plants. "What happened to his father?"

"I don't know." Rachel pressed her palms to the top of the cupboard and hoisted her body up onto it to sit. The pulpy base of her thumb pinched between two panels of wood and she winced, inspecting the white line of raised flesh left behind.

Her mother looked pained. "I know your dad and I aren't perfect, but we've always tried to be good parents to you."

"You are good parents, Mom. It has nothing to do with being bad parents." Rachel rubbed her sore palm with intensity. "I just want to know where I came from."

Her mother flicked aside a clump of soil to reveal a whitish-green shoot protruding from a faint trench in the dirt.

"I'm going to take a DNA test," Rachel confessed.

Her mom lifted her chin. She pulled gardening gloves over her delicate hands and began pruning the tomato plant, the steel blades cutting the flesh of its stalk.

"You're a lot like your father." She removed a glove and thumbed the plant's wet wound, then looked up at Rachel. "I've always thought so, at least." She leaned one hand on the edge of the potting table and put the other on her hip, turning to face Rachel directly. "Do you remember when you used to bring me things from the Easton's barn for my flower arrangements? Old bicycle wheels, tin cans, mason jars, things like that?"

Rachel shrugged. "Sort of."

"You did. You always had a way of finding something beautiful."

Emotion fizzled across the bridge of Rachel's nose into her sinuses.

Her mom looked up at the roof of the greenhouse, one hand moving to her neck. "We'll help you find out whatever you want to know, sweetheart. You deserve answers. I just—" Her bare hand jumped to her face, covering her nose and mouth as her brow crumpled. She looked about to burst into a sob, but the gesture was instantaneous, and with one quick sniff her hand was back on her hip, her face fully recovered.

"What is it? What's wrong, Mom?"

She shook her head.

"Mom." Rachel's voice was pleading now. "Please. I need to know."

She let out a long, shaky sigh. "Scoot." She approached Rachel and motioned for her to get down off the cabinet. "I have something I want to give you." She reached under the planting box and picked up a false rock—a key hider—and removed its bottom. Rachel's heart leaped. Her mom stuck the little key in the small padlock on the door to the tool cabinet Rachel had been sitting on. Inside, her mother reached past a stack of terracotta pots and took out a small book with no cover, its navy blue spine worn and frayed. There was a rubber band wrapped around it.

"I want you to have this. It was my mother's." She held the book in both hands, chest-height, and moved a hand across its cover. It was a book of poetry verses by Sara Teasdale called *Rivers to the Sea*.

"Why do you keep it out here?"

She looked confused. "This is my place, I suppose." She removed the rubber band, opened the book, and flipped to a marked page. "They're lovely poems."

"Poems." Rachel's shoulders fell. She had expected something more significant, less sentimental.

"Listen to this: *For I shall learn from flower and leaf / That color every drop they hold, / To change the lifeless wine of grief / To living gold.*" She closed her eyes and smiled sadly. "I just love that one." She shut the book, held in a high breath, then released the air from her lungs. Then she placed it in Rachel's hands like a birthright.

CHAPTER 10

VIRGINIA

JULY 2005

Mom, please. I need to know.

Vivian could still hear the yearning in Rachel's voice. She knew that kind of desperation; she had felt it herself many years ago—lying in bed for weeks on end, trembling from the loss of lifeblood and the little blue pills Dr. Wexler had prescribed after her second miscarriage. She remembered her bloody jeans on the bathroom floor, balled-up and banished behind the hamper—a relic whose stain would never come out.

She should have been preoccupied with what was happening with Rachel, but all she could think about now were the babies she didn't have, the feelings she'd never acknowledged, the questions she didn't ask. Did all women hide such secrets? Vivian sat at the kitchen table flipping through the pages of *Rivers to the Sea*. Rachel had left the book on her bedspread when she went back to the city. Her apathy stung Vivian in a way she had grown accustomed to over the years. She paused to skim a line from her favorite poem, "Barter." *And children's faces looking up / Holding wonder like a cup.*

Vivian recalled the first time she'd seen the garnet clots in the toilet water. She thought of the nursery she'd so foolishly prepared, years before it became Rachel's room, and how it sat empty and cold as a tomb at the end of the hall. Her mother's callous words: *When you have children of your own someday.* She'd become angry with the doctor, who questioned her ability to have children at all, sparking the delicate debate between her and Jonathan as to whose body was the culprit. Fertility testing was expensive, and Jonathan had deflected their efforts to adoption, so their childlessness was presumed to be Vivian's failing, and she had taken the blame without protest.

That second time, she'd called for Jonathan from the greenhouse. She'd been cutting tulip stems when she was overcome by the familiar cramping. He'd averted his eyes from the blood, but he consoled her in the months that followed. Her grief doubled; her sanity suffered. The anguish lived in her body, a spiraling convalescence, and in her soul, in the deep, sacred absence of her lost children. Jonathan had brought her back to the world, set an expectation of resilience to which she could rise.

At least that's what she'd told herself at the time.

Now, though, as the memories came back to her, it seemed as though he'd never allowed her any space to grieve.

Through the bay window, she watched two squirrels scramble feverishly across the backyard. She had the greenhouse memorized from this angle; she could paint a picture of the sunlight on its curved panels with her eyes closed. Along the side of the house, the road stretched up the hill for half a mile, intersecting with the route Rachel's school bus used to travel. The postal truck turned down it toward the house now. She thought of Rachel as a child descending the school bus steps, her rosy lips parting in excitement, the afternoon sunlight buttering her skin.

"Tell me the story of where I came from," Rachel would request each night after they'd recited prayers, tucked into bed with her little blanket, freshly bathed in pajamas, her wet hair combed. Vivian could still see her sweet face, her soft cheeks and dark lashes illuminated by a Holly Hobby table lamp. Such perfect features.

"It was a beautiful summer day," Vivian would murmur. "And the leaves were starting to change early that year." As Vivian recounted the story, she'd embellish Daphne's description of the baby girl found that morning—*brilliant, magnificent, perfect, sent from the angels*—always spinning enough fiction into the narrative to build a beautiful world for Rachel to inhabit, taking great care to add ambiguity to the abandonment. Rachel's birth parents were always just out of reach, vanished but still scarcely there in a way that bordered on magic.

"Where was I before that day?" Rachel would ask, and Vivian would look around her childhood bedroom: the quilted bedspread, the books, the clothes, the toys. The proof that Rachel belonged to them.

"You were with the mommy and daddy who made you," Vivian would say quietly, because by then the adoption had been finalized, and she was no longer panicked by the tenuous foster care period.

"But where are they now?"

"I don't know, sweetheart. I think they must be angels. Angels who asked God to send you to Daddy and me."

Vivian had done all of this for them—for him, for her. She'd created their life, raised a beautiful daughter who never seemed to flourish. Rachel dismissed the many boys who'd taken interest in her during high school, as if her own desire was a shameful indulgence. How convenient for a father to have a daughter who resisted intimacy and pleasure, who seemed to be infinitely waiting for someone to merit her attention.

The photo of the woman with Rachel's face returned to Vivian's mind's eye now. Her features, her smile, her name: *Lorena.*

Vivian carefully turned the page of the poetry book and flattened its spine. She skimmed the first couple lines of a poem called "Chance."

How many times we must have met / Here on the street as strangers do . . .

She hadn't been bold enough to show Rachel what else these pages contained, the artifact Vivian had preserved over the years like a tear in an elixir bottle. Rachel had taken no interest in looking. Perhaps she'd learned that from her mother.

Vivian slid it out now and positioned it on the kitchen table: a single piece of expensive-looking stationery embossed with the header *Helena Silva,* and a note that followed in a woman's handwriting.

Graciela Ruiz
(54 11) 45 44 2000
Agradéceme después
Besos

She picked up the paper and rubbed it between her fingers as though
to validate its existence, the same way she'd done decades prior when
she found it face up in the wastebasket in Jonathan's den.

Some wives would have confronted their husbands upon finding a
note like this. *Besos.* Perhaps she should have made a scene, demanded
answers. But Vivian was not this type of woman. She was a loyal girl
from rural Virginia who had anchored her future to the reliable shores
of Jonathan's thick uniform and gold buttons. If he wasn't the man she
thought he was for so many years, she hadn't wanted to know. If he
failed her, it would have been her own failing too.

Besides, there was a practical matter to exposing his infidelity. He
would have no choice but to tell her something: a truth, a lie—it didn't
matter. Nothing would ever be the same between them again. She had
a duty as his wife; they had a child to raise. It was a selfish indulgence
to dig through his secrets. She wouldn't want him to dig through hers.
He was never returning to South America again. He'd left whatever he'd
done there behind long ago. Overlooking his indiscretions was a small
price to pay to keep their family intact.

So Vivian waited.

She waited for signs he didn't love her, that he no longer wanted his
life with her, but they never came. In the bay window, she caught her
faint reflection: an unremarkable woman in her midfifties, graying blond
hair cut to the same length it had been for decades, a plain cardigan
draped from her thin shoulders. She was insignificant, nearly invisible.

She never asked questions. She always tried to offer him the comfort
of not having to talk about any of the things he'd seen and done, and
she was glad she didn't have to bear the full weight of knowing. There
was a level of culpability by association that came with being married
to a man who had taken the lives of others. They called it "shell shock"

back then—a kind of war neurosis. Years ago, Vivian had given him a brochure she'd picked up from the wire carousel at the grocery store checkout entitled *The Soldier's Heart*, but Jonathan never read it. She soothed him through every flashback, each memory like a piece of debris from an explosion site cleared one pebble at a time. She didn't need to know the details of his sins.

Vivian examined the piece of stationery on the table. She couldn't imagine Jonathan bringing a baby back from Argentina, certainly not by himself, but he seemed to have had a lover there, maybe more than one, and he'd hidden it from her. What else was he capable of?

He'd been so eager to return to South America for that second tour, as if he couldn't wait to get back. Vivian still remembered the day he left, the clink of his car keys in his pocket, the fabric name patch on his lapel: *SPRAGUE*. She pretended she didn't sense his guilty relief to leave her alone with the emptiness of her own body. She hadn't wanted him to leave—the weight of their brokenness was meant to be shared. They'd been married for five years at the time, but a vacancy had already entered their lives, one that threatened to grow like a fungus if it wasn't filled properly. Who were they if not the dutiful couple in the third pew of St. Vincent's with empty space on the left for the little heads God intended them to create? Who was Vivian if not the wife of a captain and future mother of his children? Without a child, their marriage would become two people whose lives stretched out through the expanse of time with no cues, no expected behavior. It had panicked her. She'd feared she had nothing to contribute to a life like that.

When he returned from his first tour, he'd insisted they put their names on the waiting list for adoption, as though he knew something was coming. He called Daphne before they'd even finished talking it through. Vivian clenched her teeth at the thought of Daphne—the way she acted superior for playing a hand in helping them adopt, as though she were some benefactor or fairy godmother responsible for Rachel's very existence. Daphne had held Rachel in her arms before Vivian had even laid eyes on her daughter, an observation Daphne only had to voice once to awaken an ugliness inside Vivian—something akin to envy, but with sharper teeth. She'd told them waiting for an infant would take forever, if it was even possible at all, but her phone call with the news of Rachel came six short months later, the very same week Jonathan returned from his second tour of duty.

And when Rachel was sixteen and asked about her birth parents, Jonathan had outsourced the search to *Secure World*, the firm where he did consulting work. That amateur PI from a family attorney in the next county handled divorces and affairs—not adoptions. She remembered the way Jonathan had looked over Rachel's shoulder, that steely detachment in his eyes as she took in the contents of her adoption file for the first time. *Look how supportive I am*, Jonathan's stance conveyed. He'd deterred her search, but Vivian never questioned why. It was easier to stay invisible than to face an undesirable truth.

She fingered the wildflowers in the bottle on the table. It was so lovely, so simple, to take root and bloom in the place you were planted, to follow the sun and absorb whatever mercies came along. Such a luxury to not have to know anything else but that.

Lorena Ledesma's face returned to her mind now. She cradled her narrow ribcage and rocked back and forth in the chair. What if Lorena had been one of Jonathan's lovers? He'd been gone for months, twice, over the span of a year and a half. It was possible. Rachel didn't look anything like Jonathan, but the man was a compilation of recessive traits, and their mannerisms often made Vivian wonder.

The screen door slammed. She jumped. Jonathan had come around the back and stood over her now, his hands smeared with dirt from the gutter he'd been cleaning. Vivian laid her hand over the piece of stationery.

His arms hung by his sides. "What are you doing?"

She didn't look up. She slid the paper toward the poetry book in her lap. He touched one corner, stopping it. His thumb left a smudge of dirt.

"What's this? You found this? You kept it?"

She sensed his defensiveness, his shame. "Jon."

"Why?" he asked, his shock distilling to something more potent—contempt, then a cruel kind of pity she'd seen before.

She looked up at him. "I don't really care who these women are unless it has something to do with Rachel. But I'm asking you now. Did you know that woman? The one in the photo?"

"Of course not."

Vivian took a long breath. "This isn't going away, Jon."

He shook his head, looked directly into her eyes. "I've never seen her before in my life. I swear to you."

Vivian straightened in the kitchen chair, mustering her conviction. "Rachel deserves to know the truth about where she came from. I'm her mother." Her throat clogged with emotion. "And I'm going to help her. We're going to help her, whatever she needs."

He crouched down next to her chair. The scent of his skin was lemony, hinted with wheat. Rachel carried this same scent after a day in the sun. "We are both going to help her. Of course we are."

"Then stop trying to make this go away and tell me the truth. Did you know her? Lorena Ledesma?"

His expression changed. Vivian saw the same debilitating fear that overcame him during his flashbacks. "No," he said quietly.

"Then who's Helena?"

"Please don't do this, Viv."

"Who's Graciela?"

"You need to stop with this." He glanced at the poetry book. "You're going to drive yourself crazy again."

"Who is that woman in the photo? Is she Rachel's mother?"

"Vivian, I've made mistakes, but they are not the ones you think."

Vivian held his gaze for a long time.

"I've always been here, right by your side," he said. "I've always come home to you. We've helped each other through. We've always been in this together. Trust me, it's better for everyone if we leave the past alone."

When Vivian finally spoke, it came out in a whisper. "Tell me the truth, Jon."

"I don't know what else you want me to say," he said.

"Did you know the woman in the photo?"

"For God's sake. I'm not doing this." He stood up, washed his hands in the kitchen sink, and headed down the hall. When he returned, he'd changed his clothes. "I don't know exactly what you're accusing me of, Vivian. But I don't *know* that woman. And I'm not doing this with you anymore." He removed his car keys from the wall hook. "I'll be home before dinner."

Vivian watched his truck disappear up the hill and then sat for a long while looking out over the backyard.

In the quiet house, her awareness was summoned to its fringes, where Jonathan spent most of his time. The sounds of his ordinary movements each evening played loudly in her mind: the back door opening and shutting, the television volume rising and fading, the occasional clink of his whiskey decanter, his gun safe locking. She got up and walked down the hallway.

The floorboards creaked with a strain she knew by heart. She entered his den, scanning the bookshelves and the desk with a heightened level of cautiousness.

On the worn desk blotter next to the *Secure World* notepad were two cheap metal keys on a silver ring. She picked them up and fiddled with them absently, then set them back down and opened the desk drawers. She leafed through the papers inside—tax documents, receipts, their marriage certificate, their passports. An old military training manual entitled *Coercive Counterintelligence Interrogation of Resistant Sources.* She skimmed the section headers—*deprivation, threats, fear, debility*—a tally of all the horrors he'd been trained to inflict.

She turned to his bookshelves, toward the Silver Star medal he was awarded after being promoted to First Lieutenant and leading his platoon through heavy fire to rescue six men from the North Vietnamese. She seethed with quiet fury for knowing this.

Across the room was his gun safe. Vivian remembered a night early in their marriage when she'd reached across the soft thread of the bedsheets and felt the smooth, cool metal of his handgun beneath his pillow. It had calmed her then, this demonstrative evidence of his protective instincts, and she'd watched him sleep, imagining him as a boy, before his innocence was tainted by a family of men who handed tempers and bruises down through the generations like heirlooms, before the molten part of him had cooled to hard steel.

It's those early hours of the morning when people are the most vulnerable, he'd said to her once, and she'd searched for tenderness in his meaning, something besides violence.

Vivian carried the poetry book back outside, where a distant storm cloud loomed above the lumpy stone wall that traced their backyard. In the garden, green tufts sprouted in neat lines from dark crumbles of earth. Flowers bloomed in harmony with tomatoes and peas. She tunneled a handful of the rich earth through her cupped fingers now— good, fertile soil—and when she released it, a few crumbs stuck to her palm. She passed the burn barrel, where dead leaves had turned to compost. A final beam of sun fell across her body before the thunderhead absorbed the light.

In the greenhouse, she locked the poetry book back in the cabinet and hid the key.

CHAPTER 11

Outside the clinic, Rachel lingered next to a Mister Softee ice cream truck near the subway entrance on Sixty-Eighth and Lex and played with her Magic 8 Ball key chain.

Is Mat going to show up?

DEFINITELY.

Will the results show that he's my brother?

MY SOURCES SAY NO.

She ran her tongue along the inside of her mouth.

Five days prior, she'd come here alone to take her portion of the DNA test. Dr. Ramel, who was shorter than Rachel with dark skin and a pristine lab coat, had snapped on a pair of latex gloves, produced a small plastic box and a handful of paper-wrapped cotton swabs. He peeled one open and handed it to her.

"Open your mouth and rub this against the inside of your cheek until I tell you to stop."

Rachel dropped her jaw to accommodate the stick.

"Other side."

When she finished, Dr. Ramel stuck the wet cotton head into a little tube inside of the plastic box. He snapped it shut, wrote a number on the lid with a black Sharpie, and jotted something on his clipboard.

"You don't need to draw blood?"

He shook his head. "This is just as efficient."

They repeated the process with a second swab, then a third. By the fourth swab, her mouth was dry. Dr. Ramel finally peeled off his gloves and collected the supplies. "We're going to do several tests." His tone was flat, and his eyes flitted away from the potential obligation of her emotional response to any of his words. "Just keep in mind that sibling tests aren't always fully conclusive. You'll only have a statistical likelihood of whether you and Sibling B—Matías Ledesma—are biological relatives."

"It's not accurate?"

He nudged his glasses impatiently up the bridge of his nose, the corners of his mouth pointed downward. "It's very accurate. It just might not be conclusive. The result will show us a DNA profile for each of you, and we'll compare those. It's not as certain as testing samples from your parents, but since they're not available, it will give us an indication. You're planning to come back with Matías for the readout?"

Rachel nodded.

"In terms of other biological relatives to substantiate the test—" He checked his clipboard. "It looks like Matías indicated having a maternal grandmother. I highly recommend that you retest against her DNA to confirm these findings."

"But she's not here."

"Do you have any other biological relatives available to substantiate the tests?"

Rachel raised an eyebrow. "No."

"Well, that would certainly give you more conclusive results." Dr. Ramel glanced at Rachel. "If it's feasible."

Obviously it wasn't feasible, she thought. Why would she be here if she knew her biological relatives? The fact that any of this was happening was scarcely believable—that Mari had managed to arrange for Mat to come to New York, and that Rachel was about to meet, for the first time, the man who could be her brother.

She looked around the street, eager, overly prepared. Her dad had insisted on running background checks on Mat Ledesma and Marisol Rey. Mat's name didn't produce a single record, and Mari's showed one infraction—a speeding ticket for going sixty-three in a forty-five on highway A1A—which only made Rachel like her more. She toyed with her 8 Ball key chain again.

"Hello."

Electricity coursed through her veins. A few feet away, Mat Ledesma stood about a foot taller than Rachel, examining her as though she were someone of great importance. He wore a T-shirt emblazoned with the word *Pericos* and an aqua baseball cap with a swooping swordfish on it. He glanced down, hands stuffed in his pockets, then lifted his head, the black brim of his hat revealing the dark, familiar expression that had haunted her from the photo. Their eyes locked, but he didn't smile or look away.

"Hi," she said.

He raised one hand. As they moved toward each other, Rachel studied his gait, his mannerisms. There was a spectral quality about him.

At close distance now, he pinched the brim of his cap and lifted it just enough to ruffle his dark hair with the other hand. A shadowy hue stained the complexion below his eyes. If he'd moved to embrace her, she would have allowed it, but he just placed his hat back on his head and glanced at his sneakers, then back up at her.

As he lowered his arm, the curve of his wrist made Rachel's stomach drop. She felt a wave of déjà vu. *Piano player's fingers.* She lifted her own hand inadvertently, then dropped it again. A passing roller blader narrowly dodged them both.

"I can't believe it." His accent was strong, his voice higher in pitch than she'd anticipated, and they realized at the same moment that they didn't have a common native language.

Rachel slipped into Spanish. "I know. Where's Mari?"

Mat scrunched his face up like he was trying to remember his lines. "She had to go back."

"To Florida?"

He shook his head. "No, to Argentina. Something came up."

Rachel felt a sting of irrational hurt. She'd somehow assumed that Mari would stay in New York until the test results came in.

"When?" she asked.

"Two days ago."

She studied him openly now—his lean build, silky hair—and smiled with curiosity and newfound pride. Mat reached into the pocket of his shorts and pulled out his cell phone, an older model with scratches obscuring the outside. He flipped it open and held the screen out in front of Rachel. He thumbed a key and, in the square window, a low-resolution image of him with an older woman appeared.

"This is my grandmother," he said, clearing his throat. "Esme. She's seventy-four." The sunlight made it difficult to see the picture, but Rachel was distracted by Mat's fingers, the knobs of his knuckles, the veins along the back of his hands, the tenderness with which he touched the screen. "She still does this walk every Thursday, searching for you."

Rachel's chest tightened. Mat snapped his phone shut and gently stuffed it back in his pocket, exhaling with a puff of his cheeks.

"What's she like?" Rachel asked.

He layered both hands on his chest. "She has a very strong heart."

Rachel smiled, then checked her watch. They had fifteen minutes before their appointment.

Mat pointed to the upper stories of the clinic building. "Should we go up?"

Rachel shrugged, then glanced at the man in the Mister Softee truck. "We could have an ice cream first."

The man looked to Mat for an answer. Mat reached into his back pocket for his wallet, ordered two cones, and handed one to Rachel.

"Thank you."

Mat licked around the base of his ice cream, a clump of rainbow sprinkles melting on his knuckles. Here, right in front of Rachel, was the most beautiful open doorway to a biological family—but to pass through, she first had to acknowledge that her own parents were hiding, lying, *involved*. She couldn't fit both truths in her mind at once. There was happiness here, in this moment, but there was also a wound. Extracting the truth from it would be excruciating; the prospect of healing seemed inconceivable. The best she could do was cauterize it and focus on the joy.

She watched Mat bite into the rim of his cake cone. If she was standing next to her brother, if she kept a forward momentum toward other new discoveries—like her grandmother—perhaps she could outpace the dread. If she just kept moving forward, perhaps she could lift off somehow and would no longer need the footing she was losing on the only solid ground she'd ever known.

They took a few steps toward Third Avenue when his cell phone rang. He glanced at it.

"It's Mari."

They stopped to linger near a brownstone. Rachel eavesdropped on his side of the conversation. There was concern in his voice; he was repeatedly asking Mari if she was safe.

Mat put the call on speaker.

"Rachel?" Mari's small voice cut through the afternoon sounds of the city, speaking English. "I'm sorry I can't be there for this."

"It's all right," said Rachel, her eyes finding Mat's. "Are you okay?"

"Oh—yes, it's fine," she said. "Everything will be fine. Let me know how it goes, all right?"

"Sure."

"Take care of yourself," said Mat. "Send everyone my love. I'll call you when I get back to the hotel." Gently, he ended the phone call.

Mat tossed the stump of his ice cream cone in the trash, and they headed upstairs to the clinic.

From the ceiling of the waiting area, jewel-colored balls hung on wire cords—like cells, Rachel thought, or whatever essential particles connected every person in the world to their ancestors. Biology had never interested her. She'd avoided family trees and medical history forms her entire life.

"Rachel Sprague," Dr. Ramel emerged. "Mat Ledesma. This way, please."

A beam of sunlight caught the green acrylic of one of the decorative balls and fell across the tiled floor they stepped on. They followed the doctor down the hallway into an exam room, where a nurse joined them. Dr. Ramel sat on a rolling stool and crossed his slender legs. He took his clipboard from the counter and lifted a page.

"Okay. Looks like we have some results."

Mat lifted a hand to the back of his neck, then crossed his arms. Rachel raised her eyes to her reflection in the metal paper towel holder on the wall, where a warped image of her own face looked back. A warm, carbonated sensation flowed through her body—this body she'd lived in for twenty-eight years, her only true inheritance—and she was filled with a sudden, private excitement she could hardly contain.

"We tested all the genetic markers we could, but the primary test was, of course, for full siblingship," said Dr. Ramel.

Rachel eyed the exam table, the crisp paper liner, and brought a hand to her mouth to conceal the grin that was forming.

Dr. Ramel tapped his clipboard with his pen. "Unfortunately, the index isn't high enough to confirm that relationship. You'll have to do more testing."

"What?" asked Mat.

A dry lump caught in Rachel's throat.

Dr. Ramel raised his eyebrows and pulled his lips into a tight, *I-don't-know-what-to-tell-you* expression. When he crossed his arms, the gesture created a chasm between them.

"Statistically, these results don't substantiate siblingship," he said.

Mat's mouth was agape.

"I don't understand," Rachel murmured.

Dr. Ramel looked at the nurse, then lifted a splayed palm as if to say, *I'm just the messenger.*

PART III

CHAPTER 12

BUENOS AIRES

JULY 1983

Esme had given Matías some *dulces* as a reward for his courage that morning, and the sugary drop filled his little mouth now, his tongue wrestling it from cheek to cheek. Esme's heart had ached when she'd lifted him onto the papered examination table, the laboratory nurse gently holding his wrist.

"I don't want to do it," Matías whimpered, resisting the prick of the needle.

Esme pushed through her mental anguish to thoughts of Ana—of the blood that coursed through the baby's veins, of her cells and flesh and bones. She needed to produce any trace of Lorena and José she could find, even if came from inside her grandson's body.

"This is going to help us find your sister, little one. Be brave."

Matías had stuck his skinny arm out valiantly and closed his eyes as the nurse drew his blood.

He sucked fiercely on his candy now as Esme took his hand. She led Matías carefully around the cardboard boxes of documents that covered her apartment floor, then slipped off her coat and tossed it over the dusty arm of the sofa. The coffee table was littered with case files the grandmothers created each time they learned of another missing child. On top of the pile, one of the parent's death certificates was paper clipped to an open manila folder. Esme shut it slowly, turned it face down.

"What are we doing here, *abuela*?" Matías asked, leafing through an open journal next to one of Hilde's ashtrays. The pages were filled with torn-out articles on blood types, a hand-drawn chart of a four-generational family tree, the word *mitochondrial* scrawled in Hilde's cursive hand.

"Just looking for something, my love," said Esme. "It won't take long. Come in here with me."

She coaxed Matías toward the bedroom and away from the space that she, Hilde, Rosa, and the other grandmothers used as a makeshift headquarters for their investigatory work. While their friendship with Alba and Reina had endured over the years, the mothers without grandchildren had taken a stronger stance against the government, focusing their efforts on resistance and protests. The grandmothers had organized themselves separately, dedicating every resource they had to finding their stolen grandchildren.

In the corridor, Matías paused to look up at the wall, where a map of the city and surrounding area was marked with tiny colored pins, each representing the address of a known adoptive family. He touched the blue pinhead that marked the home of an affluent military officer who'd adopted an infant girl the month after Rosa's daughter, Ines, was due to give birth. Poor Rosa. She'd been casing that house for years, even considered going to work as a cleaning woman or delivering a package to the door just to catch sight of the girl. She'd followed the adoptive mother into a nail salon once, where she'd overheard the woman talking about her young daughter named Patricia and how much the girl loved butterflies. Rosa glimpsed the couple getting into a car with the child one afternoon. Patricia was the spitting image of Ines. If only they could prove it, Patricia could be the first of the stolen babies whose identity had been restored.

What concerned Esme, though, was the damage being done to Patricia's psyche. Even if the girl had been adopted in good faith and raised lovingly, she was being denied her identity. How would she cope with that once the truth could no longer be hidden from her? And what if she chose to deny the truth and stay with the people who stole her?

"This way," Esme said now. "Don't touch." She nudged Matías into the bedroom, where she opened the top drawer of the jewelry dresser and removed a few strings of beads and a colorful scarf. Matías sat on the bed. She handed him the scarf, which he smoothed out across the bedspread.

It had been Hilde's idea to pursue the blood testing. She'd seen a show on television about paternity tests and began writing letters to an Argentine researcher at the United Nations, a human-rights activist who studied genetics. It had never been done before—scientifically proving a relationship between a grandparent and a grandchild in the absence of the parents' blood—but Hilde became obsessed with finding a researcher who would take on the impossible work of modifying the paternity test for the grandmothers. After countless letters, Hilde had found an American scientist from Stanford University—Dr. Mary-Claire King—who'd agreed to help create the first "grandparentage" test. Dr. King was building a repository from the grandmothers' blood samples, and Matías's blood was meant to be tested against Esme's to validate the research.

Matías traced the print of the scarf with his fingertips. He was small for seven, slight like his father, and artistic, observant, a deep thinker. Lorena had been creative at his age, too, but she'd been a far stronger child, her loud voice echoing across the same neighborhood yard on which Matías kicked his soccer ball in solitude.

"I'll just be another minute, dear," Esme told him.

She removed a few trays and reached into the back of the drawer, distracted by thoughts of little Patricia and how important her case could be if Dr. King's test succeeded. Obtaining a blood sample from the girl would be a public relations disaster, of course. Everyone knew now that the junta had taken babies from pregnant prisoners, but the adoptive families were seen by the media and the general public as the children's "families of the heart." The grandmothers, with their stubborn memory and unwillingness to let go of the past, were portrayed as attempted homewreckers—and now they were out for children's blood.

Esme recognized the same weary sentiment on the face of every neighbor: *Enough already. Let it go.* They wanted to move on from the ominous past, from the fear and terror that was only now just beginning to subside.

But Esme's conviction to find Ana was bone deep. Dr. King had explained that parents' chromosomes crossed over with each new generation, but the mother's ova held more certainty about a child's identity. The seeds of Esme's grandchildren had once existed inside her own body—in the tiny eggs embedded in Lorena's womb when she was still a fetus—and every piece she had left counted for something.

In the drawer, Esme found the small burgundy box etched in gold foil and breathed a sigh of relief.

"Did you find what you were looking for?" asked Matías.

Esme smiled. "Yes, my love."

You see, Gustavo, she prayed silently. *Sometimes it pays to be a sentimental woman.*

She opened the box. There, scattered on the velvet lining inside, were six of Lorena's baby teeth.

As the dictatorship crumbled, the truth emerged in stark patches. A mass unmarked grave known as "the pit" was discovered in Córdoba, where hundreds of executed bodies were found. A national commission began collecting testimony from former officers, surviving prisoners, witnesses, and family members of the desaparecidos—there were thousands across the country—and published the documented cases in a collection entitled *Nunca Mas*. There was a raid on Navy headquarters, where falsified documents showed that hundreds of adoptions had been ratified by the military dictatorship.

The mothers and grandmothers insisted that the remains of every found body be exhumed, autopsied, and inspected for identifying features. Dr. King had become part of their forensics team. She managed the collection of blood samples and bone fragments from the excavations. When the body of Hilde's daughter-in-law, Julia, was found in the pit, the forensics team confirmed that Julia's pelvic bones had shifted—she had most certainly given birth before she was killed—but despite being buried along with a teddy bear, no bones other than Julia's were found. There were no remains of a baby.

Hilde's son was also identified among the bodies. Hilde was devastated, but there was something enviable about the closure it brought her—the finality, the permission it gave her to fully grieve the loss of her child. Esme couldn't grieve without first accepting that her search was over, that Lorena and José were dead. Without any physical proof, she didn't dare mourn yet.

And closure was not the same thing as justice. Certain members of the junta were prosecuted for their war crimes, but within a few years, the convictions came to an abrupt halt when the new president passed a law called *Punto Final*—"Full Stop"—capping the number of cases that could be brought to trial. A second law, "Due Obedience," protected all the officers who were "just following orders." Those who hadn't yet been prosecuted received amnesty, allowing them to walk free.

Two weeks after the body of Alba's son, Ernesto, was found brutally tortured in a shallow grave, Alba's husband walked by a former lieutenant in a local subway station. The man was infamous for being the head torturer in the naval school where Ernesto had been imprisoned. Alba's husband followed the former lieutenant on the Subte and rode in the same car with the man for six stops, watching as he brushed the rain from his expensive coat sleeves, read his newspaper, wiped a splash of muddy water from his leather shoe.

Early the next morning, Alba's husband committed suicide.

The sky was overcast the day of the funeral services, a cold light rain misting the air. Matías, dressed in a suit that was too snug, tugged at his necktie as Hilde handed him a mint from her purse. A chill penetrated Esme's black blouse. She'd worn all the black in her closet recently.

When Alba emerged from the church, her face was hardened into the expression Esme had first seen years ago: *Let them take me. Let them kill me.* Esme blinked away tears. Everyone knew the amnesty laws had put Alba's husband over the edge. Justice would be unattainable until the laws were overturned. It was too late for Alba's husband, but the grandmothers had a plan to do just that, to circumvent the amnesty laws and grind the wheels of justice back into motion.

Lorena had been missing for three thousand nine hundred and thirty-four days when the grandmothers held a press conference. Esme wrestled with the retractable gate of the elevator in the old office space the grandmothers had leased in Monserrat. They'd outgrown Esme's cramped apartment and managed to raise enough funding to cover the rent and some of their legal expenses. Esme slid her dripping umbrella into the stand, then tilted her head back to examine a hairline crack growing in the high plaster ceiling. Matías took off his coat. Members of the media, civilians, and a few public officials packed into the humble office space, standing room only. Esme sat down at a long table between Rosa and Hilde. Matías lingered at the nearby window, tracing its sill with his finger. To the right of Rosa was their new attorney, a soft-spoken man named Tomás whose brother was also a desaparecido. Camera bulbs flashed.

"We understand you've been working to exploit a loophole in the amnesty laws," one of the journalists called out.

"The guilty can't be punished for only part of their crime," Rosa's voice wavered through the microphone.

"Testimony from former members of the junta confirms that babies were taken," Tomás said, covering Rosa's hand briefly with his own. "The junta are protected from being punished for their war crimes, but kidnapping isn't covered by the amnesty laws. And under international law, kidnapping is a crime that has no statute of limitations."

Esme had learned not to get her hopes up too high. It was still a long road to the Supreme Court. Tomás was trying to convince a federal judge to write a ruling on this paradox—that the military was protected from prosecution for murder, but they could still be criminally punished for "saving" the life of a baby—and attempt to revoke the amnesty laws based on his argument. It was a longshot, but if he was successful, former officers could once again be prosecuted for the full extent of their crimes rather than abduction of a minor, which alone carried a lighter sentence than auto theft.

After the crowd diminished and the news cameras had gone, Rosa handed Esme a flier.

"Do you remember this one?" Rosa asked.

Esme skimmed the flier, a brief paragraph printed below a photocopied image of a young woman:

WHERE IS FLAVIA?

On August 3, 1976, my wife FLAVIA GUTIERREZ REY was kidnapped by men in plain clothes from a café on the corner of Avenida Olazábal and Bucarelli in the town of Villa Urquiza in the province of Buenos Aires. She was five months pregnant at the time, and the baby was born in captivity on December 14th 1976. Flavia was seen alive in January 1977 when the junta escorted her and her child to her mother's house, where the baby was left. The authorities have denied all knowledge of this. Until the Argentinean government officially recognizes the arrest and detention of FLAVIA GUTIERREZ REY, it is not possible for her to exercise her right to apply for the option of political exile, guaranteed by the Argentine Constitution in its Article no 23.

Esme had seen the flier once, long ago, in Alba's archive. In the span of a decade, the document had gone from contraband to artifact. She handed the page back to Rosa.

"I remember," said Esme.

Rosa nodded toward the window, where a man stood with two young girls. The younger girl played with a ribbon, curling it around her hand and wrist. The older one, who looked about Matías's age, gazed up at Esme from beneath unruly curls, thoughtful and serious.

"The family's been in exile," said Rosa. "It's their first time back on Argentine soil since the dictatorship."

The curly-haired girl tugged on her father's shirtsleeve. The man crossed the room and approached Esme and Rosa.

"We appreciate the work you're doing," he said to Rosa. He glanced down at the flier in her hand and turned to Esme. "Two men in street clothes brought my wife back to her mother's house that day in January with the baby."

"That was unheard of at the time," said Esme. "God gave you a miracle."

He nodded. "Flavia left a letter with her mom—mostly formula instructions for Marcela." He rested his hand on the smaller girl's head. "And they let her see Marisol for a few minutes before they took her away again. We knew she was still alive, so I couldn't give up. I distributed that flier from abroad, had it translated into twelve different languages." The man cleared his throat. "But my wife's body was found in 1979. And they were after me. I'm the reason they took her."

The older girl looked up at Esme, her eager eyes shining from beneath her curls.

"Are you going to find justice for my mother?" asked Marisol.

Esme's throat constricted. *Justice* seemed too big a word for this preadolescent girl, but she gave a shallow nod.

"You hold on tight to your sister," Esme said.

The girl nodded with sincerity.

Matías neared, lingering at Esme's side, and a crashing sadness came down upon Esme. What deficiencies was she inflicting upon her grandson, raising him so entrenched in her search? She'd made him a crusader, surrounded him with women and activism and grief. Matías had the kind of void that was often supplanted with venom. How would he navigate love when he had no parents to look up to? What injustice had been done to *his* psyche? There was no psychologist in the world who had case studies the likes of his—a child whose sibling had been raised in a lie, their natural identity erased by their own "parents" and country.

Esme watched Marisol wave a splayed hand at Matías. His dark lashes guarded his eyes as they flitted toward the girl. When she smiled back, he dropped his head, stuffed his hands in his pockets, and stiffened. But when he looked at Esme, his face was lit up with a kind of easy bliss she hadn't seen there in years. Perhaps God would find a path for him after all.

Several months later, on a warm morning just after Matías had left for school, the phone rang. Esme set down the kettle she was filling and lifted the receiver. It was a worker from the forensics laboratory.

Esme drew in a breath. *Please, God.* The samples she and Matías had provided to validate Dr. King's test had remained with the lab.

The man sounded concerned. "We've been testing the samples collected from remains," he said.

"Yes," said Esme. "And what have you found?"

"One of the bodies that washed up on the Uruguayan coast. A man."

Esme drew her breath in deeper. "What? Who is it?"

"We ran the sample against our repository, and there was a positive match."

"To whom?"

The man cleared his throat. "Matías."

Before Esme could speak, she envisioned José standing before her, fixing a drink. She heard his calm voice, felt the warmth of his skin as he leaned down to kiss her cheek. Her son-in-law, Lorena's husband— washed ashore. Gone.

"I'm so sorry, Esme," said the scientist.

Esme coiled the phone cord around her finger. She swallowed a hard lump of fear to clear her vocal cords.

"Was he—the only one?" she asked.

"Yes. There were no other matches. But we'll keep testing."

When Esme hung up, her chest was empty. The knowledge that Matías had lost his father—and the prospect of telling him this—eclipsed her own grief. She felt a disturbing sense of relief that it hadn't been Lorena, but now she was overcome by a rational and intensifying apprehension: If José had been killed, the chances were slim that Esme would ever see Lorena alive again either.

CHAPTER 13

"Rise and shine, cow," said Lentil Eyes, kicking the bed. "It's time for your exercise. Doctor's orders."

Doctors in the prison, just as Flavia said. The junta had established a full institution inside these walls.

Lentil Eyes led Lorena to a room in the basement with a metal table in the center. He didn't remove her blindfold.

When the junta discovered Lorena was pregnant, they started calling her names—*Trotsky whore, cow*—and regarded her with a brand of disgust she found preferable to the predatorial stares they cast over the bodies of other female prisoners. By the time the baby began sliding against the inside wall of her uterus, tiny lumps of movement traveling across Lorena's belly, she knew in her soul that it was a girl. She thought incessantly of Flavia's story. If she could just stay alive, her baby could be safe, too—with Esme—and Lorena could see Matías again, if only for a moment.

It's all right, my girl. Lorena murmured a silent prayer to her baby. *I'm here.*

"Put your hand on the edge and walk around it fifty times. Go."

Lorena did as she was told, walking around the table, dragging her fingers along its surface. All the while, she thought about what Flavia had told her. Maybe the baby would save her life.

"Keep walking."

The concrete floor was gritty under the soles of her feet. She counted the laps. *Twelve, thirteen.* She sensed that Lentil Eyes sat nearby, watching as he always did when she "exercised," his face surely hardened into the same disinterested expression she'd caught glimpses of from underneath her blindfold.

"Keep going," he said, bored.

Thirty-eight laps. Forty-one. Forty-two. Forty-three.

As Lorena navigated the next lap around the table, a warm fluid wet her inner thighs. The slipperiness made its way down one of her legs, reaching the top of her right calf. Her heart started pounding. It was happening.

Forty-eight. Forty-nine.

A faint cramp took hold of her uterus, then subsided. The wetness grew.

Fifty.

"That's enough," said Lentil Eyes in a gruff voice. From the hall, another officer's voice summoned him. Chair legs scraped against the concrete floor as he perked up.

"Stay here," he said.

Outside the room, the men's voices were deep and muffled. She smelled cigar smoke. When Lentil Eyes returned, he pulled off her blindfold. She startled, clearing her throat.

"It's your lucky day, Rabbit House," he said.

She despised this stagecraft, the way the junta infused power into a crust of bread or a pitying gesture, only to snatch it away again.

A young officer trailed in and took hold of Lorena by her bicep. When she looked directly at him, a clear display of insubordination, he hesitated. She could sense his youth, his intense focus—something big was on the line for him. He jerked her by the arm, irritated.

"Let's go," he said.

He brought her into another concrete room with two tables and a pile of dirty cushions on the floor.

"Wait here." The heavy door slammed shut.

Lorena sat on the cushions and cradled her belly, wrists still cuffed. She contracted the muscles in her pelvic floor. What would they do to her?

There was a movement in her womb, and she took deep breaths, restoring what little strength she had to the places that needed it to keep her baby contained. Whatever they were about to do to her, they couldn't take her baby away. She was prepared to fight to the death to make sure of that.

It seemed like hours passed before a surge of commotion erupted. Four men barged into the room with such urgency, Lorena had a flash of hope that something greater was underway. Was the building being attacked? No. Because there, among the uniforms, was a white doctor's coat. Cold terror spread through her chest. She didn't trust them with her body or her baby.

The junta forced her onto the table, removed her wrist cuffs and took off her clothes. She scanned their faces for some sign of humanity, but their eyes were distant, unreachable. A young officer fastened her wrists to the table with leather straps—she was face up now, completely exposed—as another tightened more leather around her ankles. She risked kicking them, but the leather wouldn't give. She finally, silently, began to cry.

The three officers exited the room, leaving her alone with the doctor. Someone new—a woman—appeared beside her. A nurse.

Lorena tried to catch her eye, but the woman wouldn't return her attention, focusing only on assisting the doctor as he examined Lorena, his fingers prodding, violating. When he was finished, he nodded to the nurse, who put her hands under Lorena's back. She lifted Lorena's right shoulder and hip, rolling her on her side, her right limbs pulled taut by the leather straps. As she pinned her down in this position, Lorena felt a cold smear on her back and the pinch of an injection there. Her whimpers were pleading; she was too terrified to resist, even to make the smallest move.

The nurse let her go and, in a rush of heat, Lorena's legs and torso went tingly. She mustered her energy and tried to kick again. They couldn't do this to her. She wouldn't let them take her baby.

"All right, calm yourself." The nurse held Lorena's shins until her legs were numb, then pressed a musty-smelling cloth over her eyes.

A clink of metal was followed by a ragged, tugging sensation across Lorena's lower abdomen, then a terrifying pressure on her belly—a sliding, an emptying. *No, no.* Her water had already broken. Why were they cutting her open? She pulled her elbows in to lift up, but the wrist cuffs were too tight. *They cannot take my baby away.* She was woozy now. From a dreamlike state, she felt something vital inside of her being manipulated, the slip of a bean from its pod, and then, from somewhere outside of her body, a shocking cry. There was more emptying, more cutting, and when the nurse removed her hand from the cloth over Lorena's eyes, Lorena shook it off her face entirely. There, above her, was her baby, tiny, coated, still connected so intrinsically to her that Lorena had the sensation it was a part of her own body in the nurse's arms, being wiped down with a towel, crying.

She pulled against the restraints to reach up for the baby, but they were too tight. The nurse flicked the rag back over Lorena's eyes. The tugging at her pelvis continued, small and tight now—the doctor was stitching her up. The baby's cry waned, moving away from her toward the other table. There were more metal clinks—the doctor rolling up his instruments, leaving—and an officer entered, unfastening Lorena's restraints and removing the rag from her eyes. She swiveled her head to locate the nurse, who held the baby wrapped in a towel. When she handed Lorena the infant, it was as though the hand of God delivered her.

Lorena embraced her baby girl against her bare body, soaking in everything about her. The child's little face was scrunched, still blooming, and she resembled Matías at birth, though much smaller. When she opened her newborn eyes, Lorena recognized her father, then Esme. Tears slipped down Lorena's cheeks. *We have to get out of here,* she thought.

She bracketed her daughter firmly in the frame of her arms. *The frame of her arms*—she'd learned the phrase during a tango lesson she'd taken with her father once. The infant suckled feebly. In the distance—just beyond this tiny, precious being—blue-black stitches tracked a jagged incision between Lorena's hip bones. Her pelvis was pink and sore, preternaturally bloated, but it didn't matter. What else could matter now except keeping her baby close?

One officer beckoned to another in the hall, who carried in a new pile of clothes and tossed them to the nurse, leaving the two women alone in the room. The nurse placed the clothes over Lorena's legs in a gesture that fell just short of compassion. They were quiet for an extended time—Lorena lying on the table, concentrating on her baby, the nurse standing near the door, on guard.

Lorena thought back to her labor with Matías, how charmed her life was then—maternity blouses, a kitchen egg timer to track her contractions. She missed José terribly. Not the injured, weakened José handcuffed upstairs, but the sweet-tasting academic in his button-down shirt who doted on his pregnant wife when she went into labor, bringing her glasses of fresh water.

Water. She was so thirsty now.

Through months of daily battles in prison, she'd grown ever more nostalgic for the civility of her old life, ever more remorseful of the way she'd dismissed José's caution. She'd spent hours shaping piles of dust into little works of art on the floor with her fingernails, longing for art, music, refinement. José had been right. Claudio was reckless and so was she.

On the ceiling above her now, two large cracks in the cement intersected. Over the past six months, she'd thought of every possible way to escape—every concrete wall, loose bolt, and metal handle—but there was only one way out of this place: through the people who ran it. Lentil Eyes was a wall of bricks, the junta a guild of apathetic faces—but now she was alone with the nurse.

———— · ❖ · ————

On the baby's outer thigh was a dark splotch—a birthmark. Lorena ran her fingertip over the tiny skin and gathered her courage. When the nurse took a cushion from the floor and gave it to Lorena to prop her upper back, Lorena saw signs of an opening. If they tried to separate her from her baby again, someone had to know this child was hers.

"She's got a birthmark here," Lorena said, her voice groggy from lack of use. "On her right thigh. You see it?"

"Hush up," snapped the nurse, but she didn't call the guards.

When Lorena's legs regained feeling, she accepted the nurse's help descending from the table, a balled-up towel clutched against her incision. Her body was tender, raw. As the nurse helped her dress, Lorena studied the woman's face again. Could she offer hope? A line of communication? It was impossible to tell. If they took her baby away, who else could ever prove she was Lorena's?

Lorena curled up on the floor cushions, bruised, and stared at the baby as she nursed for some time. Without looking up, Lorena dared again to speak.

"My name is Lorena Ledesma. My mother is Esme Arias. Please, I beg you. Tell my mother I'm here. Tell her she has a granddaughter."

"Be quiet," the nurse hissed.

"My name is Lorena Ledesma," Lorena whispered, still looking down at the baby. Then she said, "My baby's name is Ana."

The nurse pursed her lips disapprovingly, opened the door, and left. *Please, God.*

When she returned, she brought two clean towels and a cup of water. She didn't speak or look Lorena in the eye. When she left again, Lorena adjusted Ana's makeshift blanket and re-dressed her own wound. For hours, she lay nursing the baby alone, drowsily watching her daughter, waiting for and dreading the next visit.

Through the room's single high window, night fell. Lentil Eyes arrived with a large amount of bread and two whole oranges on a metal tray. No blindfold, no cuffs. He didn't look at Lorena or the baby.

She ate shakily, and when she pulled Ana from her breast, it was a relief to see the yellowish colostrum in the baby's tiny cat-mouth. Lorena's lower body ached, but at least she could nourish her daughter.

In the morning, two officers slammed open the door, one wheeling a mop in a bucket of gray water. The nurse stood outside in the hall behind them.

"The maternity ward is closed," he yelled. "Clean this place up."

The nurse entered, crouching down, and tried to take the baby from Lorena, but Lorena shook her head fervently.

"I'll hold her," the nurse said. Then, more quietly, "I'll hold Ana."

Lorena looked up at the officer, who glared back. "Clean it *up*."

She rose from the cushion with the nurse's help, pressing the towel over the place where they'd cut her open. The nurse coaxed Ana from her arms, and the baby started wailing. Lorena shuffled over to the bucket, lifted the mop, which was heavier than she anticipated, and began pushing it across the cement floor with one hand while clutching the towel against her abdomen with the other. Blood and gray water smeared into puddles. The more insistent Ana's cries became, the faster Lorena tried to clean. She dragged the mop around the cell, under the tables, where its yarn collected small snips of blue surgical thread and one veined, bloody mass—her placenta, she realized. When she couldn't manage another stroke, she lifted the mop into its wringer and felt a muted pop along her incision. She buckled, retreating to the cushions. The nurse gave her the baby, who quieted immediately and latched on to Lorena's breast. She pulled her legs in close to her body to ease the pain.

"You're a shitty maid," said the young officer, wheeling the mop away as his companion laughed.

Alone again in the room with Ana, Lorena held the towel tight to her abdomen, but before long, she had bled through it. Ana started to cry. She was so tiny—too tiny. Lorena massaged her breasts with her free hand, coaxing her milk, which had yet to come in. Her nipples were chapped and raw.

When the nurse returned, she poured a cold, stinging fluid over Lorena's incision and taped a new swath of gauze over it.

"You're going back upstairs soon," she said. "You need to feed her so she stops crying."

"My milk hasn't come yet," Lorena said. *It was almost time. Why did they cut me open?*

The nurse gave her a reproving look, then left.

It took a long while for the officers to get Lorena back upstairs on foot. When she finally arrived, José was nowhere to be seen. Lentil Eyes didn't cuff or blindfold her. She lay on her side, coddling the baby and pressing against the gauze, which she'd bled through again. Ana's tiny lips were dry, her cry a flat line of hunger.

"Shut that baby up," grunted Lentil Eyes.

"She needs milk," said Lorena, courageous enough without the blindfold to speak. Lentil Eyes glowered but didn't immediately retaliate. When he returned with the nurse several minutes later, the woman reached for Ana. Lorena recoiled, recalling the night she'd handed Matías to Esme.

"I'll bring her back," the nurse assured her.

Lorena stared at the nurse, desperately trying to make an impossible assessment. Her breasts ached, and there was a troubling heat growing near her wound. When she wiped a matted lock from her forehead, the sudden coolness against her exposed skin caused her to shiver abruptly.

"I'm just going to feed her," said the nurse. "That's all. Then I'll bring her back to you."

Carefully, Lorena handed her baby to the nurse.

Ana fussed when the nurse took her away, her cries abating as they crossed the room and disappeared downstairs. Lorena lay on her side. The coldness surrounding her sharpened Ana's absence. Before long, Lorena shook with chills, sobbing. What had she done? How could she have let them take her baby?

Time stood still. She was freezing. As her shoulders quaked, pain stabbed at the place where the doctor had cut her open. Bloody fluid had seeped through the gauze again. In time, she fell into a fitful state that never quite reached sleep. She woke up in a sweat when Lentil Eyes kicked her bed frame.

"Get up," he said, setting a tray on the bed—a large helping of rice and bananas. He pulled a pen and notepad from his pocket. "You're going to write a letter to your family. Your baby's going back to them. You're going to be transferred."

Lorena blinked, taking the notepad. She studied Lentil Eyes through a cold lens of distrust. Was anything he said true? He handed her a pen. She hadn't held one in over six months.

"What do I write?"

He shrugged. "Whatever they need to know. How much milk to give, that sort of thing."

"They'll give this letter to my mother?"

He nodded deeply. "We have all her information on file." This was the longest conversation she'd ever had with him.

Lorena propped herself up on one elbow and rested the notepad on the mattress. She wrote: *Dear Mamá, her name is Ana.* As she formed the words on the page, an ugly pang of jealousy flared. If the junta killed her, it would be Esme, God willing, who would raise her babies. She needed Ana to be safe, but how would Esme raise her daughter when she'd always tried to suppress Lorena's fervor? It should be Lorena who held her own babies, touched their soft skin, watched them grow, sang them songs. It should've been Lorena with Matías now, hearing his voice, putting him to bed, watching him smile. A mother should see her child looking up at the sky.

Lentil Eyes watched with anticipation and—she caught a flash of it then, just behind his eyes—amusement. She put the pen down. Even if the letter made it to Esme, there was nothing else she could say that would make a difference.

"Go on," he urged.

She looked him in the face, a blatant encroachment, and noticed a scab on his cheek where he'd nicked himself shaving, maybe just this morning, in some finely tiled bathroom of some spacious home some-where, out there in a world in which she was nothing more than a task that required handling.

She picked up the pen again and wrote: *I'm still here. Love, Lorena.* Then she pushed the notepad and pen to the edge of the mattress and rolled over.

Lentil Eyes picked up the note and, as punishment for her brevity, the full tray of food, taking both away with him when he left.

A long stretch of time passed.

"Are you all right?" The nurse had returned, holding Ana. Lorena reached for her baby—Ana was safe, her pink lips plump and hydrated—and immediately started to sob, almost as much for the miracle of the nurse's fulfilled promise as for the reunion with her daughter. As she quietly cried, a tingling sensation ran down her neck and chest, coursing through her breasts, which began to throb. Her milk was letting down. *Thank God.* Ana latched on, nursing heartily, and Lorena took a breath of relief. Her baby could stay with her now. She wouldn't cry. No one would take her away again.

CHAPTER 14

It had been a long day in a painful season. Everything happened in seasons now—seasons of grief, seasons of hope. That very morning, Esme lifted the receiver of the black rotary phone in the grandmothers' office, and its thick click preceded a man's flat voice: *There's a bomb in your office. You're all as dead as your children.*

There were people who despised the grandmothers—their relentless memory, their mandates for blood samples, the way they reminded people to remember the truth and learn who they really were, whether they wanted to know or not. It didn't deter Esme. She had come too far and had too far left to go to be thwarted by empty threats. She and Matías had lived for nearly a decade without Lorena. Every missing grandchild they found felt in some way like Esme's own, and even if she'd lost Lorena forever—God, would she ever even know?—she would never stop searching for Ana.

Besides, something else preoccupied Esme as she made her way home from the office in the warm afternoon air, the wide concrete slabs of sidewalk passing under her feet. After two years of waiting, President Alfonsín's administration had finally agreed to discuss the grandmothers' proposal for creating a national center for genetic information—a data bank where they could put all the samples Dr. King and the forensics team had helped them collect over the years. A place where anyone who doubted their identity could go to find out if they were the child of a desaparecido. It was a small concession in comparison to the grandmothers' broader requests of the government, but if done properly, it could work. If the search for Ana extended beyond Esme's lifetime, her granddaughter needed to be able to find her genetic family.

She couldn't get too hopeful. There was so much to negotiate and so little chance they would prevail at the scale they needed. Who would pay for the costs, the equipment, the staff? The city of Buenos Aires? The Ministry of Health and Social Action? The government would merely throw scraps, but the grandmothers would persist. It had to be done.

Esme's key ring jangled as she searched for the mortise key that would open the new front gate she'd had installed to protect the house. She was distracted by her thoughts, engrossed with working the new gate key into its hole, wiggling the unfamiliar thing until she felt it latch. Even as it clacked loose and the gate door released, she was immersed in a contemplative haze, scarcely conscious of the tall presence appearing at her side. Startling to her senses, she gripped the wrought iron of the gate with one fist and felt the fear course through her veins, cold and familiar. *You're as dead as your children.* Still clutching the metal, a long-awaited dread overcame her, and she was suspended in this moment of panic, unable to fully surrender to its inevitability. Finally, she turned her body to face the man, braced to scream for her life.

"Esme," he said. "It's me."

Esme's eyes gained focus as she studied his face, his pale forehead moist with perspiration, the damp, coarse locks of his hair, his brown eyes red-rimmed. She was flooded with terror, confusion, a flash of fury—and then, a thrill.

"Claudio?" Pink, chapped patches marked the apples of his cheeks. He looked gaunt. "What in the devil—?"

"I know," he said in a low voice, his shoulders slumped. "I . . . please, can I come in?"

Aghast, Esme quickly assessed her options. She had never been scared of Claudio, but his presence now invoked a residual fear, one deeply instilled by the dictatorship: the risk of contracting his subversion, the contagion of his danger. The junta wasn't watching anymore. Argentina had been a democracy for years. And yet.

"No," she said.

Here was Claudio, alive in front of her—but where was Lorena? She wanted to rail against him, to physically assault him. Esme wanted to say the words that would hurt him the most, kill what was left of him, whatever wasn't already dead inside. Here he was, right here in front of her. How satisfying it would feel to tell him what he already knew. *You should've been more careful! You should have protected her! If it weren't for you, Lorena would be here with me—with her son!*

"Please," he said.

Esme noticed the thinness of his legs beneath his jeans, the way his knee quivered as he stood, how one arm hung limp at his side. There was nothing she could do or say to him that hadn't already been done or said. It was the same way with the military officers who were finally being convicted, only to be given paltry sentences in white-collar prisons. How terribly unsatisfying, doling out justice upon the vulnerable and weak, when what was truly needed was a reversal of time, a fair fight with a stronger, more viable version of the enemy, one who wielded the same power and wrath they'd once had.

Esme would never get a fair fight.

"Why did you come here?" she said.

"I needed to ask for your forgiveness. I needed to know what happened to them. It's destroyed me, all this time. Please, Esme. May I come in?"

Esme shut her eyes tightly. There was so much that had happened since she'd seen Claudio last. She'd scaled so many mountains of hope and descended into so many valleys of grief, she couldn't possibly explain it to him. She had no idea where Claudio had been, with whom he affiliated himself or what he wanted from her, but there were only two choices now: open the door and move forward or close off the past and let it rot away.

She pushed the gate open.

"Hurry up," she said.

Inside, Claudio took the maté she offered, holding it with both hands like a precious gift. He bowed his head. From where he sat on the floral sofa, he answered her questions quickly, softly, as though reciting a penance. He'd been imprisoned in Córdoba and tortured for several months. At some point, for reasons he couldn't explain, he received supervised freedom. A "recuperation project," the junta called it, implemented as the dictatorship was beginning to fall apart. Claudio had tremors and still couldn't fully lift his right arm, a result of the torture.

"Did you see them while you were in prison?" Esme asked.

He looked down and shook his head.

"Where have you been since?"

"I went into exile after my final release." He'd been in Cuba, then Spain for close to a decade, living with a woman he'd known from the Montoneros.

"Are you married?" asked Esme. She envisioned him passing the years in some foreign land by the sea, and the anger suddenly flared up in her chest again.

Claudio shook his head, stared at the carpet. "It didn't work out." When he raised his eyes to Esme's, they were wet and desperate. "Did they ever find her?"

Esme sighed. "They found José," she said. "Never Lorena." They sat quietly for a long time before Esme spoke again. "A person can only go on so long without answers before they have to find their own. I've gone years now, but I won't make Matías go on like this forever. I have to believe she's gone. A mother should know when her child has left this earth."

Claudio pulled his lips in, turned his head, and gazed up through the living room wall.

"I know it means nothing to you now," he said, "but I loved her too. Lorena was a fighter. She wanted to do something. She wanted to help."

"She didn't want this. Not for me. Or her boy." Esme wiped her eyes and straightened up. "She was pregnant, Claudio. She had a baby girl in prison. The child's name is Ana. I'm still searching for her—for my granddaughter."

"Ana?"

Esme nodded.

Claudio set his maté down on the coffee table and put his head in his hands. Without hesitation, he started to sob. Esme reached for a box of tissues.

"Here," she said, suddenly embarrassed for him. Esme felt a wave of fatigue, irritation. Claudio's unexpected presence surfaced a pain she would need to tend alone. She didn't owe him any condolences.

Claudio sniffed. "Esme, I'm sorry. I beg you to forgive me."

"God help you, Claudio. I think it's best if you go."

Claudio nodded, stood up quietly. "I'm not asking for anything. I have a place just outside of the city. You don't have to see me if you don't want to. But if you find Ana, please promise me you'll let me know. I'm begging you, Esme."

"All right," Esme said noncommittally.

On his way out, Claudio paused in front of a drawing Matías had done of a cityscape, architectural and abstract, hanging on the wall.

"What's he like?" asked Claudio.

Esme hesitated. She reached for a framed school photo of Matías and held it up to show Claudio. She gripped the frame tightly, prepared to slap Claudio's hand away if he reached for it. He could see Matías, but he couldn't touch him.

"He's just like José," said Esme.

Claudio stood before the picture with both arms hanging at his sides, reverent.

"Can I send him a letter?"

Esme tensed. "How can I stop you? You already know where we live."

———— · ❖ · ————

Claudio's first letter to Matías was postmarked from La Plata. A birthday card, three weeks early. The next came several months later and included a few sheets of soccer-themed drawing paper and a bookmark. After that, the letters came more frequently, once with a memory game that Matías was far too old to be interested in, another with a magazine article about a rock band. Claudio addressed the envelopes to Matías directly and signed them *Tío Claudio*.

Esme put all the letters in a desk drawer. When they filled it, she moved them to a box on the floor of the closet. Then, one Thursday afternoon when Matías was a teenager and Esme was spring cleaning, she threw the entire thing in the waste bin on the side of the house. By then, the letters had stopped coming altogether.

Matías turned on the radio and flopped onto the sofa. He was going through a growth spurt, becoming tall and lanky like José. Esme tied her white headscarf under her chin. She was headed out to the Plaza de Mayo to meet Hilde and Rosa.

"I'll be back in time for dinner," said Esme, "but you can get it started if you're hungry. The meat is in the refrigerator."

"Why do you still go there, abuela? What's the point in walking anymore?"

Esme paused in the doorway and met Matías's eyes, still too wise for such a youthful face. She recalled holding him, back in the early days, just after Lorena and José were taken. She remembered rocking him, telling him stories while he sat on her lap, showing him pictures of his parents. Those wise brown eyes, looking up at her.

Matías will find his baby sister.

When she spoke now, her voice was full of conviction.

"Because we're still searching, Matías. You know that. We haven't found your sister yet, and it's up to us to make sure people remember."

He looked wounded. "I know," he said.

As Esme made her way toward the plaza, the cloudless sky stretched above the cathedral. A statue of the Virgin Mary sent an ache of longing through her. Another season was coming; more change was on the horizon. Matías was becoming a man, and Esme still had plenty of unanswered prayers. She'd heard that her old priest had left the parish recently after so many years. Perhaps she would go back to mass on Sunday and find out for herself.

CHAPTER 15

VIRGINIA

AUGUST 2005

Vivian's hands shook as she filled the sink basin with water and swirled the dishrag across the surface of the last plate. She set it in the drying rack and turned toward the backyard. It had been Jonathan's idea to host Daphne and Greg for lunch, and he'd spent the better part of the meal touting the unreliability of DNA testing and denouncing Rachel's childish decision to breach the privacy of her own genetic information. He was so steadfast, so believable. There were moments when Vivian wanted to wrap his words around her like a comforter. A part of her wanted to wrap Rachel in them too.

But then, after her in-laws had gone home and Jonathan had left for the VFW, Rachel had called with the results of her DNA test.

Seventy-three, Rachel had said. That was the relationship index between Rachel and the boy.

Vivian hadn't been able to get the number out of her head since she hung up the phone.

Seventy-three. It wasn't enough to prove that they were full siblings, but it confirmed a high statistical likelihood that they were biologically related.

"The doctor thinks we share the same mother," Rachel explained. "And that we may have different fathers."

There was a long silence before Vivian let out a quivering breath. "What happens now?" she asked.

"They want to confirm our results by testing against a sample of Mat's father's DNA at the National Genetics Bank in Argentina. And a sample from his grandmother—*my* grandmother, maybe, since she's Lorena's mother." Rachel's words came out slowly and with enormity, like the deep, low groan of a starting engine that would accelerate to a colossal speed and force. "So I'm going to Buenos Aires."

Vivian touched her stomach with her fingertips. "That seems impulsive."

"I know. But I want to go."

"You just got the test results. People should wait to make decisions after they get big news, honey."

"Maybe."

"Don't you think you should talk to someone first?" Vivian's heart was racing, but she'd already heard it in Rachel's voice: a slow immovability, like the calm face in the photo of Lorena Ledesma.

"I will, Mom."

"It could be dangerous, traveling on your own."

"I'll be okay."

Vivian relaxed the focus of her eyes. Through the kitchen window, a few wispy clouds draped across the open sky. Something stirred within her—courage, relief.

She dried her hands on the dishtowel and walked to the front door. She peeked out the glass pane for Jonathan's truck, but the road was empty. She straightened up the living room, arranged the throw pillows, and placed the TV remote on the end table near Jonathan's recliner. For once, she would stop looking away.

On top of the folded newspaper were two little keys—the cheap metal keys she'd seen on his desk blotter. She picked them up and held them for a moment. Her skin tingled. She moved quickly down the hall into his den.

Without hesitation, Vivian crossed the tufted carpet to his gun safe. She entered the combination, Rachel's ascribed birthday—061077—and when she spun the handle, the heavy door glided open. Small shelves above his bracketed rifles held boxes of bullets, his shoulder holster. She removed a small metal cashbox, her heart quickening a bit, and tried unsuccessfully to pop it open. The first of the two little keys unlocked the box.

Inside, a manila envelope was folded in half and sealed with a string fastener. Vivian glanced at the clock; she had no idea when Jonathan would be home. She worked nimbly to unlace the string. From the envelope, she slid a substantial packet of carbon-copy pages pinched together with a warped paper clip. A dog-eared business card fell out from between them. On it, the name *Coronel Mayor Ricardo Preita* was printed next to a blue-and-white coat of arms. She let her eyes graze the shadowy words that filled the pages in Jonathan's cramped handwriting: his full name, Vivian's name, their wedding date, religion, residence, income, an old bank account, their church, and their medical history. Here it was. It had always been right here. All she'd ever had to do was look.

Short of breath, she skimmed to a section populated in a different hand, a different language, and made out what she could: *Baby's sex: female.* An entire section titled *registros hospitalarios* had been slashed by the tip of a pen, another had been scribbled over entirely with the words *Estados Unidos.* The red ink of a rubber stamp stained several pages: *Ejército Argentino.*

There was a power in these adoption papers, something she'd never held in her own hands before. This was the secret over which she'd been an unwitting guardian. She dropped her eyes again to the papers and ran her thumb along the printed letters.

Parents' names: NN.

She thought of that vivid summer day when Daphne called, the garden in full swing, the sun illuminating a shock of premature autumnal foliage in the yard. *It was summer, but the leaves started to change early . . .*

"She was left right outside, the poor thing," Daphne's voice had broken through the receiver. "She's teeny-tiny, but she seems healthy—and just beautiful, Viv."

Yellow leaves had speckled the trees as Vivian pulled up to the Joy & Light Family Center that morning. There wasn't a house for half a mile in either direction, but the day Rachel was found, there'd been social workers, people from the Department of Health and Human Services, a county commissioner, local cops. Even an ambulance out front. It wasn't every day that a newborn baby was abandoned in Howell County.

Vivian thought about what it would be like for Jonathan to have left Rachel on that porch. She closed her eyes, remembering the first time she'd seen Rachel open hers. Vivian had wept, a rush of urgency overwhelming her to bring the baby inside her home, to claim her, to make her belong. *There*, Vivian remembered thinking, once the baby was in her arms, looking up at her as though there had never been anything in the history of the world that required forgiveness. *There, there.*

All this time, Rachel had been part of a continuance. Vivian understood the magnitude of this connection, the connectivity of mothers and children, the links of a generational chain. Remnants of it had lingered with Rachel as an infant that morning, and when Vivian tried, she still felt it toward her own lost babies.

How fortuitous for Jonathan that Rachel's mother had been from Argentina. If it had been Vietnam, there would have been far more questions raised, but Rachel, with her beautiful brown hair and fawn-colored skin, might belong to any nation in the western world. And perhaps she carried something of Jonathan in her already, even before he had made her purely, unquestionably *theirs*.

Vivian fell to her knees. She wrapped a hand over her mouth to mute her sob and stared down at the papers until the words blurred with tears.

She had been a part of it—the perfect accomplice. She'd spent twenty-eight years asking no questions and making no waves. She passed the time with her flowers and her homemaking and the gift of her daughter, pretending she didn't need to grieve, pretending she wasn't terrified. She'd ignored her suspicions. All she had ever done was raise someone else's child.

She sniffed, wiped her eyes. A small steel seed took root in her heart. Because she still had that one thing.

She was still Rachel's mom.

It was the only worthwhile thing she'd ever been, and it was all she could be now. It meant something: the fact that she'd tended to Rachel—held her, fed her, taught her, made her a home. Vivian did it well. She'd played the part, created a world that was safe and happy for Rachel. Now her daughter was grown, and the lens had panned out far beyond the picture Vivian had once painted. The view was as big and complex as the world itself, and it included all of Vivian's failings, but there was still time. Rachel still needed a mother.

It was Vivian's job to be there for Rachel when she went to Argentina to try to make sense of her past. Vivian had lost her own babies once, and there was no one on the planet who could tell her where their tiny souls had gone or how or why. She couldn't keep those same answers from Rachel.

"What are you doing?"

Vivian gasped. Jonathan stood in the doorway, one hand on his hip, the small top button of his Henley shirt undone. The papers seemed to sear her hand.

"I—" As she spoke, a bubble of fury rose in her throat, scorching and unfamiliar.

"Vivian." He walked toward her slowly, one hand outstretched as though she were holding a loaded gun instead of a ream of papers. He smelled faintly of beer. Vivian was blazing with rage, although she wasn't sure if it was toward Jonathan or herself. The closer he got, the clearer her vision became.

Jonathan reached for the papers. "Give those to me, please."

Vivian retracted her hand, her skin fiery. "She needs to know. You're not going to lie to her."

"All parents lie to their children," he said evenly. "Hand those to me."

"She needs to see this. I had no idea you did this."

He locked eyes with her, a challenge. "Now is not the time to act righteous, Vivian."

"I didn't know you took her."

"You were never interested in the details."

"Then why would you keep this hidden from me? Why would you keep lying?"

"I never hid anything. It's all right here. I didn't lie to you." He lowered his voice. "I was just trying to protect Rachel."

Vivian shook her head in an attempt to break free of his influence. "We have to tell her. She's going to Argentina alone. Aren't you worried for her?"

His expression revealed a fear, but it wasn't for Rachel. "Yes."

Vivian looked down at the papers again, at her name, *Vivian Sprague*, written right next to his. Hot tears filled her eyes. Jonathan stood close enough to embrace her.

"We need to be with her." Vivian's words sounded like a plea.

Jonathan slid the papers from her hands and wrapped an arm around her shoulders. He kissed the top of her head. "It's going to be all right."

She hated the comfort she felt when she wilted against his chest. She looked up into his face. If Jonathan was Rachel's biological father, he might have more entitlement to her than Vivian did. Vivian had everything to lose.

"If you don't tell her about this," she said finally, "then I will."

"Vivian," he said. "I did this for you. Don't you understand that? Everything I did was for you. It was for all of us."

CHAPTER 16

MIAMI, FLORIDA

AUGUST 2005

Fat drops of rain splashed the steamy tarmac. Through the floor-to-ceiling airport windows, thunderheads loomed above the lush landscape.

Now boarding. Flight 1107 to Buenos Aires.

Rachel hurried through the loose crowd toward the announcement. Her connecting flight from JFK had been delayed. She navigated around passengers at a neighboring gate, where a young mother corralled her toddler as she rushed by. The gate agent repeated his announcement in Spanish. When she dug into her tote bag for her boarding pass, her hand brushed the silk binding of her blanket and a wave of relief washed over her.

She reached the gate and scrambled to open her passport, then paused, momentarily distracted by her own photo. Her closed smile, dark hair just past her shoulders. She smoothed her thumb over the surface of the image. This little blue booklet could validate her identity to anyone in the world, but it held no answers as to who she really was.

Attention passengers, please move quickly to your seats once on board. We're going to try to get out ahead of this storm.

Maybe the plane would crash. Maybe this was the bargain she was making with God for challenging the official version of the truth without having complete certainty.

She let out a shaky breath and surrendered her boarding pass to the gate agent.

"Have a nice flight, Miss Sprague."

Here name sounded forced, a staked claim. Outside the window, the asphalt darkened with each new drop. She wondered what she would find if this plane landed in Argentina and who her biological father was if she and Mat didn't share the same father. Perhaps he'd been a member of the junta. Perhaps her life had begun under the vilest circumstances imaginable. She shut her eyes tightly. Rachel needed to get closer to that place. It was going to hurt, but it was the most necessary thing she'd ever done in her life.

She closed her passport and reached down to touch her blanket again, rubbing its fabric between her fingers for comfort. Raindrops pelted the roof of the jet bridge. Rachel stepped carefully along the thin carpet of its metal floor, aware of the distant ground below, of the predicament of being suspended only tenuously above the earth's shifting surface, and of moving forward anyway.

PART IV

CHAPTER 17

Esme's fingertips were cold as she paced around her house, but she hesitated to turn up the heat any higher—it would get too warm once everyone arrived. Perhaps another degree wouldn't hurt. She could always open a window.

She'd been fully dressed for hours in what she hoped was the right outfit—a light blue sweater and brown slacks, the pearl studs Gustavo had given her as an anniversary gift years ago, a coordinating brooch pinned to her scarf. It was too early to start preparing lunch or *merienda*, but she put out a tray of *medialunas*, arranging them nervously. Did Ana prefer ham or cheese?

Rachel. Her granddaughter had been called Rachel all her life. Perhaps one day she would go by Ana, the name Lorena had given her. Esme chastised herself for thinking this: it didn't help to jump ahead with such silly hopes. For now, she should just be grateful.

After all, it had taken Rosa's granddaughter seven years after her DNA test to even acknowledge her grandmother—and then, for a long time, Patricia pushed Rosa to the side, treating her like some kind of shameful secret to be kept on the outskirts of her life.

"It has to be in her own time," Rosa repeated. Indeed, over an excruciating amount of time, Patricia finally came around. It didn't hurt that Rosa had gotten a dog.

And when Hilde was reunited with her adult grandson in recent years, Esme watched time melt the age from her friend's face as she held the grown man in her arms. Through tears, Esme recognized the woman she'd met years ago—Hilde's gold eye shadow, her youthful skin, her pretentious air at Café Tortoni. If only Alba had still been alive to see it. They'd been through so much loss, but every child they found was a wound healed; every completed search filled Esme's heart as though the grandchild were her own.

Presente, presente, presente, the young people chanted now for the mothers of the desaparecidos when they gathered at press conferences or demonstrations. Young people like Mari and Matías, who were carrying on the grandmothers' search armed with memory and truth, made the slow push through time toward justice, calling out the identity and presence of those who no longer had a voice of their own.

And here was Esme, mere months after first reading the transcript of a witness's testimony that would lead to Mari traveling to New York, preparing to welcome her long-lost granddaughter into her home. Preparing to host a dinner with her beloved friends and family, to celebrate the restoration of identity of her very own granddaughter, Ana.

What difference did it make what the girl called herself? Gratitude was the only appropriate response.

By now, Esme had washed and dried every breakfast dish, put them all away, and wiped down the spotless counter twice. Matías had said ten o'clock, but flights could be unreliable.

In the four-tiered wire hanging basket near the kitchen window, Esme arranged the fruit by color: six red apples in the top basket, eight oranges in the next, four lemons and a bunch of bananas in the third, and finally, pears, limes, and green apples at the bottom. She studied the rainbow. It had been ten thousand four hundred and sixty-five days without Lorena. She could still see the light on her daughter's face in the hallway that night when the junta broke in. When she lifted a hand to reposition an apple in the bottom basket, Esme could still feel the skin of Lorena's cheek.

We're coming back . . .

When Matías called from New York with the DNA test results, Esme had to dig through the letter holder on the wall to find the slip of paper on which she'd written Claudio's phone number years ago. It was a lingering paranoia, but Esme still couldn't bring herself to write his name in her gold-embossed address book, as though the junta might find it, even now, and come after her for it.

"Claudio," she'd said into the receiver after a decrepit beep. "It's Esme. We've found Lorena's daughter, Ana. She's in the United States, but she's coming to Buenos Aires. I told you I would let you know."

She hadn't heard back from him yet. She wasn't sure she ever would.

The doorbell rang now, followed by a knock. Esme startled. Her heart swelled as she moved through the foyer and reached for the door handle. Matías had already started to open the door from the other side. He forged in, beaming, and hugged her, his winter coat puffing up around them both. Over his shoulder, Esme recognized Mari's curls. They brought in the smell of the wind, of travel. When Matías finally let her go, Esme embraced Mari and closed her eyes, for she wasn't ready yet to see the person who would be standing behind Mari. Even with all the knowledge she had in her mind, Esme's heart still needed proof.

Mari pulled away, smiling, face to face with Esme. Then she stepped aside.

"Hello," said the girl, smiling Lorena's smile.

I'm coming back, Mamá . . .

"Oh," Esme said. She moved slowly toward her. When Esme embraced her, she thought her heart would explode. Her *granddaughter.* A part of Lorena was here, in Esme's arms, pressed against the beating heart in her chest. Ana had come all the way here—home to Esme— and she was letting Esme hold on to her now. She was hugging her back.

Esme's eyes welled and spilled over.

"Oh," she said again.

Then she stood back and looked at the girl for a long time.

Ana.

The resemblance to Lorena was there, but it required time for Esme to validate what she saw. Her eyes traveled over the girl's features. Her hair matched Lorena's in color, though it was coarser in texture than Matías's—he'd always had José's silky locks—but it was only hair; it didn't mean anything. The same couldn't be said for the shape of her jaw or the natural curve of the lips, slightly downward at the corners. Esme couldn't ignore the straightness of her brow bone. Her granddaughter had the face of her Lorena, but the features of someone else entirely. As with so many truths she'd first learned in her heart throughout the years, it was just a matter of time before the proof arrived for the rest of the world to see.

CHAPTER 18

Rachel felt as though she were floating alongside her body. Here was the truth, spread out before her in three padded gingham photo albums with yellowed Scotch-taped labels, the ink from a decades-old felt-tip marker bleeding into the paper. *1973, 1974, 1975*. A set of archival photo boxes printed with pink orchids.

Esme opened one of the albums. "This was Lorena and José's wedding," she said. Her words were unhurried. Mat stood above them now, one arm crossing his body and the other held to his lips in a fist, half-masking his expression.

Esme looked younger than Rachel had expected. Her grayish-brown hair was set into soft curls. She wore rimless bifocals and carried a scent of bergamot. Her lace-collared blouse was layered under a chenille sweater, the creases in her slacks crisp, and her leather loafers had a gold embellishment at the toe. She had a strong figure for a woman in her seventies. It was hard not to notice—Rachel had no other reference for what she might look like as she aged, until now.

As Esme handed her the photos, Rachel absorbed the images of Lorena as a young girl: at her First Holy Communion, as a teenager holding a stack of books, as a young woman sitting at a picnic table with several other people holding her baby boy. Rachel studied every detail of the photos: the stitch of Lorena's jeans along her thighs, the curve of her wrists, her jaw, her hair, her breasts, her eyes. She longed to touch this woman, smell her, become small enough to climb into the pictures and nestle on Lorena's lap.

Sorrow should have arrived, tears should have overtaken her, but Rachel was still floating along—fascinated, intrigued, propelled forward. Lorena was everything she'd dared to imagine when she opened her mind to the possibility. *Before that day, you were with the mommy and daddy who made you.*

Mari took a seat in a floral armchair across from them. Rachel was suddenly aware of the room—the woodstove, the little star-shaped pins lining the upholstery of the chairs, the stacks of music albums filling a bookcase against one wall: Duke Ellington, Nat King Cole, Benny Goodman, Beethoven. She breathed in the warm cinnamon smell of this modest house in Buenos Aires with its clay-tiled roof and iron gate. She'd missed out on this.

"My husband—your grandfather, Gustavo—he loved music," Esme said in Spanish when she caught Rachel's gaze landing on the vinyl records. "He didn't play, but he loved to listen."

Rachel nodded tenderly.

"Your ancestors were from southern Italy and the Basque region of Spain," Esme went on. "Gustavo had a bit of German on his side too."

"Here." Mat emerged from the kitchen, set down a tray on a clear spot on the coffee table, then perched on the arm of the sofa. "Now that you're in Argentina, you have to learn the proper ritual of maté." He filled the maté with crushed dried leaves, then carefully poured in hot water and placed the metal straw. He sipped and passed it to Mari.

Rachel took a sip from the metal straw, and a bitter tea warmed her tongue. She handed the gourd to Esme and pointed to a photo of Lorena smiling up at a dark-haired man from a lawn chair.

"Who's this?"

"That's Claudio," Esme said.

Rachel studied the deep set of the man's eyes in the photo and Lorena's expression as she looked up at him, full of something wild and knowing.

Esme set down the maté and stood up. She walked over to the letter holder hanging from the wall, its stenciled green vines winding around a little clock at the top. Hanging from a key hook below the bottom pocket were rosewood rosary beads, a plastic Jesus glued to the wooden crucifix. Esme pulled out a piece of paper from the letter holder, unfolded it and flattened it against her chest.

"Claudio was a good friend of your mother and José," she said. "They all went to university together. He was very active, politically, during the junta's reign. Lorena always had a calling toward activism too, like her father, and I think Claudio brought that out in her." Esme folded both hands over the paper, then shook her head. She looked at Mari, deliberated a moment, then put the paper back in the holder.

Rachel reached into her bag and took out a journal in which she'd hastily stashed several of her own favorite photos.

"I brought these," she said. "I thought you might want to see them."

"Oh." Esme touched her glasses and took them gratefully, setting them down one by one on the glass coffee table. Rachel recalled the kitchen table in Howell Grove, strewn with the contents of her adoption file, but pushed the memories aside as images of her own life mixed with Lorena's before her eyes.

"Oh," Esme repeated, touching her lips. She looked up at Rachel in awe, then back at the photos with an awkward blend of sentimentality and remorse. Mari handed her a tissue. "Look at this."

"I was about five years old in that one," said Rachel, pointing to a picture taken in the backyard, her arms splayed out to the sides. "Pretending to fly, I guess. This is where I grew up."

Esme marveled, shifting through the photos slowly. She stopped at a high school graduation photo—Rachel's hair loose beneath the mortar board, lips closed in a smile—and set it down next to the photo of Lorena that Mari had first showed Rachel.

Esme beamed. "Oh, *niña*," she breathed.

"The resemblance is incredible," said Mat.

Rachel felt proud, like she'd done something remarkable just by living her life.

At the end of the pile was a photo of Rachel as an infant in a bassinet, her tiny arms reaching up toward her mom's yellow hair. Esme stared at it for a long time. Rachel had a flash memory of the dresser drawer in her childhood bedroom where she'd kept the photos. It was filled with other things she'd left behind: a picture of her dad standing in the driveway in full military attire, squinting as the sun glinted off his buttons; a clipped newspaper article from one of her high school soccer victories; a crayoned, sticker-encrusted Easter card she'd made at six or seven that read *I love you, Mommy and Daddy, Love RACHEL.*

A lump formed in her throat.

"May I use the restroom?"

Esme nodded, pointed down the far hall.

Behind the closed bathroom door, Rachel ran warm water from the spigot and splashed it on her face. She cupped her hands and filled them repeatedly, staring at the flowers painted on the chipped tile. A tiny, delicate spider made its way down the wall of the standing shower. She unbuttoned her jeans and slid them down her thighs, pausing to run her palm over her birthmark.

When she stood up to wash her hands, Rachel half expected to see Lorena appear in the mirror behind her. Her strong, beautiful mother who hadn't abandoned her after all, a mother for whom Rachel had always been enough. Indeed, she felt an intimate presence here now, as prominent as her angels or the blond ghost. It was what she was looking for.

She followed it down the hall into a small bedroom like a child wandering through a stranger's house on a visit. She was still floating— she'd been awake for nearly thirty hours—and the crisp bed looked like a welcoming fantasy. On a rack of wooden pegs near the closet door, a collection of colorful printed scarves hung sorted on rings. Rachel lifted them one by one: a cream-colored silk with nautical designs, a green chiffon, nearly weightless. One had a ladybug, another a spray of hibiscus. Some were solid, others vaguely floral, a medley of hues bleeding into fabric. She felt the presence intensify.

"They were popular in the seventies," said Esme, appearing in the bedroom doorway.

Rachel startled.

"Lorena always liked to wear them. She had a good sense of style. Simple, but confident. Some of these are mine, but many of them used to be hers." Esme pulled an oblong caramel shift from a loop. "This one, for instance. This was one of Lorena's favorites." She took the scarf and draped it around Rachel's neck. "It was the color of her eyes. And yours."

Rachel touched the fabric. She watched Esme fold a navy silk into a triangle, tying it around her head. "I always wore them like this after going to the beauty parlor. I still wear these on Thursdays." She pulled two large white squares from one of the last hooks.

"What's that bible verse?" asked Mari, appearing beside them and twisting a purple scarf. "'Wear the world like a loose garment' or something?"

"That's Saint Francis of Assisi," Esme corrected.

Rachel sat down on the bedspread, holding both ends of Lorena's scarf around her neck.

"There's something you should know, dear," said Esme. She walked over to where Rachel sat and took her hands. Esme's skin was dry and warm. "Lorena gave you a name when you were born. She named you Ana."

"Ana." Rachel spoke the name for the first time, letting it live in her mouth for a moment, then breathing it in and out. *Ana.* She wondered if it was possible to have a wound so deep, so long-standing, that it required an entire second lifetime for healing.

"Poor thing," said Mari. "She hasn't slept."

"Feel free to rest, child," said Esme, gesturing to the bed.

Rachel laid her head against the pillow sham's perfumed scent. The scarves hung in her line of sight, waterfalls of color. She felt the presence approach once more, and everything around her seemed loose, slippery, temporary. Even her name.

—— · ❖ · ——

The splendors of Buenos Aires swirled like a carnival outside the taxi windows. The driver pointed vaguely in the direction of Recoleta Cemetery and Evita Perón's tomb, then the Japanese gardens and the Casa Rosada. As the cab jerked and jostled through San Telmo to La Boca, tango dancers stroked the cobblestone with their bodies in an open courtyard flanked by buildings as colorful as tropical birds. A man in a coat was making a barrel fire; a woman's ankle bracelet jingled as she panhandled, shaking her cup to a singsong "por favor."

In the backseat, Rachel toyed with the cotton ball a nurse had taped to the crook of her arm with a Band-Aid after two vials of her blood had been sent off to the genetic bank at Durand Hospital for testing. Her body swayed alongside Mat and Mari as the driver wove through the city.

"Do you still want to see El Olimpo?" asked Mari. "It's right near my sister's apartment."

Rachel's stomach lurched with the taxi's brakes. "Maybe tomorrow?"

"We've seen enough already," Mat mumbled.

Rachel pinched the sleeve of his jacket and tugged gently.

"Are you mad or something?"

"Why would I be?"

"I don't know. I just—it's not my fault the test results came back the way they did."

"I know."

"I didn't know we might have different fathers."

"I didn't either, obviously." Mat scratched his chin. "I just feel like I didn't know anything about my parents now."

Rachel lapsed into English. "How do you think I feel?"

"It's no one's fault," said Mari. "It's just life." She pulled Mat's arm onto her lap and laced their fingers together. Mat looked out the window.

"Do you know how lucky I feel," said Mari, "that my sister Marcela and I got to grow up together with our dad? I don't know what I would do if I didn't have my sister."

Rachel pulled in her lips.

"I just think you should hold your family close, no matter what the circumstances."

———— · ❖ · ————

Dinnertime arrived with the restorative sensation that an entire nation of women had been waiting to welcome Rachel home, that she'd somehow wildly exceeded the expectations of every guest who embraced her. Esme served salad, tender cuts of steak so rare they formed thin puddles of blood, and homemade empanadas. Plates were passed across a concert of conversations. Rachel sat next to Mari, sipping Malbec and trying to catch each word as the mothers and grandmothers reminisced. Esme's friend Hilde picked stray flakes of pastry dough from the tablecloth with her polished fingernails.

"It didn't start out as political," Hilde explained in quick Spanish. There was a controlled ferocity about her. "When we first started demonstrating, it was just a grief walk. We had to do something. Remember, Esme?"

"We try to document everything they know and remember," Mari whispered to Rachel. "The Abuelas are our living archives."

On the other side of Rachel sat another found grandchild, Patricia. She leaned over to Rachel and spoke in slow, broken English.

"It took me a long time to understand that my grandmother just wanted to know me. She loved me, that's all—she wasn't trying to take me away from the family I grew up with. My father was in the navy, but he's a good man. He's no villain. He's been a good father to me."

"There are still hundreds of grandchildren out there," said Mari. She looked around the table. "If we don't find them soon, they'll never have the chance to know their grandmothers."

Rachel drew in a deep breath and caught Mat's eye as he quietly cut through a piece of steak. She wanted to be closer to the part of Lorena that lived within him. Mat had touchstones to the past—scents, melodies, familiar locations—but she had nothing to guide her except her own instincts.

"What is it?" she asked. She didn't want him to reject her. She didn't want to do any of this alone.

Mat chewed thoughtfully, then shook his head. "I was just wondering if you had any plans for Christmas."

Marcela, Mari's younger sister, lived in an apartment that felt like the type of place Rachel would have lived had she grown up here—light peach walls, melon-scented candles, scattered paper lanterns throughout. Perhaps that was why she finally began to reinhabit her body upon entering it. From the silver stereo on the living room floor, a Lenny Kravitz song played at a low volume.

"I heard you have a sweet tooth," said Marcela.

Rachel watched from the kitchen table as Mari's younger sister steamed milk in a silver pitcher, then poured it into two mugs, a chocolate bar melting in each. "You'll like this." Then she held up a bottle of dulce de leche liqueur and winked, pouring it generously into two shot glasses.

"Los Pericos, por favor," Marcela called to Mari, who sat on the futon couch with Mat several feet away. "And turn it up."

The music stopped. Moments later, a reggae beat filled the apartment. Marcela bobbed her head. "One of these guys is the son of a disappeared parent."

"In the band?"

Marcela nodded. A flourish of brass lifted above the melody. She topped off the drinks with foam and sprinkled them with chocolate shavings. Then she fixed a little tray of *alfajores* and placed the cookies and the mugs on the table in front of Rachel. On the counter, an unopened miniature cereal box of sugary Zucaritas flaunted the familiar face of Tony the Tiger on a blue backdrop. Marcela followed Rachel's gaze, picked up the box, and placed it down on the table in front of her.

"You like these?" said Marcela. "Take it."

Rachel smiled at her lap. "Thanks." The small kindness overwhelmed her.

Marcela sat down in the chair beside her.

"I went to that excavation site once," she said, sipping her chocolate. Her black rhinestone earrings danced below her curls, which were just like Mari's but short and asymmetrical. "It was so depressing. Seriously. *Qué quilombo.* Why would my sister want to take you there?"

"I want to learn more about my mother." Rachel touched the scarf draped around her neck. Lorena's presence seemed to linger all around, just out of reach. Rachel sipped the drink, creamy and delicious. "Weren't you curious to see the place you might have been born?"

"*¿Por qué?* It's too tragic. You should be celebrating instead. You just found your brother."

"What are you filling her head with?" Mari called from the futon.

"I'm just saying." Marcela got up to retrieve the liqueur glasses and handed one to Rachel. She did a little dance and raised a toast before swallowing it. "There's plenty of despair if you go looking for it. Remember when they found bones in a trash can outside the naval school?"

"God," said Rachel. She sipped the liqueur.

"I'm serious," said Marcela. "I've seen those cell walls. There's an engraving on one of them—it looks like a prisoner scratched into the cement with their fingernails—that says '*Ayúdame Señor.*' I'm telling you, it's no good for you to see that."

Rachel imagined herself as an infant in Lorena's arms, crouched in some dark, hidden place.

"Believe me, I get it," Marcela went on. "I got to grow up with my dad and sister, thank God, but I still go to therapy once a week. Most of the people in your situation—the ones who were lied to—they have to be really careful about their mental health. You're not the only one. A lot of adopted people didn't know their real parents were desaparecidos."

"How many of them didn't even know it happened?"

Marcela shrugged. "Look, you can feel bad if you want to, but you're better off looking toward the future, in my opinion. You're more than just the lies people told you. You found your truth now. You should do something with it."

The words buoyed her; they seemed familiar. "Like what?"

Marcela stirred her coffee. "Your appropriator, the guy who stole you. He was in the military, right?"

Rachel opened her mouth. Marcela made her dad seem distant, like a foreign criminal.

"Yes."

"Well, no offense," said Marcela, sipping, "but fuck that guy."

"Marcela," scolded Mari.

"What? I'm serious. He did all this, lied to you, and then he threatens Mari? The guy's bad milk."

Rachel felt a hitch in her gut. "What do you mean, he 'threatened' you?"

"It was nothing," said Mari, rising to approach the kitchen table. "It was just a phone call, that's all. It could've been worse."

A fury far beyond anger or rage surged in Rachel like a stark white light, blocking everything out. She thought of Mari's business card and heard her dad's voice in her head that day on the porch: *It's impossible.*

"What did he say to you?"

"It wasn't a big deal." Mari put her hand on Rachel's shoulder. "We expected it might happen. He knows what he did—he was probably just trying to get a feel for the extent of what we know—but he positioned it as though he was protecting you. Leaving New York early was just a precaution I took." She glanced over at Mat. "We thought it would be safer, given the circumstances."

"He'd be in the oven if he ever came down here," said Marcela.

Rachel's skin was hot. She clenched her teeth.

"Come on," said Mat, standing up. "Finish up the coffees, let's head over to the *escuela*."

"Forget about that place," said Marcela. She pulled a flier out from beneath a banana-shaped magnet on the refrigerator door and slid it across the table toward Rachel. "Where you should be going is to the *escrache* with me."

On the flier was a photo of a clean-cut man in a suit, his eyes dark as black beans. He looked polished, successful—like some executive at a midtown investment bank. Beneath his picture was his name and a list of his affiliations: he'd been a military officer and part of two operational groups at clandestine prisons—Club Atletico and El Olimpo. Across his face was the word GENOCIDA, printed like a rubber stamp.

Rachel tipped her mug to swirl the last of the melted chocolate at the bottom and polished off the drink. Anger coursed through her veins like a drug. She flipped the flier over. On the back, in large font, was the header: *If there's no justice, there's ESCRACHE!*

"What's *escrache*?" Rachel asked.

Mari took the flier and folded it in half. "It's an event organized by families of the desaparecidos—mostly the kids. It's a way of calling out the officers who have never been held accountable for what they did."

"They go to the torturers' houses," said Mat.

"And what do they do there?"

"Make a statement," laughed Marcela.

"It's all completely sanctioned," said Mari. "They have permits and everything. But we're still not going."

"It's just a way of not letting the junta forget what they did," said Mat.

"Like a shaming?"

Marcela nodded excitedly.

Mari narrowed her eyes at her sister. "Marcela takes after our mother," she said. "It's a bad idea."

Marcela turned to Rachel. "Don't you want to do something? You should take your life back. It's yours now."

Rachel just wanted to move forward, to be closer to Lorena. Maybe this was what Lorena would have done. The liqueur shot had taken hold. If Rachel went to this man's house, perhaps she could get just a little bit closer to her mother somehow.

"I want to go," she said.

"I don't think you'd feel comfortable there," said Mari. "It can get a little crazy."

Mat nodded. "You may not be ready."

"Besides," said Mari. "I have an appointment at the Abuelas' office this afternoon."

But Marcela was already putting the mugs in the sink, slipping on her jacket and handing Rachel hers conspiratorially.

Rachel took her Magic 8 Ball key chain out of her backpack and shook it. "Should we go to the escrache?"

WITHOUT A DOUBT.

Marcela shrugged. "Put your batteries in, Matías."

Mari looked at Marcela warily. "Take her if you want, but stay out of trouble."

A destructive buzz lifted Rachel as she trailed Marcela and Mat down the street. Near the university, a hydrant trickled icy water into a large puddle on the sidewalk. Commuters exited the Subte silently as the group descended into it, their steps falling in rhythm with a pan-handler shaking a can of pesos.

They got off at the last station and took a bus through an up-scale residential neighborhood, disembarking just as the sun broke through a cloud. A large banner tied between two telephone poles announced: *If there is no justice, there is* ESCRACHE*!* To the right, a landscaper dragged thick branches of a lime tree to the curb, ripe fruit still dangling like Christmas ornaments. Mat plucked a lime as they walked by and handed it to Rachel. She sniffed it, then put it in her backpack. In the distance up ahead, music from a radio was drowned out by snare drums and brass. Gilded drummers in full regalia—double-breasted turquoise tailcoats, marching band hats, gold-trimmed satin pants, shirts covered in sequin patches in the shapes of peace signs, butterflies, and little white headscarves like those the grandmothers wore—lined the gathering crowd. The far-ther they walked, the denser the crowd became. A stilt-walker had a barrel suspendered around his waist and painted with the words *Anda Suelto*—on the loose.

The crowd chanted: *Alert, alert, alert the neighbors! Next to your home lives an assassin!* Next to Rachel, a woman about her age wore a tight black shirt that revealed the underside of her pregnant belly, painted with WE REMEMBER. Her pace fell in line with the crowd. This street carnival-parade-protest—full of noise and energy—would bring her closer to Lorena somehow. Exhilaration took hold.

"Are you okay?" asked Mat.

She nodded and linked her arm with his. She was propelled in the direction of instinct, her feet keeping time with the drumbeats. A young man with a can of spray paint crouched on the asphalt nearby. He stenciled large fingerprints on the street, then painted the torturer's name followed by the words: *You're surrounded.*

Two girls ran up ahead of the crowd as it progressed. At each telephone pole, they took turns boosting one another up, like cheerleaders doing a stunt, attaching yellow metal traffic signs to the pole with wire and string. *Warning,* the first sign said, *In 500 meters lives a genocidal man.* They posted another at 400 meters, then 300. The snare drums rolled.

She imagined leading the parade to her house in Howell Grove, the home of the blond ghost. *You're surrounded,* she thought. She tripped over a shallow curb, then regained her stride.

At 250 meters out, a kid with a small sponge roller brush and a can of yellow paint wrote neatly on the cobblestone street: *A torturer lives at 1955 Condarco Avenue.* Rachel looked around at the crowd of hundreds. Someone dressed as a clown carried two signs that read *Basta Yanquis* and *Patria sí, Colonia no!*

At 200 meters, the girls posted another sign, then another at 100 meters. Police barriers were erected along the sidewalks as they drew nearer. Behind them, uniformed officers stood in a line. In front of the barriers, mere feet away, a group of people held a cloth banner across the line of cops: IN SERVICE OF IMPUNITY.

Oh, sung the crowd. *Que se vayan todos . . .*

"You doing okay?" Marcela yelled.

Rachel shrugged. "I'm fine."

Marcela smiled. "You should come work at the Archivo with us."

The chants grew louder as the two girls posted a sign for 50 meters out. More police officers were present—a line of female cops who, to

Rachel's relief, looked amused, as though they didn't personally object to the display.

Look at yourselves, you're all a part of it! The crowd chanted. *It's not just the cops, it's the whole institution!*

The two-story house at the torturer's address was covered in plastic tarps. A member of the crowd fired a paintball gun; red paint splattered at a tarp's center. An older woman, one of the mothers of the disappeared, approached the barrier wearing her white headscarf.

"You had the balls to torture and kill," she cried, "but you don't have the balls to come out now? Show your face, you bastard!"

"Is he in there?" asked Rachel.

"Hell no," said Marcela. "He knew this was happening today. Probably took his family to his country house or something. We're nothing but an inconvenience to him."

Another paintball bullet was fired, and a splash of white paint stained a tarp.

Marcela chuckled. "So let him get a little cramp."

Oh, sung the crowd. *Que se vayan todos . . .*

Rachel approached the police barrier. A gust of wind caught one of the tarps and lifted it briefly away from the house, revealing a glimpse of the interior through a downstairs window. She'd grown up in a house not much different from this one, the daughter of a military officer—yet she'd been born in a prison, daughter of a victim. The person who lived beyond this window could be Lorena's torturer or her father's colleague and friend. A twisting sensation suddenly gripped her core. Did she belong outside this house or in it?

A group of preteens banged pots and pans with wooden sticks. The cool metal of the police barrier warmed beneath her grip. Inside her eyelids were images of sequins and splashes of paint.

Colonia, no! Someone shouted with fervor. A wave of vertigo hit. Something was wrong with her ears; she was losing her balance. The sugary liqueur rose in her throat as she spun through the crowd, disoriented, swiveling from one face to another until she found Mat's. The previous weeks caught up to her in a flash—Mari's call, Lorena's photo, her dad's face that morning on the porch, the test results—and she landed in her body with full force, as though she'd just disembarked from an intense roller-coaster ride. It was all happening at once. She caressed the fibers of Lorena's scarf with her thumb and forefinger. Nausea came like a storm surge.

"I think I'm going to be sick."

Marcela tugged her expertly through a crowd of bodies, tennis sneakers and boots to a miraculous patch of open grass. In an instant, Mat was at her side, his hand on her shoulders. The drumbeats carried on. They moved together to the fringes of the crowd and headed back down the street toward the bus stop. Mat draped one of her arms around his hunched shoulders.

"I'm sorry, girl," said Marcela, rubbing her back. "I shouldn't have made you come. You don't have to be part of this fight just because of what happened to you."

"Shh," Mat said. "Just let her be."

Rachel eased all her weight onto the cold metal bus stop bench.

"It's not your fault," Marcela said.

Rachel looked up at her, grateful. Marcela answered her ringing cell phone just as a bus was arriving.

"Yeah, she's here," Marcela said. She looked at Rachel, then lifted the phone. "It's Mari. She wants to talk to you."

Rachel took the phone. "Hello?"

"Rachel? I'm at the Abuelas' office with Tomás, one of the attorneys. Can I put him on?" Mari's voice was hastened, breathy. The bus lowered in front of them with an exhalation of exhaust, and the door flapped open.

"Okay," said Rachel.

Through a muffled transition, a man's nervous voice emerged.

"Miss Sprague?" a voice said in English. "We received your DNA results from Durand. Are you able to come by the office so that we can share them with you?"

Rachel looked up at Mat. "They have the test results. Can we go there?"

He glanced around. "Let me find us a cab."

"Yes," Rachel said. "We'll come now."

"Very good," said Tomás. "And there's something else, Miss Sprague. I'm afraid it's a bit urgent. You'll want to get here as soon as you can. There's a woman here—she showed up unexpectedly, arrived at the office by herself this morning. She says she's looking for her daughter."

CHAPTER 19

BUENOS AIRES

JUNE 1977

In the entryway to Helena's luxury apartment building in Recoleta, Jonathan rang the buzzer twice to no avail. The elevator was under repair, so he took four flights of stairs up from the lobby. At the top of the spiral staircase just outside her apartment door, Helena stood with one hand on her hip. She wore a silk blouse and skirt and had a freshness about her that seemed incongruous to the hour.

"Come on in."

He followed her into the spacious apartment, took off his coat, and draped it over the arm of a plush sofa.

"You want wine? Whiskey? Tea? I have plenty of everything."

"I'll have a glass of that one Ricardo drinks."

She ducked briefly out of sight and reemerged in the kitchen doorway holding up a bottle with a familiar label. "You can put on music if you like." A peaty scent filled the air as she poured. "I spoke with Graciela. She applied for a passport, and I told her you'd make all the airfare arrangements. We agreed to two hundred and fifty thousand pesos."

"And she has experience with children?"

"Three of her own."

"You trust her?"

Helena walked over to her writing desk and jotted Graciela's number on her personalized stationery. "She's been cleaning my house for eight years." When she handed it to him, she smiled as if to say, *You see how easy that was?*

"Thank you." He folded the paper and put it in his pocket.

The building heat cranked on suddenly with a loud revving sound. A gust of warm air from the overhead vent filled the room. In an instant, like a waking dream, Jonathan could see the bolts in the metal plates of a helicopter's interior fuselage all around him. A South Vietnamese attachment was interrogating two prisoners seated on the floor. The interrogator hoisted the first by an arm and thrust him out the open door mid-flight to get the second one to talk.

When Helena touched his shoulder, Jonathan startled so abruptly that the glass of whiskey in his hand spilled, the amber fluid sloshing onto her blouse. She gasped. He blinked his eyes. He was back on his training mission with the Montagnards, rifling through corpses for ammunition, lifting a Viet Cong body by the strap of his rucksack, then jumping back when the dead man appeared to gasp audibly, expelling the air left in his lungs after death.

He handed his glass to Helena, then closed his eyes and squeezed his head with both hands.

She guided him to the couch, pulling him lightly by the arm in his altered state.

"I'm sorry—" His voice was hoarse.

She shook her head fiercely. "No. It's all right. Here. Make yourself comfortable." She slid her pumps off and curled her stockinged legs up underneath her.

He sank back into the cushions next to her. She handed him the remaining whiskey, pinching a section of her damp blouse away from her body to air the spill.

———— ·❖· ————

Jonathan sat, his knee bobbing, in one of the Louis XVI chairs the secretary had made such a fuss over when she'd first given him a tour of
the embassy. He stared down at the rotary dial on the black desk phone.
He picked up the receiver and held it in his hand, assessing its weight,
then tapped the switch hook, its thick click triggering a low tone on
the line. He glanced at the clock. His brother, Greg, would still be on
duty at this hour, but Daphne would be home, presumably alone with
his nephew. If Ricardo came through for him, Jonathan would need
Daphne's help in coordinating the international adoption.

When he finally rotated the dial, it was his brother's number he
called.

"Jon!" Daphne said. "I wasn't expecting your call. How are you?" The
sound of a children's cartoon played on the television in the background.

"I'm fine. Everything's fine."

"You'll be home soon, won't you? I saw Viv last week." She lowered
her voice. "She looks terrible."

Jonathan envisioned Vivian's face, sorrow setting the slope of her
brow as the years passed and the waiting continued. "Daphne," he said.
"I need to talk to you about something." He paused. "I want you to
walk me through how things would work, exactly, with an adoption."

"I told you already. You're next on the list with us. It may be an
older child, though—that's much more likely in Howell County—and
the courts will look to establish permanency first, so you'll have to do
foster care for a time and all that—no, sweetheart, no, please don't put
that in your mouth—but you are next on the list, like I said."

"And what if there was a baby outside of Howell County?"

"Well, we take inbound referrals if we get them, of course, but we
only have so many resources." Daphne sighed. "Listen, Jon. If you have
your heart set on a baby, you're better off going through Catholic Char-
ities and finding a birth mother. I've told you and Vivian that from the
beginning. Sweetheart, get down from there." There was a clatter through
the receiver. "You know how we work at the center. We accept any child
in need with open arms, whether they've been neglected, abused, or-
phaned, abandoned—"

Jonathan straightened in the chair. A thought entered his mind, a tightly packed idea that had the density to expand and explode, splintering off into a thousand tactical obstacles. *Wait. Not yet.*

"I understand," he said.

"If your hearts aren't open to loving any child God may send your way, maybe you should consider another option. We've been over this a hundred times. There are no guarantees. But I can assure you that if a child does come into our care in need of a good home, you and Vivian will be my first phone call."

"I appreciate that." His mouth was open, but his thoughts obstructed his words. There was still time. He didn't have to tell her anything yet.

"I'll be over at the center on Thursday to make sure all your paperwork is still in order," said Daphne. "I'm glad you're coming home soon. I'm sure Viv will perk up once you get here."

Jonathan hung up and let his gaze climb the gold-trimmed molding toward the twenty-foot ceilings. His eyes fell on the crystal chandelier in the embassy hall. The thought swelled like a ripe fruit ready for the taking.

He signed off on the completed enrollment paperwork for Ricardo's nephew, Pedro, and faxed it to Fort Leavenworth, then put on his coat.

———— · ❖ · ————

A cold afternoon sky stretched out above Jonathan as he headed through the entrance of the Casa Rosada. He unzipped his coat as he made his way down the corridor, where campaign posters combating rising allegations of human-rights abuses proclaimed, *Los argentinos somos derechos y humanos!* Outside Ricardo's office, Camila was packing up her purse. She waved Jonathan through the open door behind her. Ricardo looked up from his mahogany desk, his brass name plaque centered before him, and removed his glasses. He reached for two tumblers and a decanter from the bar cart as Jonathan sat down. Camila's high-heeled footfalls faded down the corridor.

The two men sipped their drinks in silence until Ricardo opened a cigar box and handed one to Jonathan.

"Congratulations, Captain," he said, lighting one of the cigars. "It's a girl."

Jonathan exhaled with relief.

"You know," Richardo said. "This is hard for me, seeing a perfectly good Argentine baby go to a gringo like you. Only for a man of your caliber would I even be willing to consider it. A favor, you understand."

"Well, that's very good of you, Colonel." The smoke snaked around them. "And if it's not too much trouble, I'm hoping you can help me expedite a passport."

Ricardo pulled on his cigar and blew a ring. "For whom?"

"Helena found someone to help with the handling. A nursemaid of sorts. I sure as hell can't travel with a newborn on my own."

"Is she Argentine?"

"Yes, and she already submitted her application. It will probably come through in time. I'm asking just in case."

"It shouldn't be a problem." Ricardo sighed. "I should tell you that the adoption fee is not insubstantial."

"You mentioned that."

"And there was an additional expense for the special arrangements to accommodate your timeline. Surgical doctors aren't cheap." Ricardo ashed his cigar. "You can't cheat Mother Nature without paying the price."

Jonathan slipped an envelope from the inside pocket of his coat and slid it across the desk. His military savings account had amassed over fifteen thousand dollars. "This should cover it. And Pedro's enrollment paperwork is already on its way to Kansas." He set his cigar down on the ashtray and leaned forward, resting his elbows on his knees. He kneaded his palms with his thumbs beneath the loose weave of his fingers.

"I want to thank you sincerely, Colonel," Jonathan said.

Ricardo shrugged. "You know how Videla sees it. Seeds of subversion have to be replanted in healthy soil. Otherwise evil grows."

"I agree."

Ricardo cleared his throat. "There will be some documents for you and your wife to handle."

Jonathan leaned back in the chair. "I haven't told her yet. She's not . . . well." It pained him to say the words aloud. "I was waiting until we had things finalized."

"I'm sorry to hear that." He picked up his cigar.

"Does she need to be a part of this?"

"I'm sure it won't be necessary. You'll work it out with the agency."

They fell silent for a few moments. Jonathan stared into his whiskey. Vivian was going to ask questions.

"And the mother?" he asked quietly.

"In custody at the *Escuela*. Scheduled to be transferred south in next week's run."

Jonathan swallowed. He'd have to explain to Vivian that the baby's parents were enemies of the state, terrorists who fought against the government. She would ask if they were still alive, and the prospect of having to answer this felt burdensome, irritating. He'd made this entire arrangement with Ricardo to fix things—their marriage, *her*—and a baby was meant to cure Vivian's grief, not add to it.

"I leave a week from Friday."

"Thank God for that." Ricardo chuckled. He put a finger on the envelope full of money, slid it toward him, and slipped it into a top drawer. "You've got a duty now, amigo. Make sure you raise that child well."

When they'd finished their drinks, the two men stood and shook hands. Jonathan lifted his coat collar as he headed out of the Casa Rosada. He walked toward the Metropolitan Cathedral, huddling up against the cold. At the center of the Plaza, a sparse group of women were circling the Pirámide de Mayo on foot at a slow pace in white kerchiefs.

———— · ❖ · ————

At the naval school, Jonathan sat across the desk from the adoption agent, a balding man with the fatigued air of a lifelong bureaucrat.

"Shall we proceed, señor?" the man asked.

"Yes, of course."

Jonathan slid his wallet from the pocket of his uniform and retrieved the cashier's check he'd brought, pausing to show the representative a photo of him and Vivian on their wedding day.

"She's lovely. I assume since she's in the United States that this will be a proxy adoption for her."

"You don't need her to sign anything, do you?"

"No. As long as you're legally married, you can sign on her behalf." He slid a packet across the desk toward Jonathan.

Jonathan filled out his full name, Vivian's name, their wedding date, religion, residence, race, information about his extended family, income, bank account, church. A description of their home. His physical condition. When his hand cramped from holding the ballpoint pen, Jonathan paused and looked up.

"This part, here?" A series of blank lined pages constituted the remaining paperwork, headered by soft essay-like questions that struck him as juvenile. *Why do you want to adopt a child? What steps have you taken to prepare for a child in your home? How long have you been waiting to adopt?*

"You can skip that," said the agent.

Jonathan signed the documents and surrendered the check, then watched carefully as the agent reviewed the application in full, including the sections previously completed by the military doctor: the baby's sex—indeed, female—and the name of its parents: NN. *Nomen Nescio.* An unidentified baby from unidentified parents. His neck flushed.

Through the entire section referencing birth certificate and hospital record, the agent drew a quick but deep diagonal line. He paused to review the section titled "Intercountry Adoptions," and Jonathan watched the tip of the man's pen follow the long list of South American countries, then hover above the brief list of western European ones, each with its own empty square check box. Finally, he slashed the list with a line and wrote across it: *Estados Unidos.* Then he inked a rubber handstamp and pressed it against several pages, one at a time. He left the room for a few minutes and returned with a large manila envelope.

Jonathan watched and waited. Nowhere on the forms was there any administrative coordination with a US agency. The representative signed the paperwork, then made a lengthy show of removing each yellow carbon copy from its individual page and layering them together to form a second packet, which he then inserted, with much effort, into the envelope.

"The original dossier will be certified by the military government," said the representative, looping the string fastener to seal the envelope. "And, as you discussed with Colonel Prieta, given the extenuating circumstances and the need for expediency in the interest of the child, we won't go through court system. This copy can go directly to the adoption agency in the United States, if you don't mind providing the contact information for the one you've been working with."

Jonathan paused.

"I wonder," he said, "if I might deliver it to the agency myself?"

The representative looked up at him with kind blue eyes, and Jonathan saw a man who, once, many years ago, may have cared a great deal about the work he did—children, adoption, social work; whatever it was that had drawn him to this vocation—but who no longer cared about those things at all. He cared about something else now, it seemed. Something far more fundamental to his survival.

God helps those who help themselves, Jonathan suddenly thought.

"Splendid," said the representative, taking the check from Jonathan and clipping it to the original documents. "Save us the postage."

Jonathan took the envelope. He had bought himself time to think.

The priest affiliated with the adoption agency had suggested they meet at St. Michael's church near Campo de Mayo out of convenience, but the fact that Jonathan was picking up the baby from a church only solidified his belief that God was on his side.

Inside the church, painted faces of saints gazed down from interior domes. In the first pew near the altar, the agency representative was handing the baby to Graciela, whose name and physical description Jonathan had provided over the phone. The priest emerged from the vestry and stood at the nearby baptismal font as Graciela adjusted the infant in a blanket in her arms. The three of them watched as Jonathan walked down the aisle toward them. The priest nodded subtly when he got close and uttered, "May this child grow in God's love."

Jonathan looked down at the baby for the first time. He waited, expecting—hoping—to feel something significant, but instead his mental assessments were clinical. She was suitable: tiny and pale, with slicks of dark, soft hair. Her eyes were closed, and her lips puckered slightly. When one of her hands crept out of the blanket toward her face, it seemed almost perversely small. As though she could read his thoughts, the baby opened her eyes and looked up. A panic shot through him. He turned away.

Graciela, to whom he'd already given nearly four hundred dollars via Helena, was smiling down at the baby, arranging the blanket around her. He reached to pick up the travel bag at Graciela's feet. In a grotto behind her, the young archangel Michael yielded a long gold sword with one hand, pointing to heaven with the other. Michael, head of the army of God, as the Catholics believed. Up close, his painted face looked vexed by the lack of an imminent devil to defeat.

———— · ❖ · ————

At the airport, a security guard checked their tickets and passports, examined Jonathan's Smith & Wesson model 59 service pistol, and nodded respectfully at his military identification.

"Just the three of you?" he asked. The guard seemed to presume that Graciela was the baby's mother, perhaps even Jonathan's wife.

"Isn't that enough?" Jonathan smirked, taking back his gun.

When they landed, the customs officer processed their entry together as a courtesy and welcomed Jonathan home. Jonathan hadn't called Vivian to tell her when he would be arriving.

On the drive from Charlotte to Virginia, his thoughts were unsettled. They stopped at a drugstore, where Graciela selected infant formula and a few other supplies, twice asking Jonathan to translate words on the packaging. They drove to a nearby Sears and waited outside the doors until the store opened. Inside, the retail clerk showed them every feature of the Dyn-O-Mite infant seat, the only one they carried in stock. Graciela nodded attentively, shushing the baby as the clerk demonstrated the adjustable handle. Jonathan purchased the seat and put it in the trunk of the car, still in its box.

The sun began to rise as they headed east on Route 27. Graciela held the baby in her arms in the front seat and gazed out the window at the mountains in the distance. A tenth of a mile down the road from the driveway to the Joy & Light Family Center, Jonathan pulled the car over near some bushes and turned off the ignition.

He rested both hands on the steering wheel and stared through the windshield for several minutes. Then he turned to look at the baby in Graciela's arms. She was the child of dissidents who would surely be executed. Her parents had been deemed invisible by a government that scarcely knew she existed.

But someday, years from now, the child would ask about her heritage, her birth parents. She might even want to go back to Argentina, and when she did, she might see through a different lens the things Jonathan wished he could ignore now: the allegations of human-rights abuses, those unsettling women in white scarves, the possibility that *Nomen Nescio* masked victims of the junta's overreach.

How simple it would be to remove this risk entirely, to erase the bothersome notion of the baby's parents as prisoners. How good it would be—how neat and clean and orderly—if he and Vivian were to adopt a child without any history at all. A child that was simply available, predestined for them.

The adoption paperwork was in his luggage. The only other copy was stashed in a drawer somewhere at Navy headquarters in Buenos Aires. No international court system or social worker was going to follow up to ensure that he and Vivian were raising this child, and even if they did, that's exactly what they'd find.

Jonathan glanced up at the front porch to the family center. There was no one on the waiting list ahead of them if an abandoned baby were to be found. He and Vivian would adopt this baby, but they didn't have to adopt her origins. This was his opportunity to protect all of them from the truth.

It was almost noon. Daphne would be getting ready to go to lunch soon.

"Help me put the baby in the seat," he said to Graciela.

Graciela got out of the car obediently, bouncing the infant tenderly as Jonathan removed the infant seat from its packaging.

Once he'd unpacked the seat, Jonathan swiped his hand over its vinyl padding—a patchwork pattern of red and yellow flowers with a little girl in a dress holding an oversized daisy, a scarf tied around her head. It crossed his mind to ask Graciela to carry the seat to the center for him, but this was his cross to bear.

Graciela hesitated, then gently put the baby into the seat, tucking the church blanket around her tiny body.

"Just wait here," he said. "I'll be right back."

He walked through the grass toward the front step of the center holding the infant seat with both hands. In the bright daylight, the baby looked up at him innocently, curiously.

He had done nothing wrong yet. If Daphne opened the door at that moment, he would greet her. *Isn't it wonderful?* he'd say. *I wanted it to be a surprise for Vivian. I've got all the paperwork in the car. I came straight here first to get the process started.*

But Daphne didn't open the door. No one did. Why would they? He didn't knock. He was quiet, leaning his weight into the soles of his boots as he set the baby seat down on the concrete slab that constituted the center's front porch. He took a step away from the baby, willing her not to cry yet. Graciela had just fed her and changed her diaper in the backseat. She couldn't possibly need anything between now and the time Daphne opened the door to go to lunch.

Blood pumped loudly in his ears. He was giving this baby a gift. No traces of subversion. No citizenship other than the one bestowed upon her. And no hassle of an explanation, of raising a child who might judge him for what he'd done. A perfect, fresh start. He looked down at the baby, her tiny eyelids fluttering shut. *This is where your life begins*, he thought. *Right here on this step.*

Jonathan stepped silently away from her, back through grass to avoid the noise of the gravel, and moved quickly, his gait lengthening. *Hurry up.* The more distance that formed between him and the baby, the more questions he would be unable to answer if anyone saw him.

When he got back to the car, Graciela was in the front seat with one hand on the dashboard and the other splayed across her chest, her brow creased with concern. The front entrance of the center was scarcely visible from behind the bushes. Through the birdsong, no baby's cry could be heard yet. A single car passed without slowing. Graciela fidgeted. The sun beat down mightily. He hadn't factored in the wait in the July heat.

"Where's the baby?" Graciela asked.

"The baby's fine. She's safe."

Minutes passed. They sat in tense silence. In the far distance, a dog started barking. Where the hell was Daphne?

"Why are we still waiting? Is the baby all right?"

"She's fine. She's with my wife." He wanted to snap at her: *Why did you put that stupid blanket on her?*

Nearly fifteen minutes passed before the front door latch opened in the distance. There was a jingling of keys followed by a woman's gasp.

"Oh!" Daphne exclaimed.

Jonathan let out a breath. Through the bushes, he saw his sister-in-law lift the infant. There was a tiny coo, then a cry. Jonathan started the engine and quietly turned the car around.

On the long ride back to Charlotte airport, he placated Graciela with the balance of her fee and her return plane ticket, then drove until sundown to get to Fort Bragg.

CHAPTER 20

The taxi's engine idled in front of Marcela's apartment. As they stood together on the sidewalk, Marcela plucked a butterscotch candy from her coat pocket and put it in Rachel's hand.

Rachel laughed. "You're an old lady."

"I aspire to be," said Marcela. "Good luck, girl. It's still just the beginning for you." She gave Rachel a quick hug and disappeared through her front door.

Rachel sat close to Mat in the backseat and clutched the hard candy in her fist until the taxi reached the Abuelas' office. She dashed up the stairwell ahead of him, taking two steps at a time to the fourth floor. When she pushed open the heavy office door, a tingling rush of blood crept across her chest.

Esme approached her first, eclipsing her view.

"Are you all right, dear?" Esme asked.

Rachel nodded into Esme's embrace, her cinnamon scent already familiar.

Mari appeared behind Esme, a worried look on her face. She stepped back, opening Rachel's view to the large parlor, where a familiar figure

perched on the edge of a high-backed upholstered chair. Rachel drew
in a sharp breath.

"Mom?"

Her mother stood up with an apologetic smile. "You look disap-
pointed."

"No, I'm not. I'm just—" Rachel hesitated, the queasiness in her
stomach returning. Her anger, which had been bitter and pungent moments earlier, took on a more complex flavor now. She glanced back
at Mari and Esme, then turned to Vivian again, suddenly eager for the
comfort and familiarity of her embrace. "What are you doing here?"

"I needed to see you—to bring you something." In her mother's
hand was a manila envelope and the poetry book Rachel had left on
the kitchen table in Virginia. She reached out her arms hopefully. "I
couldn't let you be here alone, honey."

Rachel's head was spinning. Esme touched her back, prompting
her attention toward the conference table in an adjoining room, where
a small old man sat waiting.

"Let's all sit down and talk, shall we?" said Esme in Spanish. She
positioned herself between Rachel and her mother like a deeply rooted
tree. Mari interjected to translate for Vivian.

"Please, come sit," Esme said again. "We need to have a discussion
with Tomás. It's important. Matías, would you bring out those *facturas*
from the kitchen, please? And let's put on some tea." Esme motioned to
where the man was seated with a folio and a laptop. "Do you like tea?"

Vivian nodded as they all moved toward the table. Mat brought out
the platter of pastries. Mari picked up a green paperback book from a
stack at the center—the Abuelas' published chronicles of all registered disappeared children—and flipped through its pages idly. Black-and-white
square photos of disappeared parents appeared next to empty gray boxes.
Baby due to have been born April 1977, a caption read. On the opposite page:
Baby due to have been born in July 1978. Hundreds of empty gray boxes.

As Rachel scooted in her chair, heaviness descended. She longed for
the levity of Marcela's presence. Esme's tone was formal as she introduced Rachel to the man at the table.

"Tomás is a dear friend," said Esme. "Who also happens to be a very capable attorney."

"Pleasure," said Tomás. He raised his eyebrows and smiled, the papery skin of his forehead wrinkling like ripples of sand at the bottom of a riverbed. He nodded politely toward Vivian, who he seemed to have already met, as she lowered herself apprehensively into a chair.

Tomás looked at Rachel now with all the care and finality of a parent explaining to a child that everyone is going to die someday.

"Miss Sprague," he said. "As I mentioned over the phone, the results from the national genetic data bank came back. May I share them with you now, in present company?"

Rachel glanced anxiously at Mat. "Yes?"

"We've confirmed your identity as the daughter of Lorena Ledesma. You've been registered as an official child of a desaparecida. Lorena was abducted in 1976, as you know, and has been missing ever since. We believe her to be deceased."

Rachel spoke quietly. "But you don't know for sure."

"We don't have proof," said Esme. "But your mother is gone, my love."

Mat cleared his throat.

"I'm sorry," said Esme, her eyes glassy. "But it's the truth. I've been coming to grips with that for nearly thirty years. I know I'll see my Lorena again someday, but it won't be in this world. Your mother is gone from this earth, my dear. I can't prove it to you, but I won't let them do to you what they did to me all those years. Lorena is gone. You mustn't keep that door open."

Rachel turned to Mari, who reached over and touched her hand softly. Tomás deferred to Esme, who nodded for him to continue.

"We also tested your DNA against a sample from José Ledesma's body."

Rachel pivoted to face Mat, who looked prepared to wince. His face was backdropped by a wall gallery of black-and-white photos of the desaparecidos.

"The result came back negative. We've confirmed that José Ledesma is not your biological relation."

Mari reached over and took Mat's hand now. He closed his eyes for a moment, then glanced away.

Tomás looked at Vivian, who was still holding the envelope and book. His speech pattern was calm, as though he were diffusing a bomb with every fragile, potentially fatal word.

"Back in April, a woman from Rosario contacted our offices with some information about her late friend, Graciela Ruiz. She agreed to do an interview with Dr. Rey." He passed a transcript across the table to Rachel. "According to her testimony, Graciela was a domestic worker at the home of Helena Silva, cousin of commanding officer Ricardo Prieta, with whom we believe your adoptive father conspired. This woman's testimony alleges that, with the assistance of Helena Silva, Jonathan Sprague hired Graciela Ruiz to help him travel to the US with a new-born infant adopted through the military."

The envelope in Vivian's lap crinkled as she tightened her grip on it. Rachel closed her eyes. A massive weight descended on her chest. Somewhere far away, Mari's hand touched her forearm.

"There are flight manifests that support this woman's story," said Tomás. "Your adoptive father was on a PanAm flight from Buenos Aires to Miami with Graciela Ruiz in July of 1977. These are facts, and they were enough to lead us to you. But our witness's story was hearsay, circumstantial at best. We didn't have any proof of what your adoptive father had done until"—he looked meaningfully at Vivian—"Ms. Sprague brought us her own testimony and the papers she's holding in her hands now."

Rachel's breath felt labored. She glanced over at the envelope and poetry book Vivian placed on the table, then up at Vivian. Vivian clasped her elbows, her thin cardigan sweater pilling. When Rachel opened the poetry book now, she saw Helena Silva's stationery. Her mother had been trying to show her this. From the envelope, Rachel tugged a narrow ream of collated papers covered in Jonathan's handwriting. Tomás nodded toward the documents.

"We now know that you were put up for adoption by the military government through an agency working in partnership with the Catholic Church."

Rachel's eyes returned to the adoption papers and shifted wildly across them. *NN*. She turned to Vivian. "Did you know about this?"

A pained expression crossed Vivian's face, and her eyes spilled over. Esme passed her a box of tissues, letting her hand linger tenderly.

"I wouldn't have been able to keep it from you if I'd known," she said.

"It was a proxy adoption," said Tomás, "which means Mrs. Sprague wasn't present or directly involved at the time. There was a representative from the adoption agency who was supposed to manage the administrative coordination with the US, but your adoptive father intervened."

Rachel squinted. "Why would he do that?"

"We believe he staged your abandonment in the United States," said Tomás.

Rachel looked to Vivian, desperate to make any part of it untrue. "But why?"

"We wanted a baby," said Vivian. "And your father wanted a certain kind of life for you." She wiped her eyes. "He was trying to protect you."

"He knew your parents were desaparecidos," said Mari.

A sudden gust passed through Rachel's chest. "No," she said. It wasn't a sufficient explanation. Her father had colonized her identity.

"Rach." Vivian touched the tip of her nose with a tissue. "Look at the life you've had. If it hadn't been for him, who knows what would have happened to you?"

Esme lifted her hand from the tissue box slowly, poised as steel.

"She could've been with us," said Mat.

Tomás cleared his throat and turned to Rachel. "Ms. Sprague, we should talk more about the DNA results. We did, in fact, confirm a match for your biological father."

The chant from the escrache still rang in Rachel's head: *Que se vayan todos . . .*

Mat shifted in his chair. Vivian looked desperately at Tomás. He slipped on his glasses and lifted a page on his legal pad.

"Your father was a registered Montonero imprisoned during the dictatorship. His name is Claudio Valdez."

Vivian let out a soft, abrupt sob.

"He went into exile for a time after his release," said Tomás, "but he lives in La Plata now, not far from here."

Rachel opened her mouth. Her heart rate caught up with her racing mind. Her biological father was alive. All this time. The air in her lungs was displaced by some invisible weight on her chest. She had the urge to stand up and run—to escape, to find him. Tears pricked her eyes.

"I don't understand," said Mat.

Esme looked sad. "I asked Claudio to provide a DNA sample," she said.

"We've invited Mr. Valdez to the office to complete the official case register," said Tomás. "Although you are under no obligation to see him."

Mat stood up and reached for his coat. "I can't be here right now."

Mari moved to follow him, but Esme touched her arm. "Let him go."

Rachel's eyes followed. She wanted to leave too.

Esme turned to her. "Are you all right, child?"

She nodded blankly, a lie. The lift in her stomach was a rising sob the size of a tidal wave, and she wasn't sure it could pass through her without causing permanent damage. She lifted a hand to her clammy forehead, compelled to move physically away from this situation, but her equilibrium was precarious, as though the slightest shift in her weight might tip the entire earth in the wrong direction.

Vivian's face crumpled again. "I know I played my part in what happened. That's the reason I'm here, Rachel. I don't even know how to begin to ask for your forgiveness, honey. I know what your father did was wrong, but—I don't know how to say this—to me, it was worth it. Having you as my daughter was so much more than I ever hoped for or deserved." Her voice broke. "I couldn't imagine what my life would have been like without you."

The words floated at the edge of Rachel's consciousness, obstructed by more consuming thoughts—of Claudio, of Mat, of how she would take her next breath or manage to go anywhere else but inside this room, which was forever stained by what she'd learned here: that every time her dad had made her doubt her own instincts, it was only a mask for his lie; that her own biological father had been walking this earth all these years. Rachel didn't have the emotional bandwidth to comfort Vivian right now.

There was a long pause.

Vivian turned to Tomás. "Will Jon be prosecuted?"

"Do you understand the implications of what you're asking, señora?"

"Please," said Esme softly. "Now is not the time to discuss that."

"What's going to happen to my dad?" Rachel asked.

Tomás looked warily at Esme, then Mari. "Well, there are Argentine laws that prohibit abducting a minor, and section 142—illegal deprivation of freedom—but these are Argentine laws. Even if we could prove he broke them, which isn't a given, he would have to be in the country to be charged."

"And there was no forgery of documents on his part, technically speaking," said Mari. The words poured forth like water.

"If any money changed hands with the junta," said Tomás, "the baby could be considered an 'article of export,' but that would be very difficult to prove. And even if those charges stuck, the sentencing is minimal. Sometimes just a small fine."

"Child abduction is a felony in Virginia," said Mari. "And so is kidnapping, but the adoption in the US was legal."

"Perfectly legal," said Vivian.

"Child abandonment would be difficult to uphold," said Tomás.

Rachel could see her own hands resting on the table in front of her, but she was no longer certain she still existed in the room. The faces of Mari, Tomás, and Vivian seemed to be floating, looking to her as though seeking permission for something.

"Did he commit a crime or not?" asked Rachel.

Esme turned to Rachel and took her hands. They were trembling.

"There are the international treaties," Esme said. "We rely on these in cases where other laws have failed us." She looked at Tomás, who began reading from his notepad.

"The UN Convention on the Rights of a Child, Articles 7 and 8, requires 'state parties to respect the right of the child to preserve her identity, including nationality, name, and family relations without unlawful interference. The child must be registered immediately after birth and have the right to a name and to acquire a nationality and, as far as possible, the right to know and be cared for by her parents.' And Article 11 requires that 'state parties must take measures to combat the illicit transfer and non-return of children abroad.' Not all of these have been ratified by every country, unfortunately, but it's enough to bring charges against him under international law."

Rachel stood up. "I need some air."

"We won't do anything you don't want us to," said Mari.

"I need to find Mat," said Rachel.

"Wait," said Esme.

But Rachel hurried past her grandmother, through the door and down the first two flights of stairs without feeling her feet touch the floor. On the landing, she nearly crashed into Patricia, who was on her way up to the office carrying a box of printer paper.

"Ana?" Patricia said.

Through the stairwell window, sunlight bounced off Patricia's tarnished silver earrings, little butterflies. Rachel forced a quick smile, then descended faster, fearing Patricia would chase after her—one disappeared child after another.

She picked up her pace down the last flight, rushed through the door to the street, and banged her shoulder against a man coming in.

"*Lo siento*," she mumbled, but the man glared hard at her, sending a scattered tingle across the back of her neck like the one she'd felt when she first saw Matías on the street in New York. She kept going without looking back, gripping the butterscotch candy in her pocket. How she wished Marcela was there. The tears that spilled from her eyes turned icy on her cheeks in the wind.

Through the cold air, she quickened her steps to escape the image of the adoption papers, the thought of international charges against her dad. She wanted to tear open her chest and step out of her skin. She'd never asked for any of this.

She ran east on Avenida Belgrano, trying to calculate the direction of Marcela's apartment relative to the Abuelas' office and her hotel. *Dead reckoning*: it was a method her dad had taught her. She would always carry his voice with her. She would never escape him.

The street opened to a wide boardwalk running along the river. Rachel clutched her bag. Inside it, along with her passport and money, she'd stashed her sacred blanket. She stopped at a metal gangway leading to a departing double-decker catamaran ferry. The mud-colored river lapped at the retaining wall below. She pulled her collar up, wrapping her coat tightly around her body. Above the water, the winter sky was sunny and clear. She could board the boat, she fantasized, and sail away until she lost sight of the shoreline. She could run away forever. It wouldn't matter who she really was. She gripped the railing and watched the ferry push slowly off into the river.

As the cold air pelted her face, a rolling grief set in. She reached into her bag and took out her blanket—sweet and threadbare—and held it over the reddish water of the Río de la Plata. The wind picked up, whipping at the white fabric.

Rachel gazed through the glinting afternoon sun until her eyes started to dry. When she closed them, tiny capillaries in her eyelids lit up like rivers carving through land. She thought of how perfectly Mother Nature repeated herself in the body and the natural world: how microscopic images of skin cells had always reminded her of rocky shoals; how, at close range, bacteria looked like giant sea creatures, and the texture of bone resembled coral. Perhaps the entirety of human history grew quietly within the flesh—dark and lush, revealing itself over time and through generations. Like a bloom bearing remnants of the secrets buried in its soil. Like the place that had been stifled within her all these years, yearning to be discovered.

She put the blanket to her face and took a deep breath.

It was still there. The scent of hydrangeas, the notes of the saxophone player on the subway platform, even the angels Vivian created for her in her childhood bedtime stories. Rachel rubbed her blanket between her frigid fingertips. It didn't matter which of these things had begun as lies. She'd always known those angels were a part of her. Now she knew their names: Lorena Ledesma and Claudio Valdez. She was their daughter. She belonged to them. And at least one of them was still alive, on this very earth.

"*¡Esa es ella!*"

The wind reached down and snapped at her coat with an angry, haphazard smack, opening her eyes to a stark awareness.

Twenty feet down the boardwalk from where she stood, Mat called to her. Beside him, the man with whom she'd collided in the entryway to the Abuelas' office stood with his hands in his coat pockets. He stared directly at Rachel. She recognized the shape of his eyes, the straightness of his brow, and, through the creases of age, the playful glint she'd seen in the photo of him looking fondly down at Lorena in a lawn chair.

Claudio.

Like a shy child, Rachel lifted both hands and covered her face with the blanket.

PART V

CHAPTER 21

Not long after the coup, Claudio came to the house for dinner and announced to Lorena and José that he was going underground.

"It's getting too dangerous," Claudio explained over the steaks Lorena made. "You probably won't see me for a while."

José waved him off. "You'll be back in a month."

"If the junta doesn't catch up with us first."

Lorena poured them all second glasses of Malbec, finishing off the bottle, and watched Claudio carefully as he ate. He spoke casually, but his tone was suggestive as he caught Lorena's eye.

"We still need help. There are plenty of small ways to support us if you change your minds."

"What can we do?" Lorena asked.

"No." José lifted his hand, shutting her down. "We've discussed this, Lorena. No."

Her skin burned, but she held her tongue, resentment simmering.

Claudio grinned. "You're so precious, José. Sitting here playing house while our people starve, while these imperialists hoard all the power."

José cut into a piece of his steak. "You think killing cops is going to help? More bombings and kidnappings—is that your answer?"

"You're on the wrong side of history, my friend."

"Leave us a number to reach you," said Lorena. "Just in case."

"It sounds like you have no reason to reach me," said Claudio, peering at José.

But later, before he left, he jotted a phone number on the notepad in the front hall and gave it to Lorena. "Only if things get bad."

Lorena waited until he was gone to tuck the number in the drawer. They heard nothing from Claudio for months.

During his absence, *el Proceso* took hold in earnest. Officers lined the streets. Takedowns became a daily occurrence. Tanks lined the Plaza, daring anyone to demonstrate, and José's urging to stay calm was a loose lid on Lorena's boiling indignation. *Calm down. Keep quiet. We have a family now. There are things you can't control.* He poured drinks for himself and made trite commentary about the bleak state of the world as she struggled to prepare dinner and chase a toddler. She became downright hostile. They stopped making love.

In September, a group of high school students in La Plata organized a protest to reduce bus fares. They were mostly sixteen- and seventeen-year-old kids, members of the students' union, putting up banners and picketing. The junta arrested a group of them for the display. The kids were publicly beaten; some went missing entirely.

The news covered the story, portraying the students as dissidents, but on her way to Esme's house one morning, Lorena ran into an old university acquaintance who knew the parents of one of the teenagers who had been taken. The junta denied knowing anything about the missing kids, she'd said, but the parents believed they were kidnapped, possibly executed. Rumor had it that one of the teenage girls may have been raped.

They showed photos of some of the students on television that evening. The girls reminded Lorena of herself as a teenager. What had been done to them? And why? Lorena followed José through the house that night, whispering so as not to wake Matías.

"How can you bury your head in the sand like this? How can you stay silent?" They were standing in the bathroom now, José brushing his teeth while she slathered face cream on her neck. "If my father was still alive, he'd be out in the streets."

José spit in the sink. "And he'd be arrested for it. Maybe get himself killed."

"At least he'd be taking a stand. We need to do something." She rubbed the remaining face cream into her hands and moved to put the bottle away. "I think we should call Claudio."

José wiped his mouth with a towel and threw it on the counter. "Is that what you think, Lorena? That's your big plan? To call Claudio?" He grabbed her abruptly by the biceps, startling her into momentary silence. She dropped the bottle of Olay. José had never laid a hand on her before.

"I'm not going to say this again, do you hear me?" he hissed. "We're not 'taking a stand.' It's different now. We have a son. You're going to shut the hell up about all of this. We're doing *nothing*, all right? Now stop talking about it. People will hear you. Not a word about it again— not to me, not to anyone."

Perhaps if she had just been willing to keep quiet, things would've been different. If only her fear had been stronger than her rage, the fault line in their marriage might never have fully fractured.

She waited until José was out of the house the next afternoon before dialing the number. The receiver shook in Lorena's hand. It rang several times before an unfamiliar woman's voice answered.

"Hello?"

"I'm trying to reach Claudio Valdez."

"Who is this?"

If she had the wrong number or said too much, the junta might come after her. She'd be on a list somewhere; she could easily be turned in to the authorities.

"It's—I'm an old friend. He gave me this number."

There were muffled sounds on the other end of the receiver. "He's not here. I'll tell him to call you back."

Lorena hesitated, then gave the woman her information. She sat by the phone in the front hall. She opened its small drawer, where José kept rolling papers and the tobacco he occasionally smoked. She rolled a cigarette and lit it, coughing a little. Fifteen minutes passed. She drew a little sketch of a Darwin's slipper flower on the notepad and smoked a second cigarette. Finally, the phone rang.

"Lore?"

A rush of warmth came at the sound of his voice—relief, validation.

"Claudio," she said. "I want to help. We need to do something."

There was a pause. "Does José know you're calling?"

Another pause, longer this time.

"Right," he said. "Meet me tomorrow morning in the faculty lounge. As early as you can, understand? I'll try my best to be there."

Her lie to José the next day came easily: she was going to visit her mother for breakfast. She took his house keys and dropped Matías off at her mother's, then made her way to the university. The junta were everywhere, but she had her story prepared: her husband was a professor. He'd left some personal effects inside. She was going to retrieve them for him now.

She arrived early enough to enter the building without being stopped. The little blue-and-white soccer ball on José's metal key ring dangled as she unlocked the faculty-room door with his key. She stood in the cramped corner, rolled another cigarette, and stood by the open window, smoking and waiting.

When the door to the lounge opened, she spun around. Claudio looked different, fitter—his hard arms filled the sleeves of a guayabera shirt and grown-out curls thickened at the base of his neck. He wore a fedora, which was both ridiculous and attractive, and Lorena stiffened, conscious of the danger his new appearance implied. Also, of being alone in a room with him. She hadn't fully prepared herself for the effect his presence would have on her when they were alone together. How the hell had he gotten in so easily?

"You look nice," he said, approaching her.

She exhaled, a little scared. "Don't . . . say that."

He put on a casual air, but beneath it, he seemed tense, alert. There was an electric kettle on the counter behind her, just inches from where she stood, and he made his way to it, filling it with water from the tap and plugging it in. An old bag of yerba maté and three gourds had been left on the counter—by whom?—and she wrapped her free arm tightly around her torso and watched him prepare the tea, trickling hot water into the packed leaves. She was close enough to catch his scent: velvety soil and a hint of something powdery.

"What the junta did to those kids in La Plata," she whispered. "The way people go missing with no answers—it's making me so paranoid. I hate them. They're everywhere. I feel like they can hear my thoughts."

"Shh," he said. "That's their intention. Don't give them the power they want."

Claudio straddled a chair and removed a tin of loose tobacco from his own pocket to roll a cigarette. Lorena stubbed hers out in a clay ashtray and sat down across from him. Morning sunlight streamed in, spotlighting swarms of dust motes in the air between them. Claudio licked the edge of the rolling paper to seal his smoke.

"So what do you want to do?" he asked. "You want to help?"

When Lorena picked up the maté, her hands were trembling. She thought of the junta she'd walked past on her way here—their boots, their guns. They would surely stop her on the way out.

"Yes, I just—I have to be careful." Her skin burned at the prospect of disappointing him. It felt so good just to be near him again.

"We all have to be careful these days."

"I have to think of Matías." She feigned immunity to the chemistry between them, the perpetual invitation in his body language. It had been years since that night in his student apartment, where he'd painted the red closet door with a crosshatched black gun and staff, a mark of his allegiance to the Montoneros. José had never known. Claudio was just as magnetic now, attracting and repelling her with the slightest turn.

"And José wouldn't—"

"No," Claudio cut her off gently. He flicked his silver lighter and stared into the tall, blue flame, holding the unlit cigarette between the tips of his fingers. He brought it to his lips, lit it, and took a deep, smoldering pull. "José wouldn't understand. We both know that." He waved his index finger back and forth between them, lassoing them together, and exhaled. "But we do."

She wondered what it would feel like to pass her hands along his skin again, then physically shook her head to rid it of the idea.

"I want to do whatever I can to help," she said, standing. "But you know I haven't been involved for years, and you know where José stands. I don't know if I'll be able to do anything worthwhile."

He stood too, locking eyes with her. Why did he seem amused? Why had he come here to meet her so quickly after she'd called when she had so little to offer him?

"I think you can do just about anything you like, Lorena. You've always been a fighter."

She was silent for several beats, wrestling with the glimmer in his eye, the magnetic field that pulled her to him. He was close enough that his shirt brushed against hers.

"I just meant—what can I do?" She studied the flecks of gold slicing his brown irises and tilted her head back slightly. When the back of her hand grazed his, he took it, lifting it between them without breaking their gaze. Her heart pounded. From his shirt pocket, he pulled a ballpoint pen and started writing on her palm.

"We can always use help with distribution," he said. "And if you can get away for a few hours, it would be good to spend time with you. Maybe we could talk, like we used to." He smiled, surrendering her hand. "Meet me back here on Saturday and bring the supplies on this list. Don't share it with anyone else. Wash it off good."

Saturday. How would she possibly get away?

"And next time you call," he said, "don't use your real name."

"What name should I use?"

He lifted his right shoulder. "I've always liked the name Ana."

On Saturday morning, Lorena fumbled with her shopping bags outside the Social Sciences building. She'd lied to José again, but not nearly as confidently. Claudio pulled up to the curb in a car. He was wearing a false mustache.

"Get in," he said, leaning over to unlock the passenger door. Panic set in, but Lorena pulled on the door handle and got in the car. Once she was in the passenger seat, he handed her a thin sleep mask.

"Put it on under your sunglasses," he said. She turned to Claudio questioningly. The fabric of the makeshift blindfold was slippery between her fingers. "It's better if you don't know how to get there."

They drove for about fifteen minutes. Lorena saw shifts of light, nothing more. When the engine went quiet, she removed her eye covering. They were parked outside a nondescript flat. His silly mustache was gone.

"Follow me."

Inside, she stood in the middle of the living area on a braided rug. Facing Claudio, she dropped the bags. The place seemed to be a stash pad—there was a couch and two tables, oddly positioned—and Lorena had a visceral sense that something of significance was being concealed in the boxes all around her. Weapons, maybe. She didn't ask.

"Good work, my helper." Claudio eyed the bags. His demeanor was abrupt.

"Did I bring enough? I wasn't sure what the occasion—"

"Shh. It's fine." He pointed to the far side of the room, where a half-dozen banker's boxes were lined up next to two larger cardboard ones. "The small ones, there. They're already packed. Just make them look as pretty as you can."

"It's safe to move them?"

"They're not bombs, Lore." He smiled at her with the familiar face of her friend from university, the courageous man she so admired, who spoke up for what was right with a force that inspired her. Why hadn't she chosen Claudio back then? She'd trusted him; she'd shared his beliefs. She'd felt every ounce of his conviction, his voice sending chills through her entire body. But unlike him, she didn't have the luxury of disregarding the practical implications of her political beliefs. As a woman, Lorena had to consider every outcome of marrying a man who risked his skin to prove his truth—both for herself and for her future children.

Or maybe that was just the excuse she made for her own fear.

Maybe she was here in this apartment because she had never been brave enough to follow her heart and it had finally caught up with her. She'd chosen safety and security over her calling, and now she had something to prove to herself. Her bottled-up passion had percolated to an explosive boil. In this one moment, she could do this one thing.

Lorena got to work, gathering the wrapping paper, foil, and ribbon she'd purchased with the loose bills she kept hidden in the faience box on her dresser. She wrapped all six boxes meticulously and tied them with bows, curling each ribbon. They were heavy—documents, she suspected—but she asked no questions. She would've wrapped them even if they were bombs.

When she finished, Claudio moved away from the window where he'd been keeping watch. He knelt on the floor beside her.

"José would hate me if he knew you were here," he said. Claudio leaned toward her and lifted a piece of stray ribbon from the floor.

"It's not you he'd hate." She'd already betrayed José; there was little risk left in speaking openly about it. "I'm so angry all the time. I feel like I'm losing my mind."

"I'm angry too," Claudio offered, dropping the ribbon into her open hand. Lorena stared up at him with wide eyes. She waited for him to say something else—that she shouldn't worry, that it would all be okay—but he just leaned his weight back on one arm, looking at her. Then he lifted his hand to her throat, touching the loose knot in her scarf.

"Maybe we're both losing our minds," he said. He untied the scarf with his fingers and let it hang open around her neck. Then he tugged at one end, slipping it off. He held it in his fingers for a moment, staring at it as though he couldn't understand how it got there.

It happened in a flurry of hushed, firm movements, an evolution of mutual surprise. Claudio dropped the scarf and lifted his hand to the back of her neck. His fingers entered her hair and made a fist of it, locking her face to his, and her entire body—which had become so utilitarian and neglected in recent months—came alive. She lifted her chin, open to his kiss, but Claudio just examined her face. There was no going back.

Lorena raised her hands to his shoulders, and he guided her to the floor, moving on top of her and pressing his lower body against hers. He parted her legs with his knees, but it wasn't until his full weight was on her bones that his mouth finally found hers. She kissed him back with all her might and was grateful that he conceded nothing, pushing back with equal force.

We can't do this, she thought briefly, but it was interrupted by the scent of Claudio's bare skin, the novelty of his body shape, his movement, now, almost inside of her. Through the window of view beneath his bicep and torso, she caught sight of her own skin, her bare thigh in the distance, moving in rhythm with their bodies.

When her sighs became audible, he wrapped his hand around her mouth, and she bit him, hard; he tucked his chin and bit her shoulder in response. He moved urgently, like a drowning man trying to reach the water's surface, as though his next breath of air was somewhere deep inside of her body.

Once they finally lay still, Lorena rose from the carpet, shocked, and fumbled to thread her foot through the leg hole of her underpants. Claudio stared up at her from the floor, eyes shining. From this angle, she recognized the vulnerability beneath his bravado, the falseness of all his flagrant dalliances with obvious women over the years—just a way of distracting from the fact that he was in love with his friend's wife. Lorena had no way to prove it, of course, and she'd never dare to say it aloud, but she knew it to be true regardless: she was the only woman Claudio had ever loved. She was his warrior, locked away in hiding. The proof was right here, in the way he was looking at her at this moment.

"Run away with me," he said suddenly. "Let's go to Tucumán, right now."

She smiled, tears pricking her eyes, then bit her lip and fell quiet for a respectful moment to let the fantasy die.

"I have to pick up Matías," she said.

Guilt crept in then, cold and serious, even though she felt more alive than she had in years.

Claudio rolled to a seated position. When he tugged on his unbuckled pants and stared up at her, she could practically see his heart breaking beneath his bare chest.

CHAPTER 22

Mat tugged gently at his sister's wrist, coaxing the blanket from her face. She relinquished her hands, exposed, and opened her eyes to see the stubble on his upper lip, the brown eyes she seemed to have always known. He glanced over his shoulder at the man who stood behind him, hands still in his pockets. She shoved the blanket back in her bag as Claudio approached.

Claudio's face was familiar, his brow bone strong, his dark hair thick despite its receding hairline. He was medium height with tense shoulders, but there was vitality in his stance. He swayed slightly toward her as though he might move to embrace her, then pulled back sharply as if he didn't dare.

"Hello, Ana."

The sound of his voice through the wind made Rachel unexpectedly giddy.

"Hi," she said.

"You're very beautiful. You look just like your mother." He looked back and forth between the two of them, overcome. "My God. Look at you both together."

Mat blinked back tears, then took a step and turned away from them both. "Let's go sit somewhere we can talk." He motioned for them to follow as he led them across a footbridge toward the nature-reserve park.

Rachel's eyes jumped to inspect Claudio—the shape of his neck, his tanned skin against the collar of his down coat, the sparse curls along his hairline. Her flesh and blood.

Mat stopped at a small metal table near a coffee cart.

"You want anything?" Mat asked her, nodding at the cart.

She shook her head and dropped slowly into a cold chair.

"Cappuccino for me, if you don't mind," said Claudio.

Mat walked away stonily.

Claudio stared at Rachel. She smiled back.

"Do you speak English?" she asked.

He nodded. "I moved around Europe for close to ten years. Bilingual, as they say. Do you know what they call a person who speaks only one language?"

Rachel raised her eyebrow. "Monolingual?"

"American."

She flushed. "I have so many questions for you."

"I'll try to answer them," he replied.

She wanted to stop time, to sit across the table from him for as long as possible.

Mat set two paper cups of coffee and a handful of sugar packets down in front of them, then handed Rachel a bottled water and sat beside her.

"Thank you," said Claudio.

Mat toyed with a sugar packet, silent.

"Did you ever look for me?" Rachel asked.

"I wasn't sure you were mine to look for, until recently," said Claudio.

"What was our mother like?"

"Extraordinary," said Claudio. He took a sip of the coffee, a dab of chestnut-colored cream attaching itself to his lip. "She had hair like yours, and she would pull it up like this." He set down his coffee and lifted the same arm to his head, his knobby hand feigning delicacy. "I don't know if she knew it, but I noticed everything about her. She had a beautiful voice, and long fingers, like you kids. She was smart. And a great cook."

Every word he spoke was like a pillar, fortifying Rachel.

Mat shifted in his chair. "What happened between you two?"

"It's complicated," said Claudio. "And all my fault, I suppose. We were young. I wasn't the marrying type, God knows. I was forty-five before I was anywhere near ready to be a husband or a father. Even now, my wife might argue with that."

"You have a family?"

His eyes sparkled. "Two kids." He pulled out his wallet with the same hand and showed a photo of two lively, dark-haired children, a girl and a boy. "That's Tatiana—she's almost ten. And Daniel, he's six."

A little bubble of elation inflated inside of Rachel at the sight of these half-siblings, but it popped when she glanced at Mat, who turned his head to the sea.

Claudio followed Mat's gaze out across the water and didn't speak for a full minute.

"They called it 'night and fog,'" Claudio said finally. "Try to imagine it. Thousands of people detained without any explanation. Completely vanished. And the president got up in front of the country and said, 'the disappeared are gone.' Not 'dead' or 'imprisoned'—just 'gone.' No one identified them by name. They didn't talk about it. They just pretended it wasn't happening. And when they finally did talk about it, even the language was a trick. They called it a 'war,' as though people like your mother were worthy adversaries. Everyone knows that no one actually disappeared, but '*los desaparecidos*' is how we remember them." Claudio shook his head. "I think people like to think they would have done something in that situation—spoken out or fought back—but nobody did. There was too much fear. Nobody really does anything in those situations, despite what they say."

"Except Esme," said Mat.

Claudio raised an eyebrow. "Yes. I suppose that's true."

Mat's shoulders loosened.

"If you'd have told me years ago that Esme would become an activist,

I would've said you were crazy. Lorena was the one who had strong beliefs. She always wanted to fight."

"My grandmother says you put my parents at risk," said Mat.

"Your mother wanted to do much more than help with a couple
deliveries of publications. That's all she did—gift-wrapped a few boxes
filled with the underground newspaper *Evita Montonera*. That was her
supposed crime. She helped prepare them for safe distribution from our
printing press. She wanted desperately to be a part of the people's fight.
The good people of this nation, the people she saw working alongside
her father every day—she watched those in power selfishly depriving
them, taking away their opportunities, their rights, their dignity. We
all wanted to stop that. Even José, God rest his soul. Was there risk?
Of course. Everything is a risk. Life is a risk. But who was I to keep the
woman I loved from pursuing her truth? She had enough of that from
her government, her husband—even her mother, if I'm being honest."

Mat stiffened.

"I'm sorry to say it, but you're both grown now, and you deserve the
truth. Esme was always a more traditional person. She wanted Lorena to
settle down and have a family, stay safe. And your father and I were very
different men, despite loving the same woman. Your mother couldn't be
stopped. She was strong, and that kind of strength—well, it would've
come out somehow, as far as I'm concerned. Whether I was involved
or not."

Mat locked eyes with Claudio, man to man. "Why didn't you just
keep her out of it?"

A sudden pain clutched Rachel's chest.

"Why would I have done that?"

"You said you loved her."

Claudio sighed. "I did love her, very much."

"Then you should've protected her."

"I would have protected her, Matías. If I'd known someone was about
to hurt her, I'd have laid down my life to stop it. She might've done the
same for me. But I would never have kept her from doing what she was
called to do. That's something different. She was perfectly capable of

making that choice herself. Preventing someone from carrying out their life's purpose is not protection."

Mat sucked his teeth, unsatisfied.

Perhaps this was just what Claudio had to tell himself, but it resonated with Rachel. She'd spent her whole life being protected from things. She'd been protected from her own identity, her history, the truth, even her own name.

"If it had been me and Mari, I never would've let her get involved," said Mat. He leaned into his folded arms on the table, his coat bulking up around him. "I just wouldn't have let her do it."

Claudio frowned. Mat's words rang false to Rachel too. Surely he had no command over Mari, who had a doctorate degree, flew back and forth between continents, and appeared to have built a successful life on her own terms. Then again, Mari had a softness to her that set her apart from Rachel in some way. Perhaps Mat believed these words; perhaps Mari let him believe them.

"Your mother supported a cause," said Claudio. "She was smart; she had good instincts. She knew when things weren't right, and she wanted to do something about it. But she was trapped in many ways, and there were things about her situation that neither she nor I could do anything about." He turned to Rachel. "Maybe it's different for you now. You're a young woman in the United States. Maybe times have changed. But back then, the least I could do for Lorena was offer her a way to help."

"Times haven't changed that much," said Rachel.

"I never would've put her at risk," said Mat.

"You're your father's son," said Claudio.

"What's that supposed to mean?"

"*Hijo*, look at you. Look at what you've done." Claudio lifted his one good hand and spread it through the air above the table. "You bring people together. You and your grandmother are healers; you're bridge-builders. Your father was a far better man than me. What I saw then as cowardice was really just caution. His cause wasn't the good of the nation, it was the good of his family."

"I know more than you think I do about my father."

"Then you know the world needs more people like him. Look at me now. I'm a useless old scoundrel. It devastated me, losing them. It was why I went to Cuba. Even if I could've stayed here, I couldn't stand the memories."

"Then why did you come back?" asked Mat.

Claudio twisted his coffee cup on the table with his finger and thumb. "Argentina and I are like old lovers. I couldn't stay away. And I've made plenty of mistakes, God knows. But in the end, Lorena and José didn't disappear because of me. They disappeared because of the junta."

Mat looked at Rachel, but she dropped her head. She didn't want to decide the fates at this table any more than she did at the one in the Abuelas' office.

Claudio pruned the shredded edges of the plastic lid to his coffee cup.

"Have you ever read Borges?" he asked Rachel.

Rachel shook her head.

"Borges referred to doubt as a type of intelligence. It's a beautiful way of describing something true, isn't it?"

Mat stood up. "You talk too much."

Rachel rose to follow her brother, whose shoulders hunched with wounded pride. Claudio followed, and the three of them made their way down the flat cobblestone, the water visible from nearly every direction. Mat's natural gait was a half-step longer than hers and Claudio's. The late afternoon sun broke out, and Rachel unzipped her coat. She adjusted Lorena's scarf around her neck, then twisted her hair into a bun.

Claudio stopped walking and took a breath. He stared at her.

"What?"

"You look just like her."

Mat slowed to a stop and turned back to face them, standing together with the ghost of Lorena for a few quiet moments before resuming their pace.

"I don't want to go back," said Rachel.

"I'd imagine you'll find yourself in a bit of a conundrum with regard to your appropriators," said Claudio.

It felt easy to talk to him, like she could say anything without consequence. "Do you have some opinion about what my adoptive father did too?"

"Oh, I don't care much about all that. I was thinking more about what you want."

"I want justice," Rachel said in a small voice.

Mat's head cocked back to assess her.

"Justice is a big word," said Claudio. "Are you sure you're not mistaking it for blame?"

Rachel slid her fingers down the scarf. Mat dropped his eyes to his feet.

"It's natural to want to blame someone," Claudio went on. "To go through the rage, to want revenge, all of that. I've gone through it, too—I was tortured in prison, you know—but it's only a place to pass through. Not a destination. Do you understand what I'm saying?"

"You're talking about forgiveness?"

"Perhaps. If you understand what you're forgiving."

They passed a tiled fountain, and Mat took a step up on its rim, then hopped back down again. "Well," he said softly. "We have proof of what he did now."

"Proof," said Claudio. "What's proof? Proof is just a basis for knowing—or changing what you know. I think Ana already knows the truth. I think you've probably known it for quite a while, haven't you, Ana?"

Up ahead of them, the path led through a nature reserve toward the Río de la Plata. A retention wall stretched along the water's edge, tapering off in sections where the cement was crumbling. A strong desire drew Rachel toward it.

"Let's go over there," she said. She tied Lorena's scarf and zipped up her coat.

A break in the seawall opened to a rocky pier that stretched into the river from shore. As they approached the water, a haunted feeling came over her. She crossed over the pier. Where the wall resumed, it grew close to twenty feet, extending around a bend where the wind pushed the river against its concrete in magnificent breaks of sea spray. A presence was luring her there.

Rachel tested the stones at the base of the collapsing wall, finding grip with the rubber sole of her boots. One hand at a time, she reached up to grab the rubble, hoisting her body upward, propelled toward the force of the jumping water.

"Where are you going?" asked Mat.

Behind her, Claudio and Mat stood at the opening to the pier, watching. With the wind in the foreground, she could only make out small notes of their voices.

Rachel succumbed to the upward pull, planting each foot tenuously on the next waterworn stone. She felt like she was floating again.

"How high are you going to climb?" shouted Mat.

She raised her face to the sky. "To the high part up there. I want to see over it."

Something was calling her from the sea, in that great expanse of air and sky. It pulled her from within. She climbed higher on the broken rocks, obeying the presence.

"You should probably sit down once you get up there," yelled Mat. "It's pretty high."

"Let her climb," Claudio insisted. "Climb, Ana!"

Rachel reached the top of the seawall and sat down, dangling her legs over the side. The wind tore across ribbons of land in the distance, erasing the voices behind her. Sea spray kissed the hem of her jeans as the waves crashed and broke against the rocks below.

She opened her bag, took out her blanket, and clutched its fabric. As the wind whistled around her, she closed her eyes to the setting sun.

Her mind seemed to split in two. One part of her conceived of the full anguish of her predicament, the agonizing lies and truths. But another part was comforted by what she'd always known intuitively: she'd come from somewhere. She'd been wanted. She had the facts of her story, even if she'd yet to process them.

Rachel lifted a hand to Lorena's scarf and felt a transference of energy. The blanket was a part of a story she didn't need anymore; it was the fabric of the past. She held two of its corners and folded it into a triangle, wrapping it around her head like Esme had shown her. She tied a knot at the base of her chin, then stood up on the wall and let the strong wind blow against her.

"Be careful!" Mat called from below.

The haunting soul of the Río de la Plata pulled at her very core, inclining her further into the wind. A bolt of fear shot through her body as the force lured her toward the frigid water, but the spirit at its depths was peaceful. She felt ready to disappear into the wind.

Mamá, Rachel whispered into the air. *It's me, Ana. I'm still here.*

She took the blanket off her head and held it up with one arm, letting it fly like a white flag of surrender.

I'm all right, Mamá. I'm here.

Her fingers parted to release the cotton fabric, and the wind carried it out into the sea. The remnants of her abandonment, relinquished. Just as it reached the point of dipping to gravity, the wind picked it up and unexpectedly elevated it again, startling Rachel with a euphoria that tugged at her chest. It bounced a few more times on the breeze, hovering, waiting.

All the sunlight in the sky seemed to pass over her, blanching her soul. She felt ready to lift off into the air. Not far from where she stood, people who loved her roamed the earth like ingredients for a unique and complicated dish with no recipe. It would take time, but she would weave together the disparate parts of her identity until something chaotically beautiful emerged. The past was a place from which she would launch, shooting off into the future in any direction she chose, like an arrow or a colorful rocket, an image she remembered reading somewhere once, perhaps in a poem. She was entitled to her history, but it wouldn't define her. She saw the full expanse of herself now, every corner lit up and open. She had been loved—and this simple truth was more than enough of a foundation on which to build a remarkable life.

Rachel glanced over one shoulder. On the ground, Mat's expression was full of concern, but Claudio was joyous, marveling. Her feet were instantly rooted, tethered by an invisible filament that ran through Mat and Claudio, back through their ancestors to the beginning of time. She thought of Esme and suddenly couldn't wait to be close to her grand-mother again.

It was Ana, not Rachel, who turned back toward the water in time to see the blanket spiral gracefully into the Río de la Plata. She sat down and watched the fabric soak into the surface of the water. She leaned to one side and rested her forearm on the wall, the cold wetness of it seeping through her jeans and the elbow of her shirt. She laid down entirely, letting her face rest against the cold rock. It felt hard, certain, timeless as the earth. She lay there for a long time, breathing in the cold sea air that sent shards of ice into her chest, then letting it out again. Three more times. Five. Ten. She released the tension of an inner storm that had begun weeks, months, years, and decades ago, sending it out to sea.

She could hear Mat climbing up the rocks behind her. He sat near her on a flat top of the wall. The waves crashed below as they both stared out over the water at the horizon. At last, she felt his hand on her shoulder, warm and firm. She sat up.

"You ready to go home?"

He was testing out the word, its palatability. *Home.* Where was that? She nodded.

The sky was a smear of indigo. Lorena's presence had dissipated now. Alongside her brother, Ana climbed down.

"Your catharsis," said Claudio once they'd taken the final jump to pavement. "A beautiful thing."

Mat rolled his eyes.

Ana looked up at the man her mother had loved, this worn-out revolutionary—her father. She leaned in tentatively and slid her arms around his ribcage. One of his arms hung limp, but the other embraced her carefully, and she breathed in a rich, earthy scent. It was new and foreign but entirely welcome. There was still so much time left.

"I should've had a pastry," said Mat. "I'm starving."

"I've got a box of Zucaritas. And a lime and a butterscotch candy."

"There," said Claudio, nodding back toward the park, where carriage lights were flickering on at a pavilion eatery. The smell of cooking poultry wafted toward them.

"I have something to tell you," Mat said as they made their way toward the park. There was courage in his voice. "I feel like now is the right time to say it."

"Go ahead," said Claudio.

"Mari and I are going to have a baby."

A happy laugh burst from Claudio's lips. "That's wonderful news, man."

Ana's face relaxed into a smile. "How do you keep so quiet about everything?"

"He's just like his father," said Claudio.

"I'm happy for you," she said, but the truth was she was happy for herself. The arrival of a new little soul would make her feel that much less alone in her own beginnings with her family.

The chilled evening air shifted to a warm scent of spices as they entered the pavilion. Ana rubbed the hem of Lorena's scarf between her fingers, snuggling it around her neck and shoulders like an embrace from a guardian angel.

CHAPTER 23

Lorena held Ana in her arms. In a faraway place, minutes and hours changed their names to days. Lentil Eyes had removed her blindfold and brought more food than ever before. Lorena memorized her daughter's milky scent, the faces she made when she awoke, the way she threw her head back and shut her eyes resolutely after nursing, the strength in her tiny hands when they coiled around the base of Lorena's thumbs. Ana's little body was warm and firm, the perfect package in her mother's hands. More than once, a coy, careful smile arrived that made Lorena's heart burst.

The baby wriggled against Lorena's neck and across her breast to be fed. She had learned Ana's cries and how to quiet them hastily. As she watched her baby suckle, Lorena prayed for every joy life had to offer this tiny soul.

But when the nurse changed the bandage on Lorena's wound, a foul odor emanated from the gauze. It stagnated with time, a yellowish fluid leaking out. The baby's cheek was cool against Lorena's palm between the rise and break of her own fevers. As she nursed Ana, Lorena's chills returned until the shivering became almost uncontrollable. The heat from her own skin made the baby's body clammy, but Lorena covered Ana with the towel regardless.

Late one night, the junta arrived for the next transfer. When she saw the white coat among them, Lorena's heart nearly stopped. The officers rounded up a group of prisoners—there was still no sign of José—and forced them downstairs as Lentil Eyes and the doctor made their way to Lorena's bedside. The doctor was holding a syringe.

"No," Lorena cried, cradling Ana tightly. "Please, no."

"It's your vaccination," said Lentil Eyes. "You're being transferred to the south. Let's go." He motioned for her to give Ana to the doctor.

"No!" yelled Lorena. Ana started to cry. Lentil Eyes leaned over her bed. He put one hand on her shoulder and the other on the crook of her arm, holding it in place. The doctor pushed the needle into Lorena's bicep. She held Ana tighter with her other arm, shushing her cries, kissing her precious slicks of dark baby hair.

Hold on, my girl. Be strong. I'm here. I'm still here.

She rocked Ana tenderly for several minutes as the rush of adrenaline faded, a phantom calm coursing through her veins. But when Lorena opened her eyes to look down at Ana, the baby was gone. Her arms were empty. Her daughter had disappeared.

How could she have let her go? How could she have let them take her?

No, no, no.

Please, God. They must have taken her baby to Esme. They had to have.

Lentil Eyes yanked a knit hat down over Lorena's head and hoisted her up off the bed, forcing her to walk. The pulling pain at her incision seemed to have gone away, though there was a warm trickling down the front of her thighs. He dragged her down the stairs and into a group of other prisoners, herding them together. She felt their warmth, their breath, their arms touching hers.

"José?"

"Shh!"

It occurred to her suddenly that she was the mother of two children. Two sweet babies, who would both be with Esme now. Thank God for her mother. Esme would take good care of them until Lorena came home again, wouldn't she?

"No," Lorena cried out suddenly.

Lentil Eyes gripped her arm and draped it around someone else's shoulders. The someone else had a much slighter build and an air of resignation—a friend. Outside, the crisp night chilled her skin. She heard vehicle engines. A steady male voice cut through the noise, high-pitched and out of place. A priest reciting a blessing.

The friend helped her into the covered back of a truck, where she sat on a bench next to someone else who was beside her friend—a long line of them, it seemed, at the end of which was a wide-open mouth of night air. The truck drove off, and Lorena's entire body fell slack against her neighbor. They drove for a mystifying length of time, the night air becoming wider. When she tumbled out of the truck, she had the sense of a vast, sprawling space around her. More engines—bigger ones, screaming and powerful—roared as someone jostled her up a platform and into another cabin. This one, too, had a large, open mouth.

There was an unmistakable rise—a new sensation, a liftoff—and they were flying away now to another place. Maybe, somehow, they were taking her back to Matías and her mother and her sweet baby, Ana. Yes. When she arrived, Lorena would set up Matías's old bassinet and give Ana a bath and dress her in one of the layettes she'd saved from when her brother was an infant. The blue one with pinstripes. She would nurse her daughter in the creaky rocking chair, the one by the window in her bedroom that overlooked the ceibo tree. She understood everything now.

Her friend was gone, the floor below her tenuous. A different type of air—a fast-moving, unforgiving vacuum—filled the open mouth. Far away, strange hands stripped the clothes off her body. The hands grabbed her up, pulled her, dragged her, and when they finally let her go, a sharp, deafening air tugged at her jowls and spread her limbs apart. Her heart slowed. She was grateful for the freedom. The openness around her was breathtaking.

Behind her closed eyes, she was in the rocking chair holding Ana, breathing in the spicy scent of the empanadas her mother cooked in her kitchen as Matías ran across the patio in his bare feet. José was there, unhurt, his sun-kissed skin tasting sweet. Even Claudio, somehow, had come back to her now to meet his daughter, his eyes shining as he stroked a piece of her hair away from her face and recited a quote: *Every day people straighten up the hair. Why not the heart?*

She wrapped her arms around Claudio, knitting his hair at the nape of his neck with her fingers, inhaling the essence of his warm skin. Like an animal maneuvering to accept a caress, he rotated his head to coax her hand to his cheek, then pressed his lips into her palm.

"You're home," he said, embracing her.

He kissed her deeply, his hand claiming her hip bone. Their teeth collided, bone on bone. She was falling now.

She reached for José, her veins pumping with the blood of her ancestors, and their touch evolved from reckless to tender as she opened her eyes.

The faintest wisp of white passed across Lorena's vision, a night cloud on the wind. In the distance, the profile of a young woman in a scarf appeared.

"Ana," she called. "I'm here."

Lorena hovered for a long moment to marvel at her daughter, her children, whose beautiful hearts were filled with more chances than the world deserved. In the seconds before impact, a drowsy smile passed over Lorena's lips. Even as her body crashed through the water's surface, even when the cold plane of the Río de la Plata broke her bones, her spirit was already descending toward every new generation yet to come.

CHAPTER 24

The last days of summer were humid and lush; the tree leaves scarcely stirred. As she made her way home, Ana was distracted by thoughts of the distant Hurricane Katrina—the powerful winds, the rising sea, the suffering. The blinding afternoon sunlight struck the East River, causing her to drop her eyes as she approached her apartment building. When a shadow fell across the concrete and hit her sandals, she stopped short in her tracks. She lifted her head to the large figure, silhouetted against the sun. She would've recognized the shape anywhere.

"Hey," said Jonathan.

Her heart pounded. She looked around.

"What are you doing here?"

"What do you think? I came to see you."

She instantly regressed, fearing his reprimands—for going to Argentina, for taking a DNA test, for uncovering his secrets.

No.

In a single instant, she pulled her lagging mind forward through time, dragging it through the crevices of every painful discovery of the past season, reminding herself of everything he'd done.

"I came home one day," he said, "and your mom had left the country to find you. And you haven't answered my calls or emails. What was I supposed to do?" His hands were in his pockets. He looked tired, sad.

"I was going to—" She stopped herself and looked past him at the sparkling river. *No.*

"Couldn't we have just talked, Rach?" he asked. "It felt like you sabotaged me."

She didn't move. His presence was punishing, heavy.

"Can we go inside and talk?" he said.

She remained completely still.

He glanced over her shoulder at the bench ten feet up the block.

"Can we at least sit, if you're not going to invite me inside?"

She tried to muster the sense of belonging she felt that day with Mat and Claudio. *I'm Lorena Ledesma's daughter*, she thought, grasping desperately at the memory of the seawall.

"You lied," she said at last.

"I did. But I was trying to do something good. For you and for your mom. Come on, let's sit down so I can explain."

Her mind flooded with glittery costumes, warning posters, the sound of chants. *He's on the loose.* "You took me away from my family."

"I was helping you."

"I didn't need your help." Her voice cracked. She cleared her throat to restore it.

"Of course you did. You were an infant. Your parents had been killed—"

"By the people you trained."

He looked down. "I was doing my job."

"How do I know you didn't kill my mother?"

"Rachel. How could you even say that? These people were—" He stopped himself.

"Say it."

"It's not what I meant. We just—we wanted you so badly. And there was no one there to raise you."

"My grandmother searched for me for twenty-eight years."

"And what do you think it would have been like, growing up with her instead of us?"

She sniffed, then reached in her bag for her keys. "I'll never know."

"Wait," he said. He moved to touch her arm, then refrained. "Don't you have even an *ounce* of gratitude for everything I gave you?" He swept an arm through the air, over the street, the land, the city, the country—as if it were his very own gift, a refuge, an empire that belonged exclusively to her. "I was trying to help you. To give you opportunities. I wanted to protect you from a hard truth, that's all."

The lump in her throat hardened until it hurt. "It doesn't work that way. You can't take people away from their family." When she swallowed, tears flooded her eyes. Her throat clogged with an impending sob, but she kept her poise. "I would have done anything for you, Dad."

His head fell. He squeezed the bridge of his nose.

"I'm sorry," he said, looking up at her sincerely.

She was supposed to forgive him now, in the movie script of this moment, but she couldn't. She knew this man. He'd been through his own suffering and torture. But here they were now, the wide world all around them both, open and free. There were no prison walls or chains on either of them—yet. He had a choice. And so did she.

"You were just a baby," he said. "We wanted a baby—we wanted *you*. I should have told you the truth about where you came from. I was wrong to have done what I did. But I'm not sorry that I made you ours."

A watery smile broke across her face. "I'm not yours." She opened the front door to the building and stepped toward her apartment without looking back. The tears flowed like a deluge. This was her life—this mess of unfinished business—and her dad was a part of it. But it was hers to live, not his. She wouldn't relinquish any more than she already had.

Jonathan grabbed the entrance door before it closed and followed her inside the building. She unlocked her apartment door, stepped inside, and turned to face him.

"I don't have anything else to say," she said.

"I just wanted the best for you," he said. "I wanted you to be safe and happy."

"I know. I know exactly what you wanted me to be. I felt your expectations every day of my life. And I could never be that person. Instead of who you wanted me to be, I wish you'd thought about who I really was."

"I know who you really are," he said softly. "I raised you."

"Yes, you raised me. And here I am. This is the person you raised, right here."

"Rachel, I tried—" His face collapsed. "I tried to be a good man and a good father. I just made mistakes."

Her heart ached. She believed him, but it didn't change anything.

"I love you, honey," he said.

"I know. And someday maybe I'll forgive you. Maybe I'll even thank you. But right now, being near you makes me angry and hateful. And right now, I'm hot and I just want to put on my slippers and fix dinner. So go home. Don't call me. If there comes a time when we should talk, I'll be the one to decide."

His mouth was open. After a minute, he nodded, bowing his head respectfully. "Rachel, I just want you to know—"

"No," she said. She took one step backward into her apartment and rested her hand on the door's edge. "My mother named me Ana."

Then she closed the door softly and latched the chain lock.

CHAPTER 25

Esme moved quickly toward the knock at the front door. Light filled the foyer and blanketed Ana, who was seated on the living room sofa reading the cover of one of Gustavo's albums. The space seemed coated in newness, the sheen cast by an outsider's lens. Esme lifted her chin with pride against the small sense of intrusion and turned the knob dutifully.

Her guest's face was eclipsed by hyacinths, hydrangeas, lilacs, pink carnations. Esme wasn't especially fluent in the language of flowers, but she recognized the illustrious gesture of motherhood, reverence, family.

"Thank you for having me," Vivian said in terrible Spanish.

Esme took the bouquet and nodded at this American woman she scarcely knew, this person with whom she'd exchanged inelegant emails over the past several months on their topic of mutual interest: Ana's well-being, her psyche, her evolving mindset. *She may have told you about her new therapist in New York*, Vivian would report. *She's very good. And her spirits seem high. She talks about coming to see you often. She's still not speaking much to Jonathan. Glad she has Marcela. They've gotten so close.* Esme knew all these things, of course—she spoke with Ana frequently—but the emails seemed important to Vivian. The woman seemed lonely.

"Come in," said Esme. "Make yourself at home."

Before Vivian could close the door, Matías and Mari appeared behind her, Matías's arms loaded with grocery bags. Esme waved them in with her free hand as they greeted one another. Marcela trailed behind.

"Leave your shoes by the door," Esme said, carrying Vivian's flowers through the foyer.

"Maybe Papá Noel will fill them with something for me," Marcela smiled.

Mari held the doorjamb for balance as she pried off the heel of each sneaker with the toe of the other. Her belly stretched her blouse more tightly than it had the last time Esme had seen her. Mari had stopped traveling to Florida and moved her things into Matías's apartment in recent weeks. Esme used the phrase "living in sin" often now, a prompt rather than a criticism.

Matías carried the grocery bags into the kitchen as Ana rose from the couch and embraced Vivian and the sisters. Their English words were a collision, sudden and rushed: questions about Vivian's trip, the flight, the quality of her hotel. The air was suddenly strewn with the name Ana's appropriator had given her. *Rachel.*

Esme abated, aware of a rising rift as she entered the kitchen, a separation that left her as alone with Matías as she'd been for years. She watched him unpack the groceries, his forehead aglow with perspiration.

"Did you get the veal?" Esme asked.

"And the turkey," Matías replied. The fibers of his bicep shifted as he lifted the poultry from the bag. He was a man now; he would be a father soon. He'd lived longer than his own father had. "You're really going all out this year, abuela."

Esme glanced at the dough-covered counter, took a brief mental inventory of the rest of her holiday menu: creamed anchovies, stuffed tomatoes, multilayered tortilla sandwiches. From one of the paper bags, Matías removed a loaf of pan dulce, which she'd serve later with fruit cocktail and nougat. She thought back to the first Christmas she'd spent with Matías after Lorena and José were taken, those early days when the sting of Lorena's disappearance was still raw. Like a mallet hitting glass in slow motion, the destruction of that night had webbed out over the years, extending through generations, shattering into shards her granddaughter could only hope to piece together now. There was still work to be done. Esme had watched Ana's heated emotions cool like wax into a delicate shell over the months, stiffening her. Some exterior layer of her had washed away, it seemed, revealing something more substantial beneath—something that would endure. Esme had to be sure she could weave together every part of the story, that the fabric of her memory would be substantial enough to soften those sharp edges for Ana.

"Have you heard anything more from his lawyer?" Esme overheard Mari's voice float eagerly from the living room.

"Not yet."

"What's the status of the charges?"

"He won't contest them," said Vivian, her voice slightly muffled.

"You talked to him?"

"Rachel did."

Esme understood well enough to recognize the constraint in Vivian's voice, the poorly masked concern.

"I answered one of his calls," said Ana. "We didn't say much. I just told him we were going through with it. He understood."

Esme swallowed hard, her heart swelling with pride at the strength of her granddaughter's psyche. A sudden gratitude toward Vivian rippled through her.

Matías set out the last of the groceries and dusted his hands together.

"All set." He kissed Esme's cheek and joined the others in the living room.

Esme stood in the kitchen alone. She lifted the dough from the counter, barricaded by her hidden guilt.

She would give it all back, she thought as she twisted the dough, pressing her thumbs into its softness. All the years of searching, raising Matías, even finding Ana—she would trade everything for that night, to be with Lorena again, to stand before the junta and hold up a light to those once-terrifying men she'd watched weaken in court proceedings over the years since. She would give anything to have her daughter back for just one moment. It felt almost unbearable now.

"Can I help?" asked Ana from over her shoulder.

Esme startled, blinked back the tears she hadn't realized were in her eyes. Ana stood behind her, inspecting Esme's working hands curiously.

"Of course, dear," said Esme, stepping aside to make space for Ana as she approached the counter. "Here. I'll show you. You must fill them first, then do like this."

Ana reached for the dough, her hands a familiar song. The shape of her nail beds, the length of her fingers, each crease of skin at her knuckles. Esme remembered those hands, Lorena's hands. Impulsively, she reached out and took one. When Ana glanced up, Esme lifted her palm to Ana's cheek, leaving a blush of flour on her granddaughter's skin.

You're still here, Esme thought.

From the living room, Marcela gasped. "Come quick!"

Esme followed Ana to where Matías and Mari sat on opposite ends of the sofa, her stocking feet in his lap.

"The baby's kicking."

Matías reached over and put his hand on Mari's belly. Vivian looked up at Esme with the familiar gaze of a yearning mother.

"She's so strong, this little one," said Mari, rubbing her abdomen.

Esme remembered Mari as a young girl with her notebook and pen, her curiosity and courage and curls.

"What will you name her?" Vivian asked.

"Flavia," Matías answered, at the same moment Mari said, "Lorena."

Esme's eyes passed over the room—the advent wreath, the nativity, the paper lanterns the local schoolchildren had made for the Abuelas and delivered to their office. A sense of comfort nudged its way into her heart like a sunrise. It wouldn't last forever. This little spotlight of favor could flicker away at any time, but she held on tightly to the moment.

"We'll have a wedding to plan this spring, too, no?" Esme asked quietly. She couldn't help herself. She was too old to relinquish all tradition.

"Abuela," Matías cautioned.

"How lovely," Vivian interjected. "What kind of flowers?"

When Esme saw Ana grin, she suddenly remembered her most important work.

"That reminds me. Would you come help me with something, Ana? Here, let's wash our hands first. It's delicate business."

In the bedroom, they stood together in front of the open closet doors.

"This is your room," Esme said. "Any time you want to come."

Ana blushed. "Thank you. I was talking to Marcela about February."

Esme smiled and nodded. She pointed to the high shelf. "Can you reach that box?"

Ana was a few inches taller than Esme, and when she extended her arms, she revealed the curve of her hips, the shape of her waist in her jeans. Lorena's body, Lorena's child. Ana slid the box from the shelf and set it on the bed, where they both sat down. Esme didn't want to go back out to the living room yet.

"Do you believe in God, Ana?"

Esme expected she might unnerve her granddaughter with the question, but Ana's eyes were level.

"I have faith, if that's what you mean," Ana said. "I know where God lives."

"Faith is belief in the absence of proof."

"Then I've always had faith."

Esme's heart was at peace. She removed the box lid carefully, pulled back the archival tissue, and lifted a piece of a crocheted layette.

"Oh," Ana delighted.

"These belonged to Matías," said Esme, laying the tiny sweater on the bedspread. "I remember when Lorena used to dress him in this one." A sweet ache permeated her chest. "I saved them because there was a time when I thought I would use them for you. I thought you might be coming back to me when you were a baby."

Ana delicately removed two ribbon-threaded booties from the set.

"Well, I'm here now," she said. "But I don't think they'll fit, so let's give them back to Mat."

Esme flushed with warmth. When they finally brought the box to the living room, Mari gushed.

"These are so sweet!" she sung, holding up a nightgown to show Vivian.

"Look at these," Ana held out the booties.

"Marcela's planning a baby shower in the spring," said Mari. "You'll come, won't you, Ana?"

"So precious," said Vivian, fingering a blanket. "You kept them all so nicely."

It satisfied Esme, as though archiving were an essential duty of motherhood, as though by keeping the layettes, she'd pinned down the past and stitched a piece of it back together somehow.

Another knock sounded at the front door. Matías lifted his head and rose to answer it.

"Looks like Christmas in here," said Claudio as he poured into the house with his brood. He made a great, unnecessary production of greeting Vivian.

His wife, a clever, sprightly woman who was too young for him, handed Esme a bottle of wine. The two kids scrutinized the artificial tree, glistening with gold decorations and red-and-white garlands. If Esme had to guess, Claudio's wife had given the better part of her heart to someone else years ago, but when she looked at Claudio now, damaged as a hungry stray, she was certain that he was more than grateful for whatever love this woman had left for him and their family.

As the introductions quieted, Claudio handed Ana a framed, unwrapped print adorned with a single bow.

"It's the one we saw at the MALBA museum," he said. "Remember? *Woman Leaving the Psychoanalyst.*"

Ana stared purposefully at the surrealist image of a cloaked, gray-haired figure dangling a man's disembodied head by its beard.

"I love it," she said, hugging him.

Esme tutted but said nothing. Ana needed all these pieces, however odd. Claudio was, if nothing else, exquisite in his lack of expectation of her. *There's plenty of time for us*, he told Ana each time he saw her.

Esme handed two little bags of chocolate nuts to Claudio's children, who clod-hopped restlessly across the warm patio.

"They're wild after that car ride," said Claudio's wife.

"Maybe we should take them outside," he suggested.

"We could go for a walk," said Marcela. "It's gorgeous outside. I could stand to stretch my legs."

"Why don't we all go?" said Claudio's wife, looking at Vivian. "You can take in some of the city while you're here."

Vivian looked up at Esme with a sort of daughterly discomfort.

"Vivian," said Esme. "Do you go to church?"

"Yes."

"Perhaps you can show her my church, Claudio. It's right around the corner, up a few blocks. The altar is dressed beautifully during the holidays. You'll see all the floral arrangements. And we have a new priest. He's young, but he seems quite good."

Vivian beamed. "I'd love that." Her Spanish was atrocious.

"Take a walk while I prepare the *vitel toné*," Esme insisted.

"I need to move," said Mari, hefting herself from the cushions.

"Are you sure we can't help you, Esme?" asked Marcela.

"No, go ahead. I'll finish the empanadas."

"I'll stay here," said Ana. "I want to learn."

Matías glanced at Mari then, who waved a dismissive hand, motioning for him to hang back. A light breeze slipped in as Esme opened the door, the family members piling onto the hot street. She stood between her two grandchildren and watched the group as they walked toward her place of faith. Esme had the momentary sensation that everything was in its place. Their figures flickered in the brazen sunlight, vanishing in flashes until they'd all turned the corner. Matías took Esme's hand, the shape of his bones familiar and warm, and in the distance, the children's voices grew fainter until the last of their shadows receded.

ACKNOWLEDGMENTS

I offer my heartfelt gratitude to the following individuals and institutions for their contributions to this book:

My tenacious agent, Jessica Faust, for believing in this story.

My editor, Marilyn Kretzer, and the talented team of professionals at Blackstone Publishing: Josie Woodbridge, William Boggess, Sarah Riedlinger, Rebecca Malzahn, Rachel Sanders, Lysa Williams, Isabella Bedoya, Nikki Carrero, and Deirdre Curley-Waldern. And to Sarah Russo, Isabella Nugent, and Laci Durham at Page One Media.

Thank you to Michael Cohen, Margarita Gutman, Simone Duarte, the Graduate Program in International Affairs at the New School University, the University of Buenos Aires, the Archivo Biográfico Familiar, and the Abuelas de Plaza de Mayo for providing access to the research and experiences that inspired this work.

To the many grandmothers, mothers, children, and family members of desaparecidos in Argentina who shared their stories and knowledge, especially Estela Barnes de Carlotto, Rosa Tarlovsky de Roisinblit, Buscarita Roa, Laura Conte, the late Monica Muñoz, Mariana Pérez, Lorena Battistiol and her sister, Flavia, Juliana García, María Inés Sánchez and her sister, Maria "Miki" Mercedes, Gastón Gonçalves of Los Pericos and his brother, Manuel Gonçalves Granada

("Claudio"), Mario Villani, and my gracious host in Argentina, the poet Graciela Podestá.

Thank you to military historian Bradley Coleman, PhD, for assistance with research.

Tremendous thanks to the early readers, writers, and editors whose feedback shaped *The Disappeared* throughout its evolution: Delise Torres, Sarah Penner, Jon Reyes, Patricia Ruiz, Heather Webb, Caitlin Alexander, Chris Serico, and the teams at Salt & Sage Books and The Spun Yarn.

Thank you to Alicia Partnoy for feedback and insight.

Thank you to Michael Scarbrough for the gift of time.

To the writing communities that nurtured this story and its author, especially the Women's Fiction Writers Association, the Rockvale Writers' Colony with Sandy Coomer, the Beautiful Writers Group with Linda Sivertsen, the Writing Institute at Sarah Lawrence College, and the Writers in Paradise program at Eckerd College, with special gratitude to Andre Dubus III for his wisdom. And to the women of Fe League: Here's to Rising.

I am eternally grateful to my parents, Brian and Nancy Sanford, for providing an inimitable foundation of love and support, and to my brother, Kevin, for cheering me on. This book honors the memory of my own grandmothers, Hilda Murray Travis and Ethel Schlick Sanford.

The names of friends, family members, and colleagues who have supported my writing are too numerous to list here, and my heart overflows as a result. Thank you.

Of all the lucky stars in the sky, Nicole, you are the most brilliant. My love for you is more expansive than the universe. And to Dan—ours is the best story. I am so fortunate to share each chapter with you. Thank you for everything.

AUTHOR'S NOTE

On March 24, 1976, Juan Perón's third wife and widow, Isabel, was removed from her troubled presidency in a coup d'état that marked the beginning of a dark period in Argentina's history.

In the years that followed, with General Jorge Videla at the helm, Argentina's military dictatorship endeavored to eradicate all forms of subversion through the National Reorganization Process that reached beyond those engaged in armed actions against the state. "A terrorist," Videla stated, "is not just someone with a gun or a bomb, but also someone who spreads ideas that are contrary to Western and Christian civilization" (*The Times*, London, January 4, 1978).

Between 1976 and 1983, human-rights groups have estimated that thirty thousand people "disappeared" in Argentina. The majority were men and women in their twenties and early thirties who posed a real or ideological threat to the military junta. They were members of leftist political organizations, militants, and activists—but also trade unionists, journalists, students, artists, and teachers. This campaign of political repression was part of Operation Condor, a US-backed coordination of intelligence between South American countries including Argentina, Bolivia, Brazil, Chile, Paraguay, Uruguay, and, to an extent, Peru.

The "disappeared" were captured, held in clandestine detention

centers, subject to torture, and killed. Information as to their whereabouts was systemically withheld. The authorities' circumvention and
obstruction of the legal process left family members of the missing with
no recourse or closure, a form of psychological warfare that was highly
effective in creating a state of terror. This period became known as the
guerra sucia, or "dirty war"—language evocative of the guerrilla warfare
preceding the dictatorship that more aptly came to describe the tactics
used by the military regime.

It was in this climate of fear that a group of mothers—the Madres
de Plaza de Mayo—risked persecution to join together and organize.
They resisted the silence imposed by the junta and demanded answers
as to the whereabouts of their daughters and sons. They gathered in the
Plaza de Mayo wearing white headscarves and held pictures of their
missing children.

Among the missing were pregnant women and young couples with
babies who were kidnapped along with their parents. The mothers in
search of missing grandchildren formed their own group—the Abuelas
de Plaza de Mayo—and began documenting the estimated five hundred
cases of babies known to have been born in captivity or captured with
their parents. These babies were believed to have been put up for adoption or given to military officers or law enforcement officials and raised
with no knowledge of their biological identity.

Since 1977 the Abuelas de Plaza de Mayo have been working
tirelessly to find and restore the identities of the children of "the disappeared," gaining human-rights support on a global scale despite
tremendous obstacles. In the 1980s they were responsible for break-
through advancements in genetic testing with the help of American
geneticist Dr. Mary-Claire King, who used mitochondrial DNA inher-
ited exclusively from mothers to show a familial relationship between
a child and its maternal relatives. The Abuelas were a driving force in
the establishment of the National Commission for the Right to Identity and the National Bank of Genetic Data in Argentina, providing a
path for anyone with doubts about their biological identity. The work of
the Abuelas contributed significantly to the repeal of the amnesty laws

that protected members of the military from prosecution for their war crimes—laws that were not declared unconstitutional until the 2000s.

The Abuelas have continued to evolve their approach throughout each phase of their missing grandchildren's lives, unwavering in their tenacity and commitment to identity and truth. They were awarded the UNESCO Peace Prize in 2010 for their "tireless battle for human rights and peace by standing up to oppression, injustice, and impunity" and have been nominated for the Nobel Peace Prize numerous times.

For over forty-six years, the Abuelas have been searching for their grandchildren, and as of this writing, they have found and identified one hundred and thirty-seven of them. Their search continues.

As a graduate student, I had the great privilege of getting to know the Abuelas de Plaza de Mayo while conducting field research for my master's thesis in Argentina. The Abuelas were celebrating their twenty-fifth year as I was celebrating mine. I worked with the Archivo Biográfico Familiar de Abuelas de Plaza de Mayo, an initiative founded in partnership with the Faculty of Social Sciences at the University of Buenos Aires. The mission of the Archivo was to collect and preserve testimony from family members of desaparecidos for the purpose of creating personalized context for adult grandchildren whose identities might one day be restored.

The intention of the archives was to answer questions a reappropriated child might ask about their parents: What were they really like? What were their favorite foods, sports teams, songs? What were their beliefs and dreams? These intimate details were gathered from surviving family members who, in some cases, hadn't recounted these stories or memories aloud since their loved ones went missing. The work of the Archivo was emotional, healing, and inherently hopeful.

Much of my time in Argentina was spent with founders of the Archivo around my own age—children of desaparecidos in search of siblings born between 1976 and 1983. Many grandmothers, mothers, family members, and adult children of desaparecidos welcomed me into their homes and shared their stories. Some had only recently been reunited with their biological families.

My research also included interviews with Federal Judge Gabriel Cavallo, whose ruling on Argentina's amnesty laws ultimately rendered them unconstitutional, Nobel Peace Prize recipient Adolfo Esquivel, former prisoner and activist Mario Villani, Argentine sociologist Daniel Feierstein, members of the musical group Los Pericos and the theatrical troupe Teatro X la Identidad, and others. I attended an escrache organized by the Hijos por la Identidad y la Justicia contra el Olvido y el Silencio (H.I.J.O.S.), the Independence Day marches of July 9 in Buenos Aires, and toured former prisons and excavation sites including Club Atletico and La Escuela Superior de Mecánica de la Armada (ESMA).

After returning to New York and completing my thesis, I remained tremendously interested in the work of the Abuelas and the experience of the reappropriated children of my generation whose identities were stolen during the "dirty war." As the daughter of a Vietnam veteran, I wanted to better understand the military involvement of the United States in Operation Condor. Over time, these explorations led to the writing of this novel.

As a work of fiction written by a non-Argentine author, *The Disappeared* offers a dramatized and reductive view of this history. I encourage you, reader, to embark on your own learning about the real events of the rich and enigmatic history of Argentina, the courageous work of the mothers and grandmothers of Argentina, and the often undertaught role of the United States in South American regimes.

RECOMMENDED READING

- *Nunca Mas: A Report by Argentina's National Commission on Disappeared People*
- *Searching for Life: The Grandmothers of the Plaza de Mayo and the Disappeared Children of Argentina* by Rita Arditti
- *A Lexicon of Terror: Argentina and the Legacies of Torture* by Marguerite Feitlowitz
- *Disappearing Acts: Spectacles of Gender and Nationalism in Argentina's Dirty War* by Diana Taylor

- *The Flight: Confessions of an Argentine Dirty Warrior* by Horacio Verbitsky
- *My Name is Victoria: The Extraordinary Story of One Woman's Struggle to Reclaim Her True Identity* by Victoria Donda
- *The Little School: Tales of Disappearance and Survival* by Alicia Partnoy
- *The Rabbit House: A Childhood in Hiding* by Laura Alcoba
- *Revolutionizing Motherhood: The Mothers of the Plaza de Mayo* by Marguerite Guzman Bouvard
- *Dirty Secrets, Dirty War: The Exile of Robert J. Cox (Buenos Aires, Argentina: 1976-1983)* by David Cox
- *Other Weapons* by Luisa Valenzuela
- *Death and the Maiden* by Ariel Dorfman
- *Open Veins of Latin America* by Eduardo Galeano

FILM

- *Our Disappeared*, directed by Juan Mandelbaum
- *The Disappeared*, directed by Peter Sanders
- *The Official Story*, directed by Luis Puenzo
- *Argentina, 1985*, directed by Santiago Mitre

You can learn more about the Abuelas de Plaza de Mayo and offer support at Abuelas.org.ar.

"We have followed events in Argentina closely. We wish the government well. We wish it will succeed. We will do what we can to help it succeed. We are aware you are in a difficult period. It is a curious time, when political, criminal, and terrorist activities tend to merge without any clear separation. We understand you must establish authority."

—US Secretary of State Henry Kissinger to Argentine Admiral César Augusto Guzzetti, June 6, 1976

"It takes courage for a society to address uncomfortable truths about darker parts of its past. Confronting crimes committed by our own leaders, by our own people—that can be divisive and frustrating. But it's essential to moving forward; to building a peaceful and prosperous future in a country that respects the rights of all its citizens. There's been controversy about the policies of the United States early in those dark days, and the United States, when it reflects on what happened here, has to examine its own policies as well, and its own past."

—President Barack Obama at Parque de la Memoria, Argentina, on March 24, 2016, in remarks honoring the victims of the Argentinian military dictatorship